I0831661

TAKEN

DANIELLE RAMSAY

Boldwood

First published in Great Britain in 2024 by Boldwood Books Ltd.

Cover Design by Head Design Ltd.

Cover Images: iStock and Alamy

A CIP catalogue record for this book is available from the British Library.

Paperback ISBN 978-1-83561-647-5

Large Print ISBN 978-1-83561-648-2

Hardback ISBN 978-1-83561-646-8

Ebook ISBN 978-1-83561-649-9

Kindle ISBN 978-1-83561-650-5

Audio CD ISBN 978-1-83561-641-3

MP3 CD ISBN 978-1-83561-642-0

Digital audio download ISBN 978-1-83561-645-1

This book is printed on certified sustainable paper. Boldwood Books is dedicated to putting sustainability at the heart of our business. For more information please visit https://www.boldwoodbooks.com/about-us/sustainability/

Boldwood Books Ltd, 23 Bowerdean Street, London, SW6 3TN

www.boldwoodbooks.com

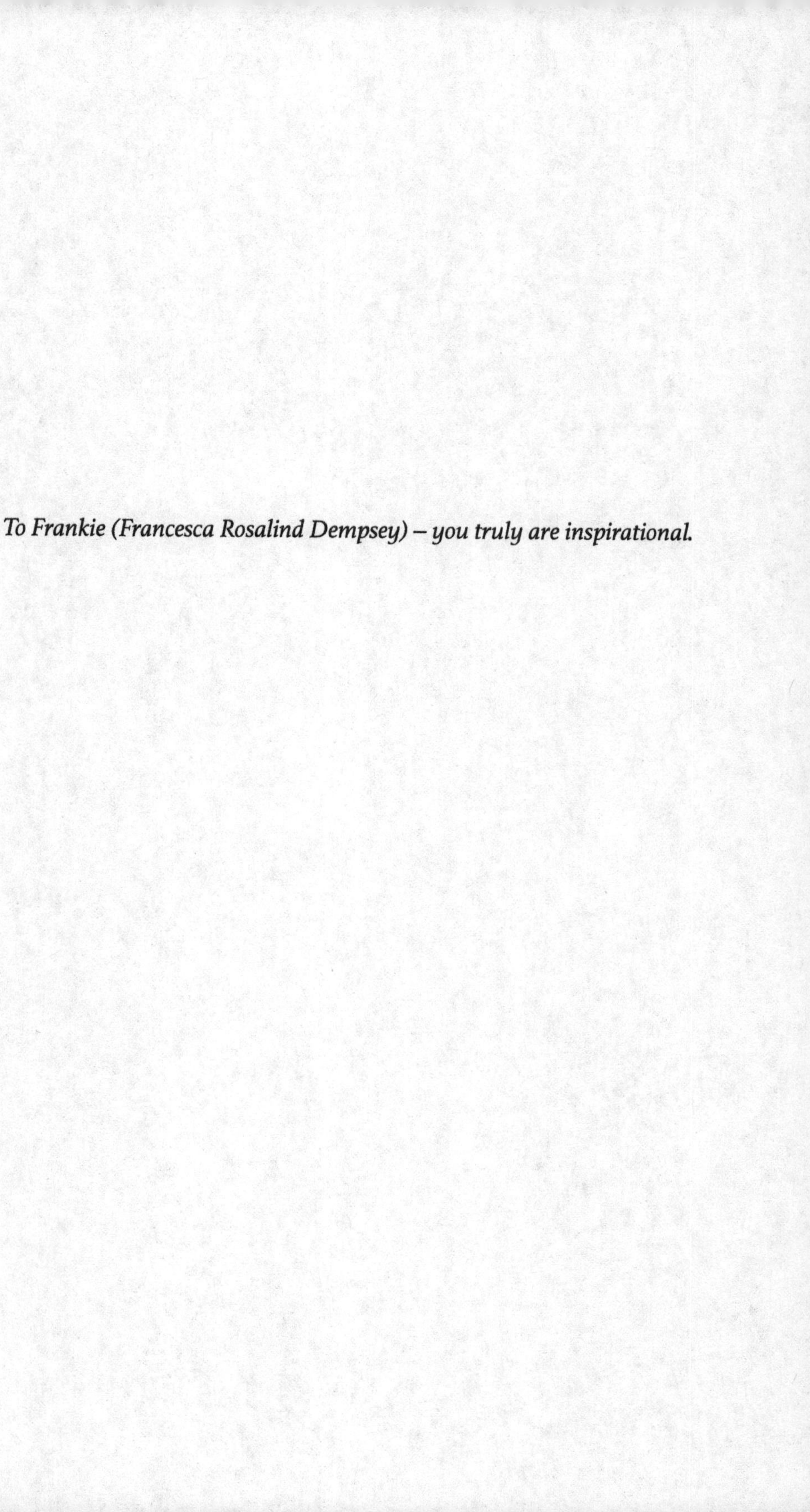

To Frankie (Francesca Rosalind Dempsey) – you truly are inspirational.

'...What loneliness is more lonely than distrust?'

— *MIDDLEMARCH*: GEORGE ELIOT

'Minds that are ill at ease are agitated by both hope and fear.'

— *METAMORPHOSES*: OVID

PROLOGUE

THURSDAY: 3.03 A.M.

I felt groggy and disorientated, unsure of who or where I was. The compulsion to descend back into the numbing black abyss I had surfaced from was overwhelming. But something didn't feel right. I gasped as I suddenly lurched to one side. I gripped onto the edge of what I realised was a wooden bed, terrified I would fall. I tried to swallow back the bile that had risen to the back of my raw throat, but my tongue was too swollen and my mouth too dry.

I struggled to open my eyes, but the explosion of fireworks in my head thwarted my attempt, the booming throbbing, accompanied by strobing white lights, making me cry out in agony. I lay perfectly still, holding my breath, fearful of another onslaught.

When the pounding started easing off, I felt myself disappearing into oblivion. But again, the feeling that something was wrong hit me – louder and more forceful this time. Confused, I tried to remember who I was. Nothing came.

WHO ARE YOU?

I am... I am...

I couldn't recall.

I tried to swallow. Again, failed.

I forced myself to think despite the flashes of searing white pain that tried to block my quest. But my mind was blank. I couldn't get the neurons to connect, to charge up and retrieve the information I needed. The electrical storm in my head had short-circuited everything. Something had happened to me. Something terrible. But what? What had happened to me? What had happened to—

Eli...

The name came to me, calling out ever so softly. Teasing me. Tormenting me. Terrifying me.

Eli... Eli... Elijah...

The room suddenly dipped to the opposite side as my stomach flipped in protest. I fought the urge to heave. Failing, I leaned over the bed and dry retched. Panting, I lay back against the pillow and wiped the spit from my lips with my hand, giving in to the exhaustion that swept over me.

Then I remembered.

Oh my God, Eli... His car seat was empty. He was gone.

Oh God... NO!

No... He wasn't gone. He was on the bed.

Remember? You crawled into bed to be near him. To hold him. To keep him safe.

Groaning with the exertion, I reached my hand out for him, fumbling around for the reassurance of his body next to mine. My stomach protested with every movement I made, as did my thumping head and feverish, aching skin. I groped blindly behind, hoping to silence the sense of disquiet screaming at me that I had committed my worst fear.

Terror took hold when my hand touched something. I snatched it away in horror.

Eli?

Sheer dread filled me as cold sweat drenched my body. Panic made me fumble for the light switch beside the small bedside unit. My hand knocked something over. I heard it hit the carpet with a heavy, dull thud before rolling across the floor. I blinked repeatedly in reaction to the bright bulb above the bed as my eyes slowly acclimatised to the painful intrusion. It took me a few moments to realise where I was, and then I remembered why.

I caught sight of the unused twin cabin bed opposite. My eyes drifted down to the floor, surprised to see an empty wine bottle and the remnants of red wine staining the light beige carpet. I felt my stomach twist and turn in revulsion at the sight. I couldn't remember drinking wine, but the bottle on the floor and plastic tumbler suggested otherwise. The empty blister pack of pills, lying alongside the discarded bottle, came into focus, adding to the incriminating evidence. I understood now why I felt so unwell, so nauseous.

Oh God... What did you do?

My heavy, barely responsive limbs and foggy, pounding head provided all the empirical evidence I needed – I had swallowed innumerable sedatives with a bottle of wine. My skin felt hot and clammy as I fought the urge to retch again.

Why? Why would you do that? Why?

It didn't make sense. None of this made sense to me.

I was perched along the edge of the bed, too terrified to turn around. The world was spinning out of control around me as I clung on frantically, praying that I was still unconscious and this was all in my cruel imagination.

It's not real. It can't be. You wouldn't have washed down all those pills with a bottle of wine. Why? Why would you do that?

But a familiar feeling began to take hold – dark despair. I could sense it descending upon me, ravenous, restless and ruthless, longing to reawaken the memory of—

I stopped myself.

Tears filled my eyes, slipping down my cheeks.

What did you do?

I couldn't bring myself to look. I already knew something was wrong. Very wrong. To look would finalise it, imprinting it to memory forever. Just like—

Again, I stopped myself.

I reached my hand behind me once more, seeking reassurance that everything was all right: that I was not fully awake and had imagined it.

Yes, that had to be it. *You imagined it.*

I had catastrophised when nothing was wrong. That the wine and pills weren't an ominous sign that I had—

I emitted a muffled sob as my trembling hand brushed against something.

His hand...

It was cold. Unnaturally so.

Eli? No... NO...

I lay perfectly still for a moment, my breath shallow, not wanting to register what was going through my mind.

What did you do, Alice?

I ran. That's what I did. I ran away. But I knew I couldn't trust myself. That Eli wasn't safe around me.

Yet hadn't Dr Samuels assured me it was all in my mind? She had said I would never act upon my thoughts.

Harmful thoughts, Alice. Own it! You obsessed about hurting him. You know that you couldn't trust yourself.

I could feel my body trembling as my mind wildly tried to assuage the suffocating guilt. I breathed out shakily, unaware I had been holding my breath. I realised my hand was still touching his smooth skin. So cold... so lifeless. So unnatural.

But still, I couldn't bring myself to look. To look would make it real. I didn't want this to be real. Not again.

What did you do, Alice? WHAT DID YOU DO?

The empty wine bottle rolled accusatorily as the room mercilessly dipped.

NO! I wouldn't hurt him. Dr Samuels had promised me. She'd promised that it was all in my head. Tricky, sneaky, poisonous thoughts that weren't really mine. That it all stemmed from what happened one year earlier before Eli.

But what were you running from, Alice? What?

I tried to block out the email on my husband's computer that I had secretly opened two days ago from a psychiatrist explaining the mental health assessment that was due to take place later today – 24 October. Horrified, I had stared at the stark, factual words addressed to him – the man I trusted and loved – detailing that I was to be sectioned under the Mental Health Act and held for four weeks against my will at a private psychiatric hospital. It described itself as a luxury retreat from the world, an eighteenth-century mansion set in acres of private landscaped gardens with a lake bordered by woodland, offering residents tranquillity and peace. However, its setting and exquisite accommodation were just a façade, hiding the brutal reality of the high-walled, gated premises with surveillance cameras and locked doors, preventing anyone from leaving. I knew the place well as I had stayed there once before. But that intervention had been a year back. So why now?

Because your husband has plans. Plans that don't involve you.

I recalled the anonymous text I'd received on Tuesday morning from a 'concerned friend'. That text had shattered my world. They knew things about my life, my husband, that I didn't know – until they told me. They informed me as a 'concerned friend' that my husband had plans for the future that didn't involve me. I was a burden to him, a problem he no longer wanted to deal with. It was an easy fix. Get rid of me on the pretext I was mentally unwell and a danger to myself and—

I stopped abruptly. I would never hurt Eli. Never. Surely he knew that? Hadn't he talked to Dr Samuels? Or maybe he had, and that was the reason for the sudden mental health assessment. Perhaps I had said something to her in our last appointment suggesting I was a threat to Eli? After all our sessions, I had undone everything she had helped me process and work through this past year. Oh God...

Is it happening again? Are you too unwell to even realise?

Holding my breath, I forced myself to turn around and look – at Eli. To prove to myself that it was all in my head, that my baby was fine. I was fine. Tom was wrong. The psychiatrist who stated I was mentally unwell and needed to be sectioned was wrong. There was nothing wrong with me.

Oh my God... Alice?

I stared and stared, not entirely understanding what I was seeing. It wasn't Eli next to me, it was—

Noah?

I let out a guttural, wounded, strangled sound as I was thrown back to that morning, precisely a year ago, when my life changed forever.

1

ONE YEAR EARLIER

'No...' I cried, holding fiercely onto him.

It felt as if the small hospital room was closing in on me.

'Please, Alice. They need to take him now.'

Unable to look up at him, at any of them, I shook my head.

'No!' I repeated with more force this time.

Tom crouched down in front of me. 'Darling, he's gone. You need to let them take him. It's time—'

'NO!' I spat, ready to fight with all my strength to keep my baby.

My baby... Oh my God... My baby...

Tom nodded at me before looking helplessly at the waiting doctor and nurse.

'Noah! His name is Noah!' I hissed.

Tom turned back to me.

'I know, honey. I know...' His voice broke.

Hot, frantic tears blinded me with the knowledge that I had to let my baby go. I had to hand over Noah, whom I had carried for nine months, only to have him with me for just eight weeks, two days, nine hours and forty-two minutes.

He was born at 12.51 p.m. after a slow, excruciating three-day labour. I had refused a caesarean section, wanting a natural birth, only to end up in the final minutes with an obstetrician intervening with an emergency ventouse delivery. The vacuum cap failed and was swiftly followed by forceps. Despite Noah's bruised, bloodied and misshapen head, he was perfect. The most beautiful baby I had ever seen, and as I held his tiny, naked newborn body against my flesh, I promised, as I stared into his mesmerising black searching eyes, that I would never let anything happen to him. No one would ever hurt him. I would protect him against everything and everyone.

But you failed him, Alice... You broke your promise—

Open your eyes, Noah... Please, just look up at me. PLEASE...

'Alice? Honey?'

But I couldn't bring myself to respond.

I knew behind the calm, collected, controlled persona of the surgeon he was that Tom, too, was being torn apart. The cracked desperation in his voice betrayed him. But my grief was so overwhelming that I had nothing to give him. I barely managed to breathe as it was, without considering how my husband was feeling. He couldn't fix this, and he was a fixer. That's what he did. His precise, steady hands could give a patient back their memories, speech, sight and ability to move – life itself.

Tom Fitzpatrick was one of the leading neurosurgeons in the UK. He had a reputation for doing the impossible, saving lives against the odds. I had fallen in love with this tall, dark-haired American with his infectious smile who had flown to London from NewYork-Presbyterian Hospital for a six-month residency. It was an immediate connection; within months, we fell in love and married.

Tom and I met when working together in the operating theatre; our eyes had lingered on each other for a heart-accelerating beat too long, followed by our fingers touching for a second more than necessary as I passed him a curette. The feeling in those moments was electrifying and beyond anything I had ever experienced.

Even though I tried to resist, the attraction was instantaneous. A few weeks later, he asked me out on a date, and despite having no intention of getting involved with anyone for fear of them learning about my past, I agreed, finding his humour and zest for life irresistible. He was the antithesis of my shy, retiring character, and somehow, we fitted together like two pieces of a puzzle that neither of us knew was incomplete. We balanced each other perfectly, yet we couldn't have been more different in all aspects, from personality to background. Tom came from an affluent, privileged environment where money wasn't an issue, with two parents who were still happily together. He had inherited a generous trust fund from his grandparents at the age of twenty-one, so he never knew what it was to experience financial austerity. He seduced me with surprise weekends in Paris, Rome, Vienna and Bruges. Not that he needed to woo me, as I fell head over heels in love with him the moment we first locked eyes. It was a whirlwind love affair, and Noah followed, much to our delight, a year after our first date. Our son made our love even more special. Now, there were three of us. Tom, as I had, promised to protect Noah. After all, he was a surgeon, and I was a theatre nurse. So how could it be possible that we, of all people, had failed our baby?

How?

But we had failed. Tom had failed. I had watched, paralysed with terror at the realisation of what was happening as my husband tried to save our eight-week-old son with chest compressions. He had failed Noah. He had failed me.

Maybe if we hadn't travelled to the United States for Tom's interview at Massachusetts General Hospital in Boston, everything would have been all right. We were here because of Tom. He had been transparent when he met me, saying he did not intend to settle in the UK. He needed to return to the States. There was no other option for him. And I had agreed, so desperately in love, to follow him.

Or was it that you were so desperate to outrun your past? To pretend it had never happened.

Noah's arrival had changed everything. Rather than returning to New York City as Tom had always envisioned, he wanted to offer our son the idyllic childhood he had experienced growing up in the small, coastal town of Marblehead, with his parents close by and Boston less than a thirty-minute commute away. Massachusetts General also offered the world's most extensive hospital-based research programme, which clinched it for Tom. So, we had flown across the Atlantic, the three of us, filled with dreams of our future in the States.

Oh God, Alice... You should never have brought Noah here. You should never have tried to outrun the past.

I gasped, unable to breathe. I couldn't go there. The guilt I felt was too crippling. And now I was paying the price. I had always feared it would catch up with me as I constantly watched over my shoulder, waiting and anticipating something happening to tear us apart. And now...

I brushed my lips against Noah's soft, black hair and pressed his body against my chest, willing him to move. To cry out. To show them – me – that we were wrong, that he was still alive. He had to be... God, please...!

But he was as cold and unresponsive as when I had reached over to wake him for his feed this morning. I had slept later than expected because he hadn't woken up as usual.

Or had he, and you hadn't heard him? Had you slept through his cries?

Tom had left us both sleeping in the guest room of his parents' large house while he went out for his ten-kilometre morning run. When he returned, he showered and then breakfasted with his parents, leaving me to catch up on much-needed sleep.

If only he had checked on Noah and you when he returned from his run, he might have realised something was wrong. But he didn't.

If only you had woken up. But you didn't.

If only you hadn't—

I blocked the torturous thought out, choking back a stifled sob, terrified if I emitted it, the sob would become a scream that would never end.

I sensed Tom standing up and stepping away.

I then heard muted, low and conspiratorial voices as Tom and the medical team huddled together, deciding how best to act. I didn't care what they said; I just knew that they weren't taking my baby away from me. I couldn't let go of him. Never.

Raw, unbridled pain tore at me. I had never felt anguish this intense, this all-consuming before. Not even when—

The memory was overshadowed by the present.

I held Noah into me, not comprehending what had happened or why. All I knew was that it was my fault. If I hadn't fallen asleep, then my baby would still be alive.

Why did you fall asleep breastfeeding him, Alice? Why didn't you place him back in his Moses basket? Maybe if you had, he would still be—

I suddenly became aware of Tom leaning over me.

'Get away!' I warned. 'Get away from me!'

I couldn't let him take my baby. Noah needed me. He was so tiny, so helpless. It was my job to protect him.

But you didn't protect him, did you?

What happened, Alice? What happened to Noah? Why didn't you keep him safe?

My chest tightened as I struggled to catch my breath, to breathe in enough oxygen to stop myself from suffocating in this claustrophobic space. My heart, now dangerously accelerated, threatened to rip apart.

I held onto Noah, filled with terror at the knowledge that they wanted to take him from me. My head felt as if it was going to explode from the despair, so desperate and dark that it now consumed me.

We were happy. Weren't we? And now?

Now? There was no now.

'Alice? Honey?'

I mumbled something incoherent.

'It's time, Alice,' my husband told me.

I nuzzled Noah's soft, delicate hair again before dragging my head up to meet Tom's dark eyes. They were filled with sadness and fear.

Fear of you, perhaps?

The medics watched silently from the doorway.

Deep guttural sobs of anguish emitted from me as I held my baby against my aching, swollen, milk-filled breasts, as I pleaded and begged for my husband not to take Noah. I couldn't imagine life without him. Not now. Not ever. All I had now was the past. The 'what if' scenarios that would drive me insane. Tormenting me, taunting me, accusing me of being careless. Whispering to me in the darkest hours that I was responsible for what had happened. That I didn't deserve to be happy. That I was a bad person.

Oh God, Alice... Now you're paying the price. You knew it would catch up with you one day.

I let out a wounded sob.

But why Noah? Why my baby? Why not me? Noah was innocent in all of this.

Without Noah, I didn't exist – I couldn't exist. I would be torn apart by anguish and regret. Regret that I had done something so terrible and now the debt had caught up with me. With us.

Without understanding how, I realised the day had disappeared, replaced by darkness. We had sped in the ambulance to the hospital this morning; somehow, it was now late evening. Outside the window, soft, glowing street lights attempted to disperse the blackness of the night. The clock on the pale blue wall ahead indicated that twelve hours had passed without me even realising.

I sobbed in desperation as Tom managed to lift Noah from my chest. I watched as he held Noah's head in his right hand, delicately cradling him.

'No… No… Tom? Give him back to me, please?' I begged. 'Just a little bit longer. I need more time with him.'

Tom didn't reply as he stared at our son. I waited as he lowered his head, raised Noah's to his own and kissed his cheek before holding him tightly against his chest.

'Tom? Please? Give him back to me!'

I jumped to my feet, but it happened so quickly that I didn't have time to react. I grabbed Tom to stop him, but I was too late to prevent him from handing Noah over to the doctor waiting by the door.

'NO! NO!'

She didn't even look at me. Suddenly, they were gone. My baby was gone.

The nurse closed the door behind them.

'Alice… Don't. Let him go,' Tom gently advised.

I ignored my husband as I tried to get past him to the door. 'Let me out!'

'Alice? Honey?' Tom implored. 'Dr Sanchez had to take him. You know that. They've given you all the time they could.'

'No! Give me back my baby!' I cried out, hitting Tom as he tried to pull me into him.

'He had to go. We had no choice,' Tom whispered as he secured me against my will, restraining my struggling body against his own.

'I want my baby, Tom. Please? Please?' I wailed.

I wanted to claw at my skin and gouge at my flesh to rip out the pain which scorched through me like flames. But Tom's powerful arms held me and his hand pressed my head into his chest as I sobbed and sobbed.

But something was wrong. I could feel it in his embrace – a coldness. I could sense his distrust.

We had been so happy and so in love. We had carelessly laughed about how nothing could tear us apart. And now?

Tom didn't need to articulate the words for me to know what he was thinking: What did you do, Alice?

But I couldn't remember. I couldn't remember what had happened. All I could remember was seeing Noah lying there.

2

THURSDAY: 3.09 A.M.

No... No! How? HOW?

I stared and stared, struggling to process what I was seeing. It made no sense. The walls of the ferry cabin closed in on me, then the room suddenly lurched. I could feel bile rising up the back of my throat.

This isn't real. It can't be. You're hallucinating, Alice. Noah is gone. Remember? REMEMBER?

This is Eli, not Noah. It has to be Eli...

I was still half asleep. I had to be; it was the only rational explanation.

The empty blister pack of drugs and the bottle of red wine came to mind. Or was I drugged? It was no wonder I was struggling to make sense of anything.

I blinked a couple of times to try to force myself fully awake. But it didn't change anything. I gasped, not understanding what I was still seeing. But I knew it wasn't Eli next to me, it was—

Noah... NOAH?

Terrified, I turned away from the motionless baby, with his eyes closed, his tiny, balled fists, next to me. He was wearing the JoJo Maman Bébé cotton blue and white striped fox sleepsuit that I had changed Eli into before we went out...

Went out where?

My mind was spinning in freefall as I tried to piece the hazy shards of my memory together. But I was scrabbling around in the dark; I had no idea what had happened to me – or Eli. The unknown terrified me as much as the known.

I dared myself to look back at him.

He's not Eli, Alice. Where is your son? Try to remember.

My mind felt as sluggish and heavy as my body, as if I was underwater unable to rise to the surface, pulled down by some invisible force.

Then it came back to me – sudden, bright and painful. I could see Eli looking up at me with his trusting, grey eyes as I strapped him in his Silver Cross car seat and clipped it onto the pram wheels. I pulled on his baby blue knitted beanie hat, fastened the buttons on his matching blue knitted cardigan and then tucked his pale blue blanket around him before leaving the cabin and taking him—

Taking him where, Alice? Where did you go?

But I couldn't remember. I couldn't force it out into the open. It hid in the dark recesses of my mind.

What time did you leave? Alice! Think!

But that fact evaded me. As did the knowledge of where I went with Eli.

I had returned to the cabin, that was obvious. But how long was I gone for?

And Eli?

I stared at the baby lying on the bed wearing Eli's sleepsuit. Horrified, I took in the familiar features.

Noah?

The last time I had seen Noah was when he was taken from me at the hospital exactly a year ago to this day. Tom had lifted him from my chest and held him, staring down at our son's unresponsive face before kissing him goodbye and handing him to the waiting medics. I'd jumped up to stop them, but I was too late. They had conspired to take him from me, refusing to give in to my grief, my primitive instinct never to let him go. And yet, here he was, lying next to me on the bed.

Alice! Stop it! STOP IT! This isn't Noah. It can't be... It's all in your head.

I reached out, fingers trembling, and touched the hair. Noah's velvety soft baby hair.

I let out a strangulated sound as I snatched my fingers away in surprise. I hadn't expected him to be really there. To be tangible. I was certain I was dreaming. Or worse, hallucinating.

I squeezed my eyes shut against the insanity of what I was seeing.

But Noah's beautiful, peaceful expression, his black, thick, fluttery eyelashes resting against his pale skin, flooded my mind. I could see the tiny white milk spots on his perfectly shaped button nose. Even the fine, fuzzy peach hair on his cheeks and forehead; stubborn remnants of the lanugo that had covered his soft newborn skin. This wasn't Eli's face. It was his brother's.

Noah? But how?

A sob escaped from deep inside me.

How was this possible?

You came back to the cabin, Alice. But what happened to Eli? Where did you go with Eli?

I couldn't remember. So much had happened since I woke up to the message on my iPhone on Tuesday morning that changed everything.

Panicking, I turned and fumbled around on the small wooden bed unit for my mobile. I yanked it from its charging cable and looked at the screensaver. Eli's face stared back at me. Those dark grey, contemplative eyes looking up at me, searching my face for answers. But I had none.

The time took me by surprise: 3.11 a.m.

How was that possible? How had I lost so many hours?

I noted numerous missed calls and voicemails from Tom that began after midnight, but my phone was on silent. I couldn't remember doing that, but I couldn't remember most of the evening. I imagined that Tom's discovery of my disappearance with Eli would have thrown him into a state of abject terror. He would have returned home, exhausted after being in surgery for over twelve hours, to the shocking discovery I was gone. I had taken Eli and the car and left, leaving no explanation of where I was heading or why.

And the texts – countless texts from Tom. A withheld number also repeatedly called before leaving a voicemail message.

The police?

A cold shiver embraced my body.

No, not Tom. Not my husband. Surely he wouldn't have reported me to the police? Eli was my son. I had every right to take him if I wanted. Admittedly, I hadn't told Tom of my plans. Equally, he hadn't confided in me the mental health assessment that was scheduled to take place today with two psychiatrists and a social worker, after which I would be sectioned against my will. I would lose everything then. For I knew that Tom wouldn't be waiting for me when I was released four weeks later – if I was released. He would be gone with Eli. But now I was the one who had disappeared with our son.

I let go of my phone, not wanting to find out if Tom had called the police.

Not that they could do anything. I was well beyond their reach now.

I forced myself to look back down at the baby wearing Eli's sleepsuit. The baby who looked identical to Noah.

How?

This isn't real, Alice. It can't be. You need to remember...

Memories started to come back to me: sudden and forceful, making me gasp.

I had felt really unwell and discombobulated, as if my body didn't belong to me. When I came back to the cabin, I felt so ill that I struggled to make it to the small en-suite bathroom in time before being copiously sick. My legs had given way, and I had collapsed on the floor with my head over the toilet bowl. I was aware of passing in and out of consciousness, unable to move my body, let alone call out for help. How long for, I couldn't say. During that time, where was Eli?

You left him in the car seat attached to the pram. Remember?

Yes... yes... he was safe...

I swallowed as I tried to tug at the delicate thread attached to the memory, fearful of breaking the tenuous connection. But I had no recollection of unclipping him from the car seat and laying him on the cabin bed.

Was that before or after you swallowed the pills back with a bottle of wine?

The thought hit me hard. Why would I take all those pills with alcohol? They weren't just any pills. I recognised the blister pack as the medication prescribed by Dr Samuels for my insomnia. I had thrown my medication together, unsure of how long I would be away. I was already taking 10 mg of diazepam four times a day to reduce my anxiety. To add what appeared to be 80 mg of temazepam into the mix was dangerous. I was prescribed 40 mg a night as my body was now unresponsive to the original dose of 20 mg.

And the wine? I knew not to drink alcohol with the temazepam. I knew that if I took more than my prescribed dose or drank alcohol, then I would fall into such a deep sleep I wouldn't hear Eli. And that was my fear, that I wouldn't hear my baby cry out for me. Worse, I could end up never waking up.

So why would I do that? I would never use temazepam when I was on my own with Eli. Not after what happened to Noah.

I choked back a sob as the image imprinted in perpetuity in my mind of Noah lying lifeless suddenly assaulted me. He had been so frighteningly peaceful that I instinctively knew something wasn't right.

Why I would take the remaining four 20 mg tablets in the blister pack was beyond me, but it would explain my dry mouth, dizziness and confusion.

Unless… It was intentional?

What happened, Alice? WHAT HAPPENED TO ELI? Why did you want to overdose? What did you do?

'Eli?' I whispered, staring at the sleeping baby lying on the bed.

Confused, I looked across at the Moses basket parallel with the cabin-bed wall for stability. I didn't understand why I hadn't laid him in his basket. Why had I wanted him next to me when I was terrified of him overheating or suffocating in bed with me? The soft blue blanket was still inside, but Eli's teddy bear, which he always slept with, lay discarded at the bottom of the basket. Struggling to understand what I was seeing, I looked back down at Eli.

But it wasn't Eli; it was Noah. There was no mistaking that fact.

I placed my fingers on his chubby hand, delicately caressing its smooth skin. It was cold, as I feared – just like before.

I dared myself to pick him up, the weight of his body surprising me. His arms flopped to his sides, unresponsive, as his tiny hands, with minute nails, remained clenched. I cradled his head as I bent down and kissed his cheek, inhaling his scent.

Noah?

But it wasn't Noah I could smell; it was Eli.

I pulled back and studied his sleeping form. At first glance, I could be mistaken into thinking this was Eli as his hair was black, like Noah's, but Eli's nose was slightly flatter than Noah's, and his lips a bit fuller, a subtle difference that only a parent's eye could see. And I could see that this wasn't Eli.

But he was wearing Eli's sleepsuit, which was why he smelled of him.

He? Noah?

I stared in shock at the baby I held, who looked identical to Noah. Even the eczema flare-up between the red and flaking folds of his neck and wrists was there.

And the milk spots, Alice. Look at them on his nose. How is this possible?

Eli's skin was unblemished. He had no dry, flaky eczema patches or milk spots on his nose. Nor did he have black peach fuzzy hair covering his cheeks and forehead, unlike this baby I was holding.

Again, my mind attempted to rationalise the situation with the suggestion I was still deep asleep or experiencing some drug-induced hallucination. But I could feel the weight of this baby in my arms. He felt real...

'What is happening to me?' I muttered.

Unsure as to whether I was imagining all of this, I knew there was one way to determine whether this was Eli.

I gently laid him down on the bed. I shakily breathed in to steady myself before fumbling with trembling fingers at his sleepsuit and vest to see whether the haemangioma on the left side of Eli's chest was there. It had appeared a few days after birth as a small crimson dot and then had grown exponentially in the following weeks to a significantly raised red lump on his skin filled with blood vessels. We were advised that it would get more prominent for the first six to twelve months and then start to shrink.

Fingers trembling, I pulled the vest top to the side. Gasping, I stared in disbelief at the smooth, unblemished flesh. There was no sign of a haemangioma. None at all.

Come on, Alice! You must be dreaming! WAKE UP!

I squeezed my eyes shut and dug my nails deep into my palms to bring myself back to reality. I waited, willing this all to be a dream.

I opened my eyes and stared back down in confusion at the baby still lying next to me. The baby that wasn't Eli and looked like—

Oh my God, Alice. What is happening to you?

Then I thought of Eli's eye colour. It was a rare dark grey – the same as mine – whereas Noah's eyes were so dark they appeared black, like his father's.

But the baby's eyes are closed, Alice...

I needed him to open his eyes. I needed to look into his deep, dark grey eyes to centre myself.

I gently shook him. But he didn't stir.

'Come on, Eli... Please? Don't scare me... Wake up,' I pleaded.

But he didn't react.

I broke out in a cold sweat as the room began to spin, making me nauseous.

I snatched him up, held him against my chest, and rocked backwards and forwards, trying to block out what was happening. I was terrified I was losing my mind. I needed Dr Samuels. I thought of calling her. But what would I say? That I had taken Eli and run. Worse, I had fled the country with my baby and was on a ship heading for Europe, and had awoken in the middle of the night to the discovery that I had lost him – Eli – and the unimaginable had happened: I was now holding Noah. But how was that even possible?

Alice, what have you done? What has happened to Eli?

3

ONE YEAR EARLIER

'How is she?' questioned Barbara.

'Shh…' hissed Tom. 'I'm just checking that she's still asleep. I don't want her disturbed.'

'She can't hear us, darling.'

I could hear them though, despite my mother-in-law's assumption. Not that I wanted to. I wanted them to go away and leave me alone in the miasma of despair that clung to my skin.

'I know. But…' Tom was then silent.

'How long will the effects of the lorazepam injection they gave her at the hospital last?'

I heard Tom give out a low sigh. 'She's slept now for sixteen hours. The dose she was given could make her sleep for two days straight. I hope so, for Alice's sake. I've never seen her like that. It was—' He broke off.

How? How was it possible that I had slept for so long? What had happened to me? My body felt so heavy, as did my head.

I tried to fit together the fragmented pieces of my memory, but every time I went back there, to the claustrophobic blue hospital family room with the clock on the wall, my mind went blank. Beyond the blue room, some unspeakable truth lurked, waiting to destroy me, to take what was left of me.

I could feel my fragility as if I were a hollow shell that would shatter into a thousand bits, pierced by the wrong word.

'Shouldn't she have stayed in hospital so they could monitor her?' asked Barbara.

'I opted to discharge her. I know Alice. It would be the last thing she would want. She needs us, and she needs somewhere safe.'

'His Moses basket and other things, though? Don't you think that will distress her when she wakes up?'

'I don't know, all right? I've never been in this situation. All I know is I lost my son yesterday. I'm trying to keep it together for you and Dad and especially Alice. She'll need all the support she can get when she finally wakes up. Christ, Mom! This... this doesn't happen to people like us. I mean... Noah was so well taken care of, so loved. How?'

A painful silence followed.

I gasped as searing white pain tore through me as the memory of what had happened to Noah – *my baby* – came back to me.

I waited to see whether they realised I was awake, even though I couldn't move my body or open my eyes. Not that I wanted to be conscious. Not here. Not now. Not ever. Not without—

Noah... Without Noah... what's left for me?

'Oh darling, I wish I could say something to make it right,' Barbara whispered. 'I... I just don't understand it either. I mean, there'll be an investigation, surely, so we'll have answers.'

I could feel her red-rimmed eyes boring into me, searching for those answers.

I knew she had been crying from her hoarse and cracked voice. As had Tom.

I couldn't cry. My body was too numb, too disconnected from my thoughts. And I knew if I started crying, I would never stop.

'What exactly happened, Tom? Did she tell you?'

I waited for his answer. Had I told him?

'No... No. She hasn't been able to talk about it. I mean... After I found her and Noah, she was in a state of shock. She couldn't accept that he was...' His voice trembled as pain punctuated his words.

Silence followed. Heavy, awkward, foreboding.

The air in the room was oppressive, which was how I knew they were still there, watching me sleep. But I wasn't sleeping. I was painfully aware.

'Her mother...' Barbara began. I could hear the incrimination in her voice.

My mother? But my mother was—

A stab of betrayal coursed through me. I realised my brother, Oli, must have said something to Tom. But when? Or had I said something? I couldn't recall. But why had Tom shared something so private, so personal, with his parents?

'Do you think what happened—'

'No!' Tom immediately cut her off, an unfamiliar edge to his voice.

'I'm just pointing out the obvious,' she retaliated.

'I should never have told you,' Tom muttered.

'Well, it's too late for that. I still don't understand why.'

'Why what?' Tom questioned.

'The rush? You and—' She faltered as if she had said too much.

Again, I felt her eyes burning my skin, peeling back the layers, searching for the unspeakable.

'You had everything here, Tom. I'm still struggling to come to terms with your decision to go to the UK. Then, to marry Alice so quickly... And as for Blair—'

'Don't!' Tom snapped.

'Alice doesn't know about her, does she?' Barbara questioned, surprised. 'I wondered why you have been so on edge since you arrived.'

I tried to recall how long we had been here. I only remembered arriving on Monday afternoon at Boston Logan International Airport. The late October sun had been so intense, it had momentarily blinded me when I'd stepped outside. The white rays had caressed my skin, filling me with joy and hope of a new beginning for the three of us.

And now, Alice? Now there's only two of you.

I was terrified to travel. I'd feared that the plane would crash over the Atlantic Ocean, plummeting into the deepest and darkest waiting water, never to be found again, taking everything from me. But we had somehow survived the non-stop seven-hour-and-forty-five-minute flight from Heathrow to Boston. I didn't question how or why. I just took it as a sign that I had outrun my past. I now had a future with my husband and baby son on a different continent. I couldn't have got further away from her if I had tried.

But it was all lies. I had been cruelly fooled into believing that I had escaped.

Noah... Noah? He's gone, Alice.

I blocked the thought.

Tom's parents, Barbara and William, had met us and taken me into their embrace and their brilliant lives as if I had always belonged. The car journey back to Marblehead had passed in a blur of excitement as the promise of new beginnings enchanted us. The Fitzpatricks' son had finally returned to them, bringing with him a wife and much-anticipated grandson.

I had been seduced into believing that this new world was safe. When the following morning had arrived, the dazzling sun had reached through the guest bedroom's glass doors to the veranda, which overlooked the tennis courts below and the Atlantic Ocean beyond, fooling me into believing everything was perfect, if only for a second. For that was all it took for me to realise that it was all lies, that something was wrong. So very wrong. And that was when? Only yesterday morning?

I recalled the empty blue hospital room. Then the panic that ensued after Tom had taken my baby from me. I was inconsolable, unable to cope with the anguish of being separated from Noah. The screams inside my body, my head were relentless. Over and over, drowning everything and everyone out.

Sixteen hours, Tom had said. Sixteen hours when I had no recollection of Noah.

Their voices infiltrated my thoughts again.

'She didn't need to know. It would have destroyed her. Alice would only blame herself if she knew.'

'Isn't she to blame?' Barbara questioned.

'No!' Tom hissed. 'Of course, she isn't. Now isn't the time, Mom.'

'And you don't think she would find out now you're back here?' Barbara continued, ignoring him. 'I mean, she's still a part of our lives, Tom. You can't just pretend she doesn't exist. What you did was—'

'I know. All right?' Tom interjected. 'I planned on telling Alice at some point. But not now... Not after...'

I waited. I had no idea who 'she' was or why he had kept her a secret.

Their floating words began to fall like burning ash upon my lifeless body. I couldn't move, even if I wanted to escape them. I wanted to fade into oblivion, where the suffocating, scorching pain of reality couldn't find me.

Perhaps this is only a nightmare... When you awaken, none of this will be true. Noah will still be with you, Alice.

'I just don't understand what happened, Tom,' Barbara whispered conspiratorially. 'Noah was a healthy baby. You're a neurosurgeon and Alice is a nurse. So how could he have possibly—'

Her sharp voice pierced me like poisonous darts, forcing me back into the present, crushing my hope that this wasn't real. Her hushed accusation hung in the air around me, circling me, goading me. I wanted to scream at her that I didn't do anything to harm Noah. I loved him more than life itself. I would do anything for him. But was I terrified I had done something wrong? That I was in some way responsible?

Oh God, Alice... Maybe if you hadn't fallen asleep breastfeeding Noah in bed, then maybe he wouldn't have—

I couldn't think it. I couldn't accept the unacceptable – that my baby was gone and maybe it was my fault.

The crashing waves outside drowned out their words. Water haunted my dreams and waking life. Ironically, I'd run to London from my childhood coastal village in Devon to escape from the torment of the Atlantic Ocean, but our rental house had overlooked the Thames. I would nervously watch when the river swelled, edging up the embankment and threatening to flood the garden and find its way into our home to reach me, desperate to pull me under and take me away.

I thought of her – my mother. Even here in Tom's beautiful hometown of Marblehead in Massachusetts, I couldn't escape her. My past had caught up with me. I could hear the ocean pounding against the rockface beyond the Fitzpatricks' tennis courts as if it had followed me here. Reminding me of her, of what had happened to her because of me.

I had never imagined that it would be my baby I would lose. Never.

But you did something so terrible, Alice. Something unspeakable.

And now you're paying the price...

4

'Alice?'

I ignored the voice, not wanting to be pulled up from the shadowy underworld I inhabited. The pain I felt when fully conscious was unbearable. Life without Noah was unimaginable. So, drifting in and out of forgetfulness was the only way I could exist. I had no idea how much time had passed.

When the lorazepam injection they administered at the hospital had finally worn off, I was inconsolable. Tom and his parents had called their family doctor and friend when it became evident that I wasn't 'coping'. I had raged at my husband that there was no way of 'coping' with the sudden and unexpected death of our son. Their doctor, a kindly, elderly, white-haired man, had deemed it necessary to prescribe sedatives. They were highly addictive and supposed to only be used for a few days to get me through the 'worst of it', or so he said. But I knew there was no end to this torture. How could there be? I had lost my raison d'être. I had lost my baby.

It was preferable for all concerned that I slept rather than battle the excruciating loss that came in waves, shocking my body with its force, taking away my breath as if I was slowly and agonisingly suffocating. The pain ripped through my heart, threatening to explode it into a million pieces, while I drowned in grief so all-consuming that it felt like my lungs were filling with black, toxic water until I was clawing at my throat for air. Without the sedatives, my mind tortured me, cruelly reminding me that I would never see my baby again, hold him, kiss him, smell him, and that I was to blame. It was that simple, that black and white. I had committed a crime so terrible and unspeakable years back that now it had caught up with me. I had paid the price with a loss so overwhelming that I had no future, only a past haunted by ghosts. By 'what ifs'. The irony didn't fail me. After all, I had driven someone to—

'Alice, it's me,' the voice persisted.

I moaned in objection. I didn't want to be disturbed. I wanted to remain in this formless wasteland. The pain couldn't find me here, nor could the guilt. If I kept my eyes closed, I could escape the truth of my unbearable reality without Noah.

'Alice, please? Talk to me,' the voice begged.

Go away, I thought. *Leave me alone. I don't want to talk. I want to disappear. I want to join—*

'Come on, Alice. You need to get up!' the voice insisted.

'No...' I protested.

'Come on! Sit up,' he ordered. 'You can't just lie there.'

'Go away,' I hoarsely muttered.

'Sit up first, and then I'll leave you alone.'

'No...'

'ALICE!'

I felt powerful hands grip my shoulders and shake me.

Shocked by this aggression, my eyes betrayed me and opened.

'Oh God...' I grumbled as the light blinded me. I shaded my eyes with my hand as the intrusive, penetrating late-autumn sun streamed through the windows, bouncing off the walls. 'Close the blinds,' I moaned.

'No, Alice. You've been lying in the dark for over a week now. It's time you got up.'

'Go away,' I ordered.

He didn't respond.

I repeatedly blinked, rubbing at my dry and irritated eyes with the heels of my hands.

He waited, silently watching me shake off my cocoon of sleep.

Finally, my eyes adjusted to the intrusion.

'Why are you here?' I asked, forcing myself to look at him.

'Come on, sit up,' he coaxed.

I ignored him.

'The sooner you sit up, the sooner I give you these,' he said, opening his palm and showing me the blister pack with two sedatives left. He held the elixir of life in those two tablets. Keeping me asleep, numb to the world around me, prolonged my life, at least until it was decided by my husband and his parents that I wasn't at risk of ending it.

It was a bitter pill to swallow. Continue on this drug-induced path, barely existing, or follow Noah's cries. The instinct to be with Noah was so overpowering that without the sedatives, I would have found a way to reach him by now. For I could still hear him crying. I would try to reach out for him next to me, only to discover he was gone.

I yearned for the tell-tale tingling in my breasts as milk threatened to leak. But I no longer had swollen, milk-engorged breasts; like my stomach, they had deflated, leaving me a couple of bra cup sizes smaller. Tom's family doctor had prescribed me two tablets of cabergoline. It had cruelly worked, quickly drying up my milk. The sudden lack of feeding had caused my breasts to become engorged and hard. Mastitis followed. I had awoken two days after losing Noah to hot, red, lumpy and intensely painful breasts, accompanied by a raging fever, symptomatic of a breast infection. When Tom had agreed to the hospital doctor injecting me with lorazepam to sedate me, he hadn't thought about the fact my body would still be producing milk, and I would surface from sedation not only in excruciating mental pain but also physically. I knew that one of the side effects of taking cabergoline was heightened fertility levels: within a few weeks after taking the prescribed drug, the risk of pregnancy increased exponentially. Not that I imagined this was a problem that Tom and I had to consider any time soon, as he couldn't bear to even sleep in the same room as me. His rejection didn't bother me. My world had ended, and I didn't care what happened to him or me.

I somehow forced my arms to push myself up against the headboard. It seemed to take forever for that one small command.

Oliver then sat down on the bed, making it creak in objection.

'Why are you here?' I asked again. 'You're the last person I expected to see.'

'You're my little sister,' he answered.

'That never mattered before,' I retaliated.

I couldn't control the anger and hatred simmering beneath the surface. I was aiming it at Oli, but, really, the fury and loathing I felt were towards myself.

I could see the hurt in his gentle eyes. 'This isn't good for you. You need to start processing what's happened. You can't stay sedated forever.'

'NO!' I snarled at him. 'You don't get to tell me how to deal with...' My voice cracked. I couldn't say it as the force of my reality stole my breath away.

'I'm sorry.'

'For what?' I threw back.

He didn't answer me, but his expression said it all.

I narrowed my eyes at him. Here sat my older brother seeking absolution from me.

'You travelled here for what? You want forgiveness? You want me to make YOU feel better?' I spat.

Silent, his green eyes held my furious glare. I hated him for the pity I saw in them.

'Who told you?' I questioned. Before he could respond, I answered for him. 'Hah! Of course, Tom would have reached out to you.'

'He's worried about you. Worried that what happened with—'

'Don't you dare go there! Don't! You have no right to say his name.'

He dropped his gaze.

I watched as he awkwardly rubbed his reddish-blond stubble. His hair had grown longer and was tied back in a man bun. Wisps of stray curls had escaped, adding to his unconventional appearance. He looked leaner and more muscular than ever. His dark tan told me he hadn't spent the past few months surfing in Devon. Oli had cut me off after I'd admitted something dark, terrible and unforgivable. I had thought he would understand; he had proved me wrong.

Neither of us spoke for a beat. I heard voices drifting up from downstairs. I recognised Tom's and his parents', but there was another voice: that of a woman.

'Did you bring someone?' I asked, realising I knew nothing of his life now.

Oli shook his head and frowned. 'Why?'

Then he heard the same voice as me. I imagined she must have been leaving as the voices came from the spacious entrance hallway below us. I glanced over at the bedroom door that Oli had left ajar.

'Oh, that's Blair,' he explained. 'She must be leaving. She's an old family friend who came by to see if she can be of any assistance. She grew up here. Her parents live directly across Bartlett Street on Spray Avenue. It's literally a stone's throw away. You can see the Worthingtons' property across the road from here,' Oli explained, gesturing to the two wooden sash windows.

The name Blair sounded familiar for some reason, but Tom had never mentioned her to me. He had told me about his childhood friends, but I knew her name wasn't amongst them. I then recalled overhearing Barbara and Tom talking, believing I was asleep. Barbara had challenged Tom about not telling me about some woman who was still a part of their lives. I vaguely recalled Barbara saying: 'You can't just pretend she doesn't exist.' I remembered waiting for Barbara to elaborate, but Tom had shut the conversation down.

Could Blair Worthington be the woman they were discussing? If so, why had he kept her a secret from me when she was still a part of the family's lives? It was odd. Tom had never struck me as someone who kept secrets. But then, I was sure he would say the same about me.

I looked over at the two windows, overwhelmed with the urge to get up and look at this Blair Worthington. But it was then that I realised that the windows were unfamiliar. Disorientated, my eyes darted around the room, taking in the sparseness. I struggled to recognise the pieces of bedroom furniture. It then hit me that I wasn't in the original guest bedroom where—

I stopped myself and attempted to swallow. I was surprised at the dryness in my mouth. There was nothing here of Noah. Or Tom. I couldn't see his clothes or the suitcase or the holdall. I glanced at the dark mahogany bedside cabinets on either side of the antique king-size bed where I lay with a beautifully ornate patchwork throw spread over me. No tell-tale phone or iPad charging cables or books. Tom was an avid reader in his downtime and insisted on being weighed down with paperbacks. But there was no trace of him in this room. Or my baby.

Right hand shaking, I reached for the glass tumbler of water beside me. I took a sip as I tried to recall being brought here, but the memory eluded me.

'Where am I?' I asked Oli.

He cleared his throat and brought his eyes, uncannily like our mother's, to meet mine. 'You're in the other guest bedroom. Tom thought it better to move you—'

'But I want to be near Noah's things,' I protested, cutting him off.

'I... I understand. But the noise of the ocean disturbed you. It added to your distress, so they moved you down to this room on the first floor at the front of the house.'

'Noah's Moses basket and... and his clothes and blankets. Where are they?'

'I don't know, Alice. I didn't ask,' Oli uneasily answered. 'I only arrived early this morning. I spent time with your in-laws and Tom, but I left them to it when Blair arrived. I've sat here for the past hour, waiting for you to wake up.'

'Where did you fly from?' I asked, suspecting from his tan that he hadn't travelled from the UK.

'California,' he answered. 'I've been based there for the past four months.'

'Oh...' I quietly uttered.

Oli had always looked after me since we were little, and yet we were only together now because of Noah's death: his nephew, who he hadn't met because our past had ripped us apart. Oli was five years older and had taken charge when our father had left when I was ten. I had come home from school one day to discover Dad had gone. He hadn't just left us, my brother, mother and me, he had left the UK. He had taken a post in Australia, ensuring there were as many miles as possible between us. I had found a letter from him on my bed, simply explaining he had been promoted and promising to fly us over when he had settled into his new job and had found suitable accommodation. It never happened. I had no phone number or address to reach my father, and I never heard from him again. I discovered the truth three years later, but by then it was too late.

'I need to let Tom know you're awake. He wants you to eat something before you take these pills.'

'I'm not hungry,' I replied.

'You still need to eat,' he answered.

'Do you know how long it's been since you talked to me?' I asked, staring at the deep sunlines etched on his face.

He shrugged.

'You didn't even visit when I had Noah,' I ventured, my voice cracking with pain.

'I've been caught up with training. I'm competing in the coming months,' Oli simply answered.

'But I had a baby,' I argued.

'I know. I didn't expect to—' He stopped, shook his head.

I suspected he was about to say he didn't expect to run out of time but had thought better of it.

I had spent the last six months scrutinising our fallout, which had been catastrophic. We had called each other out on our bad behaviour. Oli had accused me of running away from Devon as soon as possible and forgetting about him, which was true. I'd left after my A levels for Kings College London to take up a place on their nursing degree, never returning. The memories were too overwhelming, and Oli's decision to remain in and renovate the family home overlooking Croyde Beach was too much of an obstacle to overcome. I never wanted to be reminded of the sea there or what happened that night when I was thirteen.

Six months ago, Oli had stayed with Tom and me in London and disclosed things he and our mother had withheld from me about our father. Things that would have changed my perception of events and my reality if only I had known. We'd had a blazing row, and he'd accused me of being responsible for our mother's death. It was something he couldn't take back. What made his allegation worse was that there was a level of truth to his claim.

I stared at Oli now. If only he had found a way to keep the truth from me, we would have been fine. But he had felt duty-bound to honour our mother's memory, whose looks and subtle mannerisms he had inherited. Whereas I had always been a daddy's girl, who adored the man I physically resembled. My existence after he had walked out on us was too much for my mother to bear. She couldn't bring herself to look at me, bitterly remarking that I was a constant reminder of him. Nothing I did could please her. Nothing I said could bring her love for me back. It had evaporated that terrible day my father left us. She had come home from work at the solicitors firm where she was a secretary to the same shocking discovery. Only there was no note for her. Her world had shattered; she had taken to bed, unable to cope, and had stayed there until—

I winced at the memory.

'What?' Oli asked, his brow furrowed.

'Nothing,' I replied. 'Can you give me my tablets, please?'

He nodded. 'Sure. Once Tom has brought you up some food.'

'I told you, I'm not hungry,' I wearily replied, sinking back against the pillows and closing my eyes. I was tired, and my head had started to hurt. All I wanted to do was sleep.

'Alice, don't repeat history,' Oli warned. 'Please? Don't be like Mum.'

My eyes flew open. 'Don't ever compare me to her! I am not our mother. She... she...' I couldn't bring myself to say it.

Oli waited. The profound sadness in his eyes caught me off guard. He then dropped his gaze to his hand, holding the blister pack. 'I wish I'd never told you.'

'So do I,' I whispered.

He nodded, unable to bring himself to look at me. 'I'm sorry, Alice. I'm so sorry for everything you've gone through and for what happened to Noah.'

I didn't reply.

'You know I'm here to support you for his funeral next week?'

Shocked, I stared at him, stunned that the funeral was going ahead without my consent.

'Tom said you won't talk about it. That you're refusing to even acknowledge his...' His voice trailed off.

'They blame me for what happened to Noah,' I stated.

'No... No, they don't. The medical examiner has ruled that it was sudden infant death syndrome. He documented that he was a healthy baby with no underlying medical issues who, for some inexplicable reason, died in his sleep.'

'No!' I fired back. 'Healthy babies don't just die, Oli. They don't! I'm a nurse, for God's sake! Tom's a surgeon. We couldn't be more qualified as parents to keep our baby safe. SIDS doesn't happen to people like us.'

Oli gave me a sympathetic look as he reached out and touched my hand. 'Alice, it can happen to any parent, regardless.'

I snatched my hand away. 'It's my fault. I know it's my fault. I should have woken up. But I was too exhausted. I hadn't slept all night because Noah was crying. He wouldn't settle, and then finally, he fell asleep in the bed next to me while feeding, and... so did I. Tom got up to go for a run. Supposedly, Noah was fine when he left us. He was still—' I stopped, unable to bring myself to say it. I swiped at the tears that had started to fall. 'Something must have happened. I must have done something. Maybe I rolled on him?'

'Alice, you need to stop this. Noah didn't suffocate. There were no signs of trauma. He was a healthy baby.'

'So why did he die, Oli? Why?'

Oli shrugged. 'I wish I could give you an answer.'

Unable to stop myself, I started to cry uncontrollably.

He leaned in and pulled me into him. I tried to push him away, but he wouldn't let me go. I let myself finally yield to him, burying my head into his chest as my body convulsed with agonising sobs. It threw me back to when I was thirteen, and he told me our mother was dead. I had hidden my face against his chest then, not wanting him to see me, for I knew I was responsible for her death. But Oli hadn't known what I had done. Or, more to the point, what I hadn't done.

5

'Hey, are you okay?' Oli whispered.

Oli and I sat together, waiting for the Fitzpatricks to join us. I couldn't bear anyone looking at me, never mind attempting to find words of consolation.

The funeral service at Our Lady, Star of the Sea Church on Atlantic Avenue, had been filled with people supporting Tom and his parents. The large stone church was unquestionably beautiful and decorated with sublime stained-glass artistry. The wispy white-haired priest who had stood at the monolithic, wooden altar with an imposing wooden figure of Christ on the cross behind him was suitably sombre and dignified. Yet, I had felt a sense of disquiet sitting on the front pew. All I could focus on was that Noah didn't belong here in the small coffin positioned in front of the altar for all to see and weep at. It had struck me as odd that neither Tom nor I were religious. Neither of us had discussed Noah being raised in a particular faith, and yet he was to be buried by a Catholic priest, the same priest who had served the parish when Tom was a choirboy. I had argued with Tom that we weren't going to baptise Noah. That a Catholic funeral was hypocrisy, but he had responded that we hadn't the time with Noah to know for definite. He had then assured me, misunderstanding my resistance, that Father Edwards, who was a close friend of William, Tom's father, had explained that when the parents intended to have the child baptised, but the child died suddenly, it was permissible to have a Catholic funeral.

I'd had no further words of objection to this statement, seeing in Tom's dark, lost eyes a desperate need for this ceremony. Whether it was for his parents or for him, I couldn't say. All I knew was that it wasn't about Noah. Or me.

'Alice? You okay?' Oli repeated.

'No,' I hollowly answered, blankly staring straight ahead.

How could I be all right? I thought as I watched strangers standing awkwardly, talking and waiting to sit. I was relieved I was wearing sunglasses to hide the blazing enmity in my eyes. I hated this spectacle, despising everyone here. I didn't want to come, but Tom had forced me, literally dressing me and pulling me out of the safety of his parents' house and into the car. I should have known the significance of today when earlier he had filled the bath, helped me climb in and knelt on the floor next to me, delicately washing my skin and shampooing my hair. I had thought it was simply an act of love. A way of trying to reconnect with me and pull me back to him, for I had lost my bearings in the shadowy underworld of grief. I hadn't washed or changed my clothes since the morning I'd reached for Noah's sleeping body, only to find he was cold to my touch. Tom hadn't spoken while carefully dabbing at my skin with the expensive, fragranced body wash his mother had left in the en-suite bathroom. The silence between us had echoed off the gleaming, white-tiled walls. When the tears had rolled down my cheeks, Tom had ignored them and continued dabbing at my goose-pimpled flesh as if it were fine porcelain. There was no mistaking that he had to force himself to touch me. I noticed he couldn't bring himself to look me in the eye, either. I wondered what horror he supposed he might find there.

Barbara had nervously busied herself in and out of the guest bedroom while Tom had dressed me, blow-dried my hair and rubbed Vaseline on my dry, chapped lips. I had started chewing them again – a childhood habit I had acquired when I was ten and had faced my first sudden loss. I had managed to break the habit when I fled Devon, but now the past had caught up with me. Barbara had attempted to add some make-up to my dull, lacklustre skin, but I had batted her fluttering, smothering hands away from me, refusing to allow her to make me look 'acceptable'. I didn't recognise my reflection in the mirror when she'd left me to stare at my pallid, gaunt face. The black and bluish bruising under my bloodshot, red-rimmed eyes, accentuating my paleness, took me by surprise. I could see why she wanted to cover up my ghost-like face and add some semblance of life. But the problem was, I didn't care what I looked like. Not any more. All that mattered to me was Noah, and he was gone.

It was as if part of me had disappeared the night Tom took him from my arms and handed him over to the waiting medics. My heart ached with such an intensity that I was waiting for it to rupture under the pressure. I could feel the surges of adrenaline repeatedly assaulting it, enough to stop the cardiac muscle from contracting normally, potentially causing heart failure. I was aware that, in rare circumstances, someone in such emotional distress could experience a heart attack-like event. I also knew of broken heart syndrome, otherwise known as stress cardiomyopathy or takotsubo cardiomyopathy, where extreme grief could affect the left ventricle, the heart's main pumping chamber, making it change shape and subsequently affecting its ability to pump blood effectively.

'Has the dizziness passed?'

'Alice? Did you hear me?'

I felt my hand being squeezed.

'Alice?'

I turned to my brother. 'Yes?'

'Do you still feel dizzy?' Oli questioned.

'No,' I answered.

He gently rubbed the back of my hand.

I wanted to snatch my hand from his suffocating grip, but instead, I turned away from his concerned gaze. Oli had barely left me these past few days, not that I had registered his presence, too blighted by the pain of Noah's loss.

It took me a moment to comprehend my surroundings. I was surprised to realise that I was no longer sitting in church but in the front row of the Fitzpatrick family plot in Old Burial Hill Cemetery in Marblehead, waiting for the inevitable. I had no memory of leaving the church or travelling to the cemetery. I recalled feeling light-headed and Oli supporting me to a seat, but that was all.

I took in the scene in front of me, one that I didn't want to be any part of, not now, not ever. Tom and his parents had made all the decisions without listening to me. I had objected and reasoned that I wanted to take my baby home, back to London. But Tom had argued that Marblehead was his home, and now our home. That he wanted his son laid to rest someplace familiar. That this cemetery was perfect, and, in time, would become a source of comfort to me, with its wooden seats on the top of the hill with its panoramic view of Marblehead and the ever-changing ocean. But this place wasn't of my choosing. I didn't want to be here. Nor did I want my son to be buried here with his Fitzpatrick ancestors. He didn't belong here. He belonged with me.

Oli squeezed my hand again, sensing my unrest.

I tried to swallow, to ease the unbearable dry sensation in my mouth. I accepted that, along with the feeling of light-headedness, it was a side effect of the alprazolam, or Xanax as it was otherwise known in the States, prescribed by the Fitzpatricks' family doctor, as a coping mechanism, to help me get through the day and be present for the sake of Tom and his family.

I could feel the anxiety building in my chest. I knew I was due another one in an hour, but whether I could cope until then was questionable.

Tom's parents had taken charge of events when it became evident that I was too lost in my grief to make any decisions. Even the simple black dress I wore, with a black cashmere wrap and black flat pumps, had been chosen for me. Not that I cared what I wore. All I wanted was my baby back. Consequently, I had become a silent bystander at my son's funeral, voiceless and powerless as the Fitzpatrick family did what they did best: take control.

I was surprised at how handsome Tom looked in his black suit, white shirt and black tie as he talked to various mourners, putting them at ease despite his grief. I marvelled at how he and his parents held it together, warmly shaking hands with people and graciously accepting condolences. I had never felt more like an interloper. I couldn't pretend and be polite. I couldn't act for the sake of protecting other people's feelings, too angry and resentful at what had happened to me – to us.

I was an oddity here, the strange, sullen British woman whom no one knew, whose baby had tragically died. I was someone to shun out of embarrassment or fear of saying the wrong thing. For what does one say to a newly grieving mother? What words of comfort can you offer a stranger you don't know? I was someone to whisper about when they thought I couldn't hear. Whereas the Fitzpatricks were a well-respected family in this New England small coastal town in Essex County. Tom's family could be traced back for centuries in Marblehead.

The smell of sea salt carried on the breeze off the ocean spray assaulted my senses, pulling me back to the present and the Fitzpatrick family burial plot. Unable to look at the small, open grave, I turned and stared down the hill at the deep blue ocean, iridescent under the intense midday sun. White yachts adorned the water in the harbour, tranquilly bobbing on the glittering surface. I recalled Tom's father telling me on our first evening that in 1915, *The Boston Globe* described Marblehead Harbour as 'one of the most beautiful views in American waters'. But the splendour was lost to me.

I chewed my lip as I considered William Fitzpatrick's conversation over dinner that first night. There were over 2,000 yachts and powerboats moored in the harbour, with over 1,000 people on a waiting list that took twenty years to get a mooring. Somewhere down there was his prized yacht. Tom had planned on taking me out sailing on it to show off the stunning coastline and his nautical skills, desperate to get me to fall in love with the scenic coastal town and what it could offer us and our family.

But what now that our tight, nuclear family was torn apart? What would become of us? Tom still couldn't bring himself to look at me as I sat here with my brother, waiting for some acknowledgement from my husband that we were together as grieving parents. That Noah's death hadn't divided and destroyed us.

I squeezed Oli's hand. I was sure he was feeling equally triggered. My eyes burned as I became that terrified, guilt-ridden thirteen-year-old who silently watched on as mourners murmured how sorry they were for our loss while Oli and I held hands as our mother disappeared into the cold, hard ground.

Everything about this place was triggering: the harsh, brutal sunlight, the ocean air, and the accusatory, crashing waves. Old Burial Hill Cemetery was too similar to Mortehoe Cemetery near our childhood home overlooking

Croyde Beach in Devon: my mother's final resting place. The inviting azure blue sea below the cliff top had mocked us that calm September day as the sun blazed down, blinding the mourners. I didn't recognise anyone that day, too consumed by guilt and grief, too shocked by the events that had led to that moment I witnessed my mother's burial.

A voice pierced my thoughts. Bright, breezy and filled with intimacy.

'Tom, I'm so sorry.'

I looked up to see my husband embracing someone. I waited a beat, expecting him to release her. He didn't. He held onto her.

His back was to me, so all I could make out was long, cascading blonde, wavy hair painstakingly styled to appear naturally perfect as she rested her head against his shoulder. Her slender fingers pulled him into her body as she hugged him hard. I noted the bright red shellac gel polish on her long fingernails, accentuating the large diamond engagement ring.

'That's Blair Worthington,' Oli confided.

I realised I had clasped his hand too tightly in response to their lingering embrace, which conveyed more than just a childhood friendship – something less innocent.

I watched her teeter back when they finally released. I hated her as soon as I saw her. Her pouting mouth had intricately applied red lipstick, coordinating perfectly with her nail polish. Her large light blue eyes had just the right amount of make-up to make her look naturally beautiful, and her high cheekbones were complemented with a subtle combination of blusher and bronze highlighter. I suspected she was roughly Tom's age: thirty-eight. Not that she looked it, but her confidence spoke of the years she had over me. I was ten years younger than Tom, but I was sure I looked much older now.

Unlike me, she bore no battle scars, only an air of privilege and entitlement. It was self-evident from her exclusive, designer black coat, dress and high heels and her tall, slender figure and perfect features, that she led an enviable lifestyle. After all, she had grown up in Marblehead like Tom, where property prices guaranteed that only the rich could afford to reside there.

My skin felt prickly and itchy in the woollen dress Barbara had bought for me. My feet nipped in the unflattering pumps, and my neck was hot and sticky under the cashmere shawl.

I gnawed at my bottom lip, unable to silence my jealousy towards this woman. As if reading my thoughts, she shifted her focus from Tom to me. I felt my breath catch in the back of my throat as it seemed her gaze penetrated through my sunglasses, burning into me. I felt pure animosity for the briefest of moments, but it was directed towards me, emanating from her.

Tom followed her gaze, twisting his head. I saw the embarrassment register on his face when he realised who she was looking at. I expected Tom to come over and introduce her. He didn't. Instead, he turned his back on me. A smile lingered across her full red lips as she looked me up and down before dismissively throwing her hair back and focusing her attention on my husband.

I cringed inwardly, feeling pathetic.

In contrast, Tom exuded such confidence surrounded by these affluent guests. My husband's wealth had never been an issue for us – for me. I had never felt out of place with him or in any way made to feel less because I didn't come from money. Tom loved me for who I was. But now, seeing him with Blair, someone who shared his entitled background, I wasn't sure what he saw in me.

'I want to go,' I said to Oli.

'What?' Oli questioned, shocked.

'You heard me. I want to go. I can't do this, Oli. I can't—' My voice cracked.

'Sure… Sure, I understand. Let me just tell Tom, okay?'

'No. I don't want him to make a fuss.'

'But Alice, this is—'

'I know what it is, and I didn't agree to it. This isn't for Noah. It's for them,' I hissed, looking towards the Fitzpatricks. Barbara and William had now joined their son and Blair's muted conversation. 'I want to go, Oli!' I insisted, hearing the strained pitch of my voice.

'Okay… Okay, let's go,' he reluctantly conceded, not wanting a scene.

I felt eyes scorching my back as we got up and left. When I turned to look over my shoulder, I was shocked to find that Tom and his parents hadn't noticed. The only person who did was Blair, who watched my sudden departure. I found it odd that she didn't alert them that I was leaving. Instead, she turned her back to me as she moved to my husband's side, putting her arm through his as she conspiratorially continued talking to my in-laws.

I stared in disbelief. This woman had usurped me at my baby's funeral. Or maybe I was being overly sensitive. Perhaps she was doing what any family friend would do: comforting Tom and his parents. She was engaged, after all; I had no reason to feel threatened by her.

Then I recalled the look in her eyes. There was no pity or embarrassment, just pure abhorrence.

6

'Why?' Tom questioned. 'It was about saying goodbye to our son together. People couldn't help but notice that you just got up and left without a word. Nothing to either me or my parents. Do you have any idea how that made me feel? How they felt in front of our friends and family? Do you?'

I worried at my lip until I tasted blood's metallic, sour taste. I had been anticipating Tom's return from the funeral. I'd heard the bedroom door being thrown open, bringing with it the sudden intrusion of voices rising from the ground floor. I had resisted looking, hoping that whoever it was would leave me alone. However, the woody, fresh citrus aroma of Aventus Cologne, which was Tom's favourite scent, had alerted me to his presence.

I reluctantly turned over to find Tom standing by the bed, waiting for me to acknowledge that he was there. His expression was cold, with an atypical hard edge. I didn't recognise the man watching me, as much as I could see from his eyes that I was no longer the woman he once knew. We were strangers to one another in an unnavigable land. Whether we would find our way back to each other was debatable. Noah's sudden death had changed us from the madly in love wife and husband who had it all, envied and admired by colleagues and friends, to a hostile couple separated by an unimaginable loss.

Tom had called Oli as soon as he had noticed that we had disappeared. Oli had tried his best to appease Tom, explaining that I couldn't cope and needed to leave. That it was all understandably too much for me to bear, considering my fragile state.

Their exchange of words had been painfully curt.

Oli and I had returned to the Fitzpatrick residence, where catering staff preparing food and drinks for the wake had let us in. Otherwise, I would have had to wait in the car until the funeral service had ended. When I'd returned, I'd run up the stairs to the guest bedroom, where I'd spent my first and only night here with my son. Oli had followed me, realising too late that I had passed my room and headed to the second floor. I'd swung the door open and stumbled into the guest bedroom, only to be bewildered by what greeted me.

'Where's Noah's stuff?' I'd screamed at Oli.

It had all been removed as if he had never existed. Tom's belongings were here, clothes laid out on the bed. Books and charger cables on his bedside cabinet, but the cabinet on the opposite side was bare of any of my possessions. I, like my son, had been eradicated.

I had felt my legs give way as I collapsed to the wooden floor. I desperately needed to hold something of Noah's. To smell him again. To know that he really existed and wasn't a cruel, twisted, fake memory. I had no idea where my iPhone was and couldn't access any photos of him. I was terrified that I was beginning to forget him: what he looked like, his mesmerising dark eyes, the smell of his delicate skin, the feel of his soft hair.

'Why?' I had howled in anguish. 'Why would they move his things? WHY? They had no right! He's my baby, Oli! Mine!'

I had looked wildly over at the open bi-folding doors and the wooden veranda with the chairs invitingly seated around the low table. I was assaulted by the fresh, salty air and the intense sound of waves crashing against rocks beyond the garden and tennis court. I was suddenly overwhelmed with the compulsion to get up and run out to the veranda and—

Before I could, I'd felt Oli's hands grab my body, pulling me into him, holding me as I howled and fought with him to let me go. Once I had exhausted myself, Oli had got me down to the guest room on the first floor facing Blair Worthington's parents' picturesque traditional New England home. He'd helped me remove my pumps and shawl, then guided me into bed, pulling the intricate patchwork comforter over me. He had briefly left me alone, returning with water and another Xanax, which I'd accepted without thought. He had tried talking to me about what had happened upstairs, but I had turned over in bed and stared at the delicate and beautifully illustrated turquoise mockingbird wallpaper. He had then closed the blinds and left me at my behest.

'Alice? Alice? Are you even listening to me?' questioned Tom now.

I looked up at him.

'You think you're the only one who is suffering here?' my husband demanded through gritted teeth as he yanked at his black tie to loosen it.

I watched as he undid his shirt's top button, his eyes never leaving mine. 'Do you? I had to bury our son without you. How do you think I felt standing there without my wife in front of all those people?'

I didn't reply. I simply held his unwavering gaze.

'You're not the only one in pain,' he pointed out.

Sighing, he sat down on the bed. I sensed the old Tom returning, overpowering the stranger who had temporarily hijacked his body.

'Alice, please? Let me in,' he begged as he reached out to brush the stray hair from my eyes.

I found myself recoiling from his touch.

The pain that crossed his eyes was unmistakable. But it was too late. I couldn't undo the action.

I tried to speak and apologise, but the words were lost to me.

'I'm not to blame!' he threw at me. 'I did everything I could to try to bring Noah back. But—' He stopped himself.

I was surprised to see tears gliding down his face. I wanted to reassure him, but again, I couldn't form the words.

'I… I should have picked Noah up and put him in his Moses basket before I left for my run. But he was asleep beside you, and I didn't want to disturb him. I knew you'd been up with him most of the night and—' He stopped and shook his head.

I watched as he tried to swallow, forcing his Adam's apple to jump.

Tom didn't understand. I didn't blame him. I blamed myself. I was responsible for what had happened to Noah.

'I stood watching him sleep,' he continued, his voice barely audible. 'He must have been dreaming as his eyelids were twitching, and he was opening his mouth, making rooting noises. I assumed he'd be awake soon to feed. I didn't realise that the next time I saw him, I would be trying to resuscitate him. But... It... I would be too late.'

I tried to touch Tom's arm.

He suddenly stood up, leaving my fingers grasping at the air.

I realised then that someone was at the bedroom door.

'Give me a minute,' Tom called out in response to the gentle tapping.

I watched as he swiped his damp cheeks with his hand. He then breathed in deeply before slowly exhaling, steadying himself.

Whoever had knocked either didn't hear Tom or didn't care as the door squeaked open.

I looked over to see someone poke their head around the door. A woman – Blair Worthington.

I winced, feeling violated.

'Tom, are you all right?' she gently questioned, her voice soft and syrupy.

I hated the sound of the seductive purr at the back of her throat when she spoke.

'Blair? What's wrong?' Tom quickly asked.

I felt the embarrassment radiating from him.

'Hey, I'm sorry. I understand you need some alone time, but your mom sent me to look for you. Father Edwards is leaving now. She wanted you to thank him for the—' She stopped mid-sentence, realising I was also in the room.

Her eyes looked past Tom, lingering on me. Her ice-blue eyes stared at me with pity and morbid fascination. I felt my cheeks burn as if she had slapped me. Then she broke away and turned back to Tom as he reached the door.

'Oh gosh, I apologise, I didn't realise,' she gushed at Tom.

She mouthed 'sorry' at him as she gestured with her eyes towards me.

'I'll be down in a minute,' he evenly replied.

She nodded, her hand sympathetically touching his arm for the briefest of moments before turning and leaving.

Shame coursed through me at the realisation that she felt sorry for Tom dealing with me on top of holding it together for his parents and being the gracious host while simultaneously being the grieving father.

I heard the self-important clicking of her heels on the reclaimed oak floor, which Barbara had told me was imported from Italy. I imagined my mother-in-law wouldn't be impressed if Blair left indentations in her expensive flooring.

I watched as Tom hesitated, his hand on the door handle. He then turned around to face me. 'Alice,' he began, 'I need to go. I'll be back later. All right? We need to talk about what's going to happen—'

'No!' I hoarsely cut in. 'I don't want to talk.'

'At some point, we need to have this conversation. Not now, but in the next few days. We need to figure out what we're—'

'I want to go home. I don't want to be here,' I interrupted.

'Alice, be reasonable. We've come here for a new start, and I have my interview at MGH—'

'It's impossible now. Don't you see that?' I questioned, unable to stop myself from cutting him off again. I couldn't believe he was thinking about the interview at Massachusetts General. After what had happened to Noah – to us. How could he even contemplate staying here after all we had lost?

I stared at his stunned expression.

'I want to go home,' I continued. 'I can't stay here. I can't. This is where... where Noah...' My voice faltered as I left it unsaid.

Tom shook his head. 'Marblehead is my home, Alice. I grew up here in this very house. We discussed this before you and I married. You agreed to relocate to the States.'

'That was before, Tom! Before we lost our son! Don't you understand that? Nothing can be the same any more,' I fired back, surprised to hear myself shouting.

Tom simply stared at me. His expression was inscrutable.

'I'm needed downstairs,' he quietly stated. 'We'll talk about this when you're feeling better.'

'There's nothing to talk about,' I answered with finality before turning away from him and staring at the wall. 'And I want my phone back!' I added.

I could feel his hesitation. 'Alice, I don't think looking at your phone right now is a good idea. Maybe wait until you're feeling a bit stronger.'

'Why do you want me to forget Noah? Why?' I cried out.

'I don't. Look, it's not that. It's—' He abruptly stopped.

'It's what?'

I heard him sigh.

'Tom?' I questioned, still unable to bring myself to look at him.

'We'll talk about it later,' he concluded.

'Can we also talk about why you continue sleeping upstairs? I'm not contagious, Tom—' I stopped, suddenly remembering what I had discovered earlier when I ran upstairs to the guest bedroom. 'And Noah's Moses basket? His clothes? Everything of his is gone. How could you do that without asking me? How?'

I waited for a response. Nothing. I wasn't even sure whether he was still there.

I then heard him emit a low sigh before quietly replying: 'I've got to go.'

I desperately wanted Tom to stay, for him to walk over, climb into bed and hold me so tight that I could feel his heart beating. I had never needed him more than I did right now. If Tom left me, then I would be lost to him forever. I physically ached for his tall, muscular body pressed hard against mine, to feel a connection to life, to feel alive again, for all I felt was a cold numbness that was slowly consuming every part of me. Leaving me alone in the black abyss to drown in my grief wasn't the answer. I needed him to reach down to me and pull me back up. To save me from my torturous self. I needed him to love me more than I hated myself.

I heard the objecting creak of the door, followed by the click of it closing. Shocked, I turned around. But he had left.

I wanted desperately to cry, but I couldn't. The tears wouldn't come. I felt cold and somehow detached from my body. I wanted Tom to take me in his powerful arms and hold me. But he was gone. Just like Noah was gone. I had nothing or no one to hold onto to stop myself from descending into a frenzied madness that was ripping me apart from the inside.

Without Tom, I didn't know if I could continue.

But I couldn't ignore the obvious: Tom was pulling back from me. I knew he blamed me for Noah's death. And why shouldn't he? After all, I had done something terrible, so unthinkable all those years ago. I knew what was happening to me was some cruel form of biblical justice – a life for a life.

Oh my God, Alice... What did you do?

I squeezed my eyes shut, trying to stop the whispering accusations inside my head. I was just a kid at the time. I knew no better.

You were thirteen, Alice. You knew exactly what you were doing...

7

'Tom Fitzpatrick! Do you hear me?' she soothingly scolded as her hand tilted his chin up so his eyes met hers.

'Why are you being so nice to me after everything I did to you?' Tom questioned. 'I don't deserve this.'

The vulnerability in his voice threw me.

I waited, holding my breath as he held her gaze. Neither one of them spoke.

They didn't know I was watching them. I had forced myself to get out of bed, follow Tom into the hallway, and plead with him to stay with me. I needed to know he still loved me. But I had no idea I would stumble upon Tom and Blair's clandestine conversation.

Icy fingers trailed down my spine. *What did he do, Alice? Is that why he's never spoken about her to you?*

The thought assaulted me, taking me by surprise.

I watched, transfixed, as Blair raised her hand from Tom's chin to stroke his cheek.

'Because I still care about you, regardless of what happened between us. It breaks my heart to see you like this. To watch you suffering. I just wish there was something I could do for you. For... For your wife...' She faltered as she stared intently up at him as if gauging the effect of her words on him.

I bit down hard on my hand so I didn't give myself away. How she said, 'your wife' made me feel uneasy, as if I were the problem. If I wasn't in the picture, then Tom would be fine, and they would be fine.

What hasn't he shared with you, Alice?

I recalled the conversation between Barbara and Tom as they hovered over me, believing I couldn't hear them because of the lorazepam injection forcibly administered at the hospital the night they took Noah from me. I tried to think back to their exchange, but I hadn't given it much consideration. Then it came back to me, Barbara arguing with Tom that he couldn't pretend that 'she' didn't exist. But it was Tom's reply that struck me: 'I planned on telling Alice at some point. But not now... Not after...'

What was he planning on telling you, Alice? Was it connected to Blair? To whatever happened between them?

I watched with sickening clarity as Blair tenderly cupped his cheek without objection as she held his gaze. I knew there was more to their relationship than an innocent childhood friendship, that much was obvious. But why had he never mentioned her to me?

'It's about what's best for you and your career. Then there's your mom to consider,' Blair said.

Tom jerked his face back from her hand. He then pulled his other hand free from her grip.

'Tom? Please?' Blair said, trying to touch his face.

He stepped back from her. 'What's wrong with Mom?' he asked, his voice barely audible.

She hesitated.

'Blair?' Tom demanded. I could hear the restrained anger simmering beneath the surface in his voice. I knew that he was fiercely protective of his mother.

'She's worried about your dad,' Blair uneasily answered.

'Dad? Why?'

'This is a conversation you should really be having with your mom, Tom. Barbara asked me not to say anything to you.'

'Blair? If you know something you need to tell me,' Tom insisted.

'Tom?' Barbara's voice called out from downstairs. 'Tom? Father Edwards is leaving soon.'

Tom turned around, bent over the spindle stair banister, and called down: 'Sure. Give me one minute, Mom.'

I quickly ducked my head back so he couldn't see me. Trembling, I dropped my hand from my mouth and shakily breathed out. I leaned back against the wall and waited a few moments for them to resume talking. I didn't want to take a chance and look again in case either one of them spotted me.

My eyes rested on the black and white photographs on the wall opposite me. I knew Barbara was a keen photographer, and these images of Tom during different stages of childhood must have been her artwork. They were breathtakingly beautiful as they captured something exquisite and intimate between mother and son, immortalised in perpetuity. I clenched my hands, willing myself not to cry. But looking at the photograph of Tom as a toddler with his huge dark eyes, long, lavish black eyelashes and thick, messy black hair as he stared up into the camera lens caught me off guard, for this was what Noah, who was identical to Tom, would have looked like if only he—

I forced my hand in my mouth to stifle the sob of despair that threatened to give away my presence. My other hand instinctively touched my flat abdomen.

'Blair! You need to tell me!' Tom insisted now.

'I'm sorry to be the one telling you this, but your dad had a TIA a few weeks back,' Blair confided.

The startling news suddenly grounded me. Oh my God... William?

A transient ischaemic attack was otherwise known as a mini-stroke, which temporarily disrupted the blood supply, and crucially oxygen, to a part of the brain.

How could we have not known? I now understood why Barbara had been so intent on Tom settling in Marblehead and securing the position at MGH. But William seemed so fit and healthy. He had recently sold the advertising firm in Boston he had built up over forty years. He now spent his time sailing, playing golf and writing the great American novel he had never had the time to begin before.

'Did he get immediate medical attention?' I heard Tom ask, the concern in his voice palpable.

'Of course,' Blair reassured. 'Hey, Tom, your dad's going to be fine.'

'Christ, Blair! I'm not one of your patients,' he snapped. 'We both know that a TIA greatly increases the risk of having a stroke in the next ninety days.'

'Barbara called me immediately to assess him as soon as he was brought in,' Blair calmly explained, not reacting to Tom's barbed comment. 'She wanted me to be his doctor, but I referred your dad to Jake Howards. You know he's the best we have at MGH. He's in good hands, Tom.'

I heard Tom let out a heavy sigh as he processed what he had been told. 'Were they even going to tell me?' he asked her.

I could hear the hurt in his voice.

'I am sure they were. But then what happened with Noah—' Blair stopped herself.

'And nothing happened the two days following the TIA?'

'I would have told you,' Blair answered.

At that moment, I realised that Blair must be a neurosurgeon at MGH. What were the odds? I suddenly felt pathetic and underqualified. No wonder she looked at me with such pity. I was a failure. It was my fault our son was gone, and Blair knew that. I could see it in her eyes. I was her antithesis in every way possible.

'Why didn't you tell me when it happened? Don't you think I had a right to know? And why now? Today of all days?' Tom questioned.

'You know why. I hadn't seen or heard from you since you...' She faltered.

I held my breath, waiting for her to say what had happened between them. But she didn't.

'Also, there's patient confidentiality,' she continued. 'Anyway, Barbara and William promised they would tell you in person. But I appreciate that they won't want to burden you with the news now. Not only are they grief-stricken, but they're also worried about you. And as for why now, I didn't know when I'd get another opportunity to get you on your own.'

'Christ, Blair, this is... It's just—' Tom cut off.

'I know,' she murmured.

I clenched my hands, digging my nails into my palms, trying not to imagine her comforting him. I resisted the urge to check whether my suspicions were founded, too fearful of what I would see. Also, I had no idea how Tom would react if he caught me creeping around spying on him. He barely could look at me as it was without making matters worse.

I chewed my bottom lip until the comforting sour, metallic taste came, willing one of them to speak, desperate to end the tortured scenes in my mind of them embracing, or worse.

I heard one of them give out a low, heavy sigh.

I waited, hating myself for filling in the silence.

Another sigh followed before Blair spoke: 'You seriously need to consider what to do, Tom. Your wife isn't coping. She needs more than visits from Dr Rosenburg to get through this.'

'What are you suggesting?' asked Tom.

I could hear the wariness in his voice.

'I'm talking about you admitting her someplace for a couple of weeks so they can help her process what's happened. She needs professional help, sooner rather than later. You can't do this alone. You know that. She's... Well, she seems to be getting worse. I hate to say it, but I overheard her before and...' She faltered. 'Well, all I'm saying is she needs more help than you can give her.'

I quickly covered my mouth to stop myself from gasping out loud. What the—

I waited for Tom to respond, to contradict her. He didn't. His silence screamed at me.

'I heard her demanding her phone,' Blair said. 'She hasn't seen those comments, has she?'

'No... That's why I've kept it from her. She isn't strong enough to cope with that,' Tom assured her.

'Good. I was worried that she had. People are sick! Why would they say those things about her?' Blair questioned.

What is she talking about, Alice? Who would be saying things about you and why?

I wondered if she was mistaken. Or perhaps I had misheard her?

'Barbara told me about your wife's mother. What happened to her. It can be hereditary, Tom. You know that, don't you?' she continued.

It felt as if a hornet's nest exploded inside my stomach. I shakily breathed out as I tried to centre myself.

'I know,' Tom quietly replied.

'Then you need to act, before something else happens.'

Oh my God! She wants Tom to put you in some institution... And then what? What will happen to you, Alice? He'll forget about you and move on with his life. With her.

8

'Alice?'

'Go away,' I murmured, wanting to be left alone.

'Come on, you need to get up.'

I groaned as the pain of my cruel reality hit.

Is this how it will be every time? I questioned. The sudden, gut-wrenching realisation that Noah didn't exist any more? In my dreams, he was with me. I could smell him, kiss him, hold him. But here, there was nothing but a loss so intense, it hurt to breathe. All I wanted to do was sleep to forget what was always there, lurking in the shadows of my mind, ready to rip me apart.

'Go away,' I repeated, snarling, desperately wanting to drift off and be with Noah.

'I'm catching a flight back later tonight, Alice,' Oli continued. 'I need to talk to you before I leave.'

I blocked out my brother's words, not wanting to talk to anyone.

'Please, Alice?'

'No!'

'I'm not leaving until you sit up,' he insisted.

'Okay... Okay...' I conceded as I struggled to open my eyes, feeling fuzzy-headed.

'I've some fresh coffee here.'

I watched as he placed it on the coaster on the bedside cabinet.

'What time is it?' I asked, squinting.

I was about to ask him to close the blinds but realised they were already closed, and it was the light from the bedside lamp hurting my eyes.

'It's late afternoon,' Oli answered, sitting beside me.

I pushed my body up with my elbows, forcing myself into a slouched sitting position.

I was surprised I still wore the black dress Barbara had bought me.

'Late afternoon...' I numbly repeated.

I then realised that the house was disconcertingly quiet.

'Have the guests left already?'

'The funeral was yesterday, Alice. You've slept straight through.'

I found myself frowning, not quite grasping what he had said.

'It's Friday,' he added for clarification.

'How? How could I have slept for so long?' I asked. 'That's twenty-four hours straight!'

Oli uneasily shrugged. 'Maybe it was something to do with the sleeping pills.'

I rubbed my eyes as I tried to recall when I had last taken some. I had taken one of the sleeping pills prescribed by the Fitzpatricks' family doctor after—

After what, Alice?

I couldn't remember. Or maybe I didn't want to remember.

Had I taken more than one?

Confused, I shook my head.

'Oh God,' I moaned as the movement elicited an explosion of pain.

'Come on, drink some coffee. It'll help you wake up,' Oli suggested. 'Then you should eat something. Barbara made you a sandwich. It's over there on the tray when you're ready,' he said, gesturing to the table by the windows. 'You had nothing yester—' He abruptly cut off and shifted his attention to the mug of coffee when I shot him a reproachful glare.

How could he possibly imagine I could even think about eating yesterday?

'Black and strong. Just how you like it,' he awkwardly continued.

My tongue was thick and swollen, covered by a furry film. I reached out and picked up the mug, hoping the coffee would wash away the texture and foul taste in my mouth.

'Hey, careful. It's hot,' Oli said. 'Your hand, it's shaking,' he explained.

'Oh,' I uttered in surprise.

I cupped the mug with two hands and lifted the scalding black liquid to my lips, blowing on it before taking a tentative sip.

'Alice, you know we're all worried about you,' Oli began. 'Tom said three temazepam tablets are missing from the blister pack he left here.'

I blew on the coffee again, avoiding Oli's accusatory gaze.

'Please... Alice, listen to me. This is serious. Tom assumed you had taken a sleeping pill yesterday afternoon because of... Well, you know, you weren't coping. So, he wasn't overly concerned about finding you asleep when he checked on you after everyone had left. But when he couldn't wake you this morning...' Oli faltered and shook his head. 'Well, he panicked. He rang Dr Rosenburg, who came by and checked on you to see whether you needed to be admitted to the hospital for observation.'

'Oh, come on, Oli! Don't you think that's overreacting?'

'Tom explained to me that an overdose of temazepam can lead to breathing difficulties, which in turn could lead to—' Oli stopped, unable to follow through.

'Christ!' I hissed under my breath.

He stared at me.

'What? I didn't take an overdose, Oli. I took one or maybe two temazepam tablets to help me sleep. I couldn't cope with the noise from all those people downstairs. I just wanted to block it out. Tom had left the blister pack on the bedside cabinet the night before. Do you really think he would do that if he thought I was at risk of taking my life?'

'Tom said he forgot he'd left them there. That he had been distracted.'

'So why didn't I take all of them if that's what you think?'

'You did,' Oli solemnly answered. 'You took the remaining three.'

'Thirty milligrams of temazepam won't kill me,' I argued. 'Sure, it'll make me sleep, but that's it. Tom knows that. So why would he bother calling Dr Rosenburg? He should have known I hadn't taken enough to hurt myself. I just wanted to sleep through what was happening yesterday.'

'He obviously knew that but just wanted a second opinion. Tom's more shaken up by what happened to—' Uncomfortable, Oli dropped his gaze to his hands.

'Noah?' I questioned, acutely aware of the bitter edge to my voice.

He awkwardly nodded.

'I know you couldn't be bothered to meet your nephew, but at least have the respect to say his name!' As soon as I said the barbed words, I regretted them.

Oli's face flushed.

'I'm sorry. That was uncalled for,' I apologised, knowing we had been here before. Lashing out was a coping mechanism for easing my own guilt. But it was a brief respite before the agony returned tenfold, as I hated myself even more for inflicting my misery on Oli.

He dragged his guilt-filled eyes up to meet mine. 'I know you, Alice,' Oli quietly stated.

I sighed, irritated that he was returning to the stupid tablets.

'Tom had every right to be worried about you.'

'I'm not our mother! All right?'

'You took an overdose,' Oli insisted.

'No, I didn't,' I argued, frowning as I looked up at him over the mug's rim. 'I… I wouldn't do that!'

But I could hear the doubt in my own voice.

Wouldn't you, Alice? You took three 10 mg of temazepam? What were you thinking?

Then I remembered why. Why I wanted to sleep so badly. It wasn't just about Noah. It was…

'Where's Tom?' I suddenly asked.

Oli didn't answer.

'Where is he?' I asked, feeling my stomach knot.

'He's on the phone—'

'Who to?'

Oli dropped his gaze.

I knew it was about me. That much was self-evident from Oli's reaction.

'No…' I croaked, my voice hijacked by terror. 'He wouldn't… You wouldn't… Oli? Tell me you wouldn't let Tom have me committed. I didn't take an overdose. I'm… I'm just struggling. It's understandable. You get that?'

Panic slipped through my veins, turning my blood to ice as I recalled the clandestine conversation I had overheard between Tom, and Blair Worthington.

'I want to go home, Oli. That's all. I don't want to be here any more. It's a constant reminder of what happened,' I hurriedly explained, the words tumbling out of my mouth. 'I... I'll get help when I get back to London. I promise. Just don't leave me here. Please? Take me back to London. I'll do whatever it takes. I'll talk to my GP about antidepressants, and I'll get some grief counselling. Whatever you want—' I faltered at the realisation of how manic I sounded. But I didn't care. All I knew was that I didn't want to be admitted to some hospital in Boston at the mercy of the Fitzpatrick family. 'I don't want to be left here. Don't let Tom take charge of what happens to me... I'm scared, Oli. I'm scared he'll put me somewhere and forget about me.'

'You're being ridiculous, Alice. Tom loves you. He would never do anything to harm you,' Oli assured me.

I shook my head. 'No... That's not true. He knows I want to go home. But he won't listen to me. He wants to stay here because of her.'

'Her?' questioned Oli, confused.

'Blair.'

'Why would he want to stay here because of Blair?'

'Because there's more going on between them!' I heatedly replied.

'Come on, Alice! That's ridiculous—'

'Is it?' I snapped.

Oli heavily exhaled. 'Look, you guys are struggling, but Tom isn't a cheat. He's one of the good guys.'

'What? Like Dad, you mean?' I threw at him. 'Isn't that what I was always led to believe? He was one of the good guys, and Mum was the problem. It was all lies! Christ! And you! You upheld those lies until—'

Oli leapt up.

'No! Wait! I'm sorry. All right? Hear me out,' I begged.

Oli looked at me. There was a familiar cold glint in his green eyes.

At that moment, it felt as if I was staring into her hard, hateful eyes again. I shuddered, trying to dispel the memory of my mother.

'Sit down. Please... Please, Oli?'

It took a moment before he reluctantly sat back down. 'I was the one who looked after you when Mum died. I could have had you put into care, but I didn't. I was eighteen. I put my life on hold to keep you in the family home and ensure you had stability and familiar surroundings to get through your GCSEs and A levels. And for what? For you to bail on me the first chance you got when you were accepted to uni in London. During those five years before you left, I not only physically supported you, but I held you when you cried at night. I endured your tirades and spiteful outbursts because I knew what you'd been through. What we'd both been through. I worked long hours in a crap job to keep the roof over our heads and protect you from—'

'I know, Oli! I know what you sacrificed for me and that you didn't deserve me leaving you behind the way I did. It was selfish, I get that. But if I hadn't got out of that place, it would have killed me.'

Oli didn't reply. But I could see the unresolved pain in his eyes that I had inflicted from walking out of his life without so much as a thank you after all he had given up to protect me.

The only time we had dared to talk about the past had resulted in a terrible argument. Dreadful accusations had been thrown, driving us even further apart.

'I'm sorry I put you through so much crap. I was just...' I shrugged.

'Angry?' Oli questioned.

I nodded. 'It was too much to cope with back then. I was just a kid. You know?'

He took the coffee from me and placed it on the bedside cabinet. He then reached out and took hold of my hands.

'I know. And for what it's worth, I bitterly regret not being around these past few months for you. And Noah.'

'You're here now,' I said. 'And that's what counts.'

'Yeah, I suppose,' he agreed.

'At least until you catch that flight back to Cali later tonight,' I said, smiling, trying to lift the mood.

He shook his head. 'No, I reckon I could do with some time in London helping you before heading back home.'

'Thank you,' I whispered, feeling my eyes start to smart.

I pulled my hands away from his protective grip, willing myself not to cry. Without Oli, I only had Tom and his parents. And I was unsure of them and my place in their perfect nuclear family. It seemed they knew more about me than I did about them. Tom had clearly omitted to tell me something about his past. Why that was, I had no idea. But Barbara was aware of it. She had challenged him about when he was going to tell me.

But tell you what, Alice? What was Tom hiding from you? Who exactly was Blair to him? And what did he do to her?

Then I reminded myself that I had secrets from my past that I had withheld from Tom. I was certain that if he found out about them, he would hate me.

You mean, hate you more than he already does, Alice? It's your fault Noah died, regardless of the medical examiner's findings, and Tom knows that.

Blair's chilling words of warning to Tom about me came back: 'You need to act, before something else happens.'

What did she mean? Had Tom confided in her that he suspected I was responsible for Noah's death?

Oh God, Alice... Have you played into Blair's hands by taking those extra temazepam? Have you given Tom the perfect reason to have you committed?

Why? Why did you do it?

Then it hit me why. Sudden, cruel and forceful, the memory resurfaced.

No... NO...

'Alice? What's wrong? What is it?'

Numb, I stared at Oli as I tried to formulate the words.

'My phone... I found my phone...' I answered.

'You didn't look at any of your social media accounts, did you?'

The anxiety in Oli's voice and Tom's reticence to give me my phone back all made sense.

I understood now why he didn't want me to check my phone. And why, in desperation, I took those temazepam tablets. I would have taken more if I could.

It felt as if the room was closing in on me as I recalled reading those hateful, horrific words on my phone. Words about me...

Oh God, Alice. Someone knows what you did... But how?

9

'What did you see?' Oli questioned.

I could hear the tremor in his voice – fear.

'Alice?' When I didn't reply, he repeated, 'What did you see?'

'Enough,' I numbly answered, recalling the moment I'd read those vile messages.

Once I had looked, I couldn't stop myself, regardless of how painful. I found myself masochistically looking at another comment about me and another. Cruel, vindictive words, all condemning me. I had scrolled down and down the rabbit hole, unable to breathe as I read their accusations, spurring one another on. It seemed that darkness attracted darkness, and the more hateful the comment, the more endorsements it received.

If only I hadn't searched for answers, I wouldn't have found out. Tom was right when he'd said I should wait until I was stronger before looking at my phone. However, I had no suspicion that this hate campaign existed against me. How could I?

'Why would someone post about me?'

'I wish I knew, Alice. Tom doesn't have any idea, nor do Barbara or William,' Oli shared.

I froze, holding my breath at the realisation they had all known about these posts and vitriolic comments. What else were they withholding from me?

I watched as, oblivious to my reaction, Oli checked his Apple watch. I assumed he had received some notification.

'When did you all become aware of it?' I asked, feeling the knot inside my stomach tighten.

Oli looked up, meeting my hurt gaze. He cleared his throat as he seemingly gauged how to answer me.

'When?' I repeated.

'Someone saw the post and told Tom,' Oli replied.

'Who told him?' I demanded.

Oli distractedly rubbed the reddish-blond stubble on his chin.

'Oli?'

'Barbara,' he finally answered.

'Tom's mother?' I cried out, shocked. 'Why would she be checking my X account?'

Oil shrugged. 'I don't know.'

I stared at him. The flush of colour in his cheeks suggested he was lying to me.

'Someone mentioned it to her, maybe,' Oli continued, trying to appease me. 'I'm not sure of the facts. I suspect someone looked you up on social media. Do you know what people are like? They're curious. Tom brings back this British wife that no one knows anything about. You're an enigma to them.'

'An enigma?' I caustically repeated. 'Christ! I lost my baby, Oli! I'm not some object for people to stare at and prod at. I... I... For God's sake! Noah died!'

'I know, Alice. I know,' Oli quietly agreed.

I shook my head, at a loss.

'I imagine someone checked your account for whatever reason and saw that post and told Barbara about it,' Oli suggested.

'Maybe,' I muttered. 'Doesn't matter now who told Barbara. What does matter is finding out who posted it in the first place...' My voice trailed off as I thought about it. 'It must have been someone at the funeral,' I mooted.

Blair Worthington immediately came to mind. Something about the way she talked to Tom and touched him didn't feel right. But did she resent the fact I was married to Tom enough to post something so reprehensible about me?

I tried to think back to who else was there. But the only people I remembered seeing were the Fitzpatricks and Blair. As for the other mourners, I couldn't recall them. No one in particular stood out to me. Not that I had been in the right frame of mind to even notice anyone else.

'Can you think of anyone?' I asked, searching Oli's uneasy green eyes for an answer. I resisted the urge to share my suspicion that Blair could be behind the post.

He shook his head. 'I've tried. But at the time, I was more concerned about you than who was there.'

Feeling exhausted, I sank back against the pillows, questioning why I had opened Pandora's box. If only I had stayed in bed when Tom had left me. I wished I could undo overhearing Tom and Blair. But I had succumbed to the jealousy their hushed talk had elicited in me and had wanted to find something on Blair Worthington to substantiate my suspicions about her and Tom. I had crept around like a criminal in the second-floor guest room, searching through the drawers, hunting for my iPhone. I had wanted to find out everything I could about Blair. Something didn't feel right about her. I had finally found it in Tom's jacket hanging in the wardrobe. I'd pulled out my iPhone charger with its travel adaptor plug from what had briefly been my side of the bed.

The pain I had felt earlier when I'd run up to the guest room and discovered that Noah's Moses basket and other baby paraphernalia had vanished was still as raw when I revisited to retrieve my phone. I assumed that Barbara had packaged everything up. Her actions had undoubtedly come from a place of kindness, but they felt cruel and thoughtless. She hadn't asked my consent or even if there was something of Noah's I wanted to keep with me, such as one of his sleepsuits or his small, soft Peter Rabbit toy that he slept with. Something to hold onto so I knew he had existed.

I had tiptoed back to my room and climbed into bed. My phone was dead, which wasn't surprising, considering I hadn't used it in over two weeks. I had plugged it into the charger and watched as it buzzed to life, oblivious to how that one act would change everything, releasing an unimaginable evil into my world. A pang of pain had torn through me as I'd stared at the screen-saver. It was a headshot of Noah taken the day before we left the UK for the States. I'd choked back the strangulated sob at the back of my throat as I touched his perfect, innocent face, smiling up at me from the screen. Swiping at the tears, I had forced myself to focus and not lose myself to grief again. I had retrieved my phone to find out who Blair Worthington was and whether my hunch that she and my husband had once been more than friends was correct.

But before I could look her up, my phone had started blowing up with hundreds of notifications. There were texts from friends and colleagues who must have heard the news about Noah. I suspected Tom had informed some of them, and word had been passed around. But it wasn't the messages of condolences that surprised me; it was the countless social media notifications from my X account. It didn't make any sense. I stared in disbelief as new notifications continued popping up. I hadn't posted anything since the evening we had arrived at Tom's parents' home. I had uploaded a couple of photos of Noah with Tom and his parents, proudly posting three generations of Fitzpatricks, but that had been on Instagram and Facebook. I rarely posted on X.

I had left my phone on the bedside cabinet that night when I'd gone to bed, only to be awoken shortly afterwards by a fractious and unsettled Noah. At some point, twenty-four hours later, when Tom and I had returned from the hospital without our son, my phone had disappeared. Not that I had been in any state to realise or care. Until yesterday.

Bewilderment had found me clicking on my X account to find out why I had so many notifications, only to fall prey to the trolls waiting for me. Then I understood what Tom had been hiding from me and why. I'd stumbled across people I didn't know demonising me. Every comment I'd read was like a razor cut to my flesh – causing me to bleed over and over again. But one of the comments that stood out cut me to the core. I had felt physically winded, unable to breathe, when I read it, as if someone had plunged a knife between my shoulder blades: one that, no matter how hard I tried, I couldn't reach to pull out.

'Tom and his parents have gone over all the guests, and we can't figure out who it could have been. It just doesn't make sense,' Oli said.

I blinked a couple of times as I focused back on him, dragging myself away from the memories of yesterday's unwitting discovery.

'But it had to be someone who was there,' I insisted.

'I agree, but it was all family and friends. Honestly, Alice, I think someone heard about what happened to Tom and his family and is using it to hurt them.'

I stared at him. 'How? By attacking me?' I incredulously questioned.

'There's no one here, you know,' Oli reasoned. 'To the outside world, the Fitzpatricks have everything, and people get jealous. William made a ridiculous sum of money when he sold his advertising business. But from what he told me, the new CEO let go of employees William had guaranteed would be safe. Times are hard, and some people believe that William didn't give a damn and sold them out. He's had to deal with accusations from ex-employees he once counted as friends. No matter what he says, they still feel he threw them to the wolves to line his pockets.'

'So why focus on me? Why not single out Tom's dad if it's about hurting him?'

Oli didn't have an answer. I knew he was trying his damnedest to allay my fears. But I was the target; no matter how much Oli wanted to deflect the truth, there was no denying that.

'Whoever posted that comment aimed it directly at me. They tagged me, Oli. *ME!* It has nothing to do with William Fitzpatrick.'

I twisted around, feeling under the pillows for my phone. Grabbing it, I pulled it out. I stared at it, fearful of turning it back on.

Oh my God, Alice... What if there are more comments about you?

I realised my hand trembled as I pressed the side button to activate my phone. I watched the white Apple logo against the black screen, terrified of what I would see next.

'Don't, Alice. Please,' Oli said, his eyes filled with concern. 'These people aren't worth the time.'

'I just want to check when the comment was first posted.'

'No. Please? Seriously, Alice, it's not a good idea,' Oli objected.

I raised my eyes to meet Oli's concerned gaze.

'As soon as I've checked, I'll deactivate my account. All right?' I assured him, looking back down at the screen.

I froze as my phone lit up with countless new notifications.

'Alice, you shouldn't be looking at that stuff. People are crazy,' he said as he reached over and tried to take my phone from me.

'NO!' I snapped, protectively shielding it from him. 'I can handle this, Oli! I just need to know when it was posted.'

'Does it matter?' he asked.

I didn't reply; I was too intent on clicking on my X app. I slowly exhaled between gritted teeth, feeling like I had been punched in the guts when I realised it had gone viral.

I focused on the post I was tagged in by someone calling themself 'Eve Truth'. When I looked yesterday, she had no followers, which made me suspect that it was a fake name and account, but now she had over 4,000 people following her. A wave of light-headedness overcame me when I looked at the number of likes her post had elicited. It was nearly 6,000, along with over 100,000 views.

How was that even possible?

But I knew the comment she had posted about me was so offensive that it couldn't help but get traction. My breathing became constricted as I reread the words:

> Too guilt-ridden to stay for Noah's funeral? Why don't you admit that you killed your baby @AliceFitzpatrick? #NurseGuiltyascharged #WatchingYou

I attempted to swallow the hard lump lodged at the back of my throat but failed. I still couldn't believe that someone could post something so heinous about me.

Not only did they know I had left the funeral, they also knew I was a nurse. How?

'When was it posted?' questioned Oli.

I realised I was chewing my bottom lip again when I tasted blood. I looked up at my brother. 'Eleven thirty.'

'That wasn't that long after we left,' Oli stated.

I nodded. I then dropped my eyes to the post and scrolled through the comments.

'You promised you would deactivate your account,' Oli argued.

'I am. But she tagged me again,' I said. 'I want to show you what she's posted.'

'It's not a good idea to look at that stuff,' Oli reasoned.

I ignored him.

'ALICE!'

'Oli, please. You'll understand when you see it,' I insisted.

Finding it, I could feel the blood draining from my face as goosebumps covered my clammy skin. It wasn't just the words that caused the hairs on the back of my neck to stiffen. There was a link to an old newspaper article from the *North Devon Gazette*. Seeing it again elicited a fear so primitive that I had to override the compulsion to throw some clothes in a bag and run. I had no idea where I would go. I just knew I had to disappear, which was the reason I had swallowed back three 10 mg tablets of temazepam last night, desperately wishing there was more in the blister pack.

I shivered as I reread what Eve Truth had posted:

> You can't keep running @AliceFitzpatrick/Alice Morgan. I know what happened when you were 13. It wasn't an accident. Nor is it an accident now. How much did the Fitzpatricks pay to cover up what you did? #Killer-NurseGuiltyascharged

10

Oli leaned into me to see what had caught my attention.

'Christ, Alice! Don't read that. These people are sick in the head!'

'Oli,' I muttered, unable to take my eyes off her comment. 'How does she know our surname? I mean, how did she know about this article in the *North Devon Gazette*?'

He didn't answer me.

'Do you know an Eve Truth?' I asked him.

'No, of course I don't. It will be a fake name, Alice. These trolls use fake accounts. She knows nothing about you. She's just—'

'So how does she know my surname? How?' I snapped, cutting him off. 'And how did she know about the article? How, Oli?'

He shrugged. 'Maybe it's someone who knew you before you married Tom. A colleague or—'

'Why would a colleague accuse me of... of hurting my baby?' I wildly questioned. 'And no one knows about what happened back then. I made a point of never discussing it.'

'But Tom knows,' Oli said.

'Yes, but he wouldn't tell anyone.'

I then recalled the conversation I overheard between him and his mom when they believed I was too heavily sedated to hear their fevered whispers.

Tom told his mom, Alice. Remember? Who else has he told?

'Could it be someone who knew you from Croyde?'

I frowned at Oli. 'Like who? Who would do that to me?'

'Someone from school? Are you still friends with anyone from then?'

'Oli, you know I had no friends! Christ! And I cut ties completely with Croyde when I left for uni.'

Oli was silent.

I had severed him from my life as well back then in a bid to distance myself from what had happened.

'How many followers does she have?' Oli asked.

I was relieved he had changed the subject instead of picking at old scars.

'Thousands. But yesterday, she had no followers. She isn't following anyone either,' I answered.

'It's a fake account, Alice. Just shut yours down.'

'But I could put a statement up saying this is all lies. That... That Noah died of—'

'No! Don't engage. That's what they want. They're sick psychos who are out to hurt you. Nothing you can say will change their opinions. Just close your account down,' Oli instructed.

I shakily nodded. He was right.

I looked back down at the phone screen. I had to deactivate my account and never look at it again. Yet, something compelled me to scroll through the responses to Eve Truth's post. Most were depraved, cruel comments, agreeing with her. But there was one reply that appeared to defend me. I stared in surprise, recognising the respondent's name: @BlairWorthington.

> The poor woman has just lost her baby. It's outrageous to post something so heinous. The Fitzpatricks are a good family who don't deserve such vile aspersions cast about them.

I felt embarrassed that I could have suspected Blair of being behind the post and was relieved I hadn't shared my misgivings with Oli.

I gasped when I read Eve's response.

'Oh my God... Oli?'

'What? Shut the damned account down. Give me your phone!' he demanded.

I shook my head as I looked up at him.

'Read it,' I said, handing my phone to him. 'Tell me I'm not imagining it.'

He took it from me and slowly read the comment from Eve Truth that I had somehow missed:

> @BlairWorthington She is guilty as sin and deserves to die for what she's done. @AliceFitzpatrick you can't hide forever behind the Fitzpatrick family. I know where you are – you can't keep running #KillerNurse-Guiltyascharged

'Oli?' I questioned as I watched his reaction. He didn't seem shocked.

He looked up at me.

'You know about this?' I asked.

He nodded.

'What? And that Blair had responded?'

'Tom said she couldn't help herself. She was so outraged at what had been said about you and the Fitzpatricks.'

Stunned that Oli already knew, I simply stared at him.

'Tom's talking to the police now,' he added.

'The police?' I numbly repeated.

'We have no idea who this person is, Alice. But they know who you are, and I suspect they know you are staying with the Fitzpatricks. It's not really a stretch of the imagination. Marblehead is a small town. It wouldn't be too difficult to track you down.'

'But...' I muttered in shock. 'I... I haven't done anything, Oli. I would never harm Noah. You know that?'

'I know,' he assured me, pulling me into him. 'Hey, Alice, we'll get through this,' he whispered as he held my head against his shoulder.

Oli didn't mention the other accusation. Neither did I. As he held me, I could feel the fear emanating from him. He knew the terrible truth of those words: You can't keep running @AliceFitzpatrick/Alice Morgan. I know what happened when you were 13. It wasn't an accident.

I hadn't clicked on the link to the newspaper article. I knew what it said, as did Oli. We had both read it at the time. The words were imprinted on my mind in perpetuity:

> CROYDE BAY TRAGEDY AS LOCAL WOMAN, 45, DROWNS
>
> Tammy Morgan of Croyde, a competent surfer and swimmer, drowned when taking a late-evening swim alone. It is believed she got caught in one of the prominent rip currents and heavy sandbars. The coroner found high levels of alcohol and sedatives in her blood, which would have impeded the experienced swimmer's reaction to the situation. She leaves behind a son, Oliver Morgan, 18, and a daughter, Alice Morgan, 13...

I had gone looking for something on Blair Worthington, only to discover I was the one being scrutinised and vilified by strangers.

I could hear Blair's sickly sweet voice in my head: 'She hasn't seen those comments, has she... People are sick! Why would they say those things about her?'

Had she believed there to be some truth in them? Had Tom? But then Blair had called this Eve Truth out about her post. Or was she simply making a public show of protecting the Fitzpatricks?

'She knew...' I muttered, more to myself than Oli.

'Who?'

'Blair,' I answered, pulling back from my brother.

'Knew what?' questioned Oli.

'She knew about Eve Truth's comment on my X account not long after it was posted.'

'Barbara no doubt told her,' Oli suggested.

And why not, I thought. I had witnessed how close Blair and Barbara were at the funeral, adding to my insecurity about my strained and awkward relationship with my mother-in-law. That first evening with the Fitzpatricks, I knew I wasn't what they were anticipating, despite the exuberant greeting when I first walked through Arrivals at Boston Logan International Airport. I had no idea what Tom told them about me, but it was evident I didn't match their expectations. Unlike me, Blair Worthington ticked all the boxes: beautiful, confident, well-educated, and a surgeon like their son. Blair and Tom looked perfect together on paper and in person.

'I wanted my phone to look her up,' I confessed.

'Why?' Oli questioned, surprised. 'I've gathered that she's a close family friend.'

'So close that Tom never mentioned her to me,' I stated.

Oli shook his head. 'Alice, this is—'

'I saw them together yesterday afternoon,' I interjected. 'On the first-floor landing by the stairs. They didn't know I could see them. It was the way they were talking. It was intimate, Oli. And she took hold of his hand and... Christ! She even stroked his face.'

'Have you considered that maybe she was comforting him?' suggested Oli. 'Yesterday must have been tough on Tom when we left the funeral. They've been friends since childhood, Alice.'

I let out a low hiss as I restrained myself from saying something I would regret. Oli was always inclined to see the best in people, even when the facts couldn't be disputed.

'He's hiding something,' I insisted.

Oli sighed. 'You're feeling vulnerable just now. It's understandable. Forget about Blair, Alice. She's nothing more than a family friend. Look, eat the sandwich that Barbara made you and then get showered. You'll feel better.'

I bit back the impulse to scream at Oli that my baby had died, so how could he even suggest essential human functions would make me 'feel better'? I didn't want to eat anything and didn't care what I looked like.

'So why did Tom ask her why she was being so nice to him after everything he had done to her?' I questioned.

'Maybe he let their friendship slide because he met you? He'd taken up a six-month residency in London, fell head over heels in love with you and ended up staying in the UK.'

I shook my head. 'No, there's more to it, Oli. Just the way she touched him. Her voice. It was all seductive... and sexual.'

'Seriously, Alice? She's engaged. Like I said, she was no doubt just offering emotional support.'

'She was offering a lot more than emotional support.'

Unconvinced, Oli furrowed his brow.

'She suggested that Tom look after his career and that he should think about having me committed.'

I waited, my eyes never leaving Oli's face.

'What? She actually said that?'

'Not verbatim. She said something along the lines of he should have me admitted someplace for a couple of weeks. Same deal,' I stated.

Oli slowly exhaled. 'And Tom? You didn't talk to him?'

'No. I didn't want them to know that I was there, and also, Barbara had called up for him, and they went downstairs shortly after that.'

I left out the fact that I had heard Blair tell Tom his father had suffered a mini-stroke a few weeks back. I wanted to confirm it with Tom first.

'Listen, Alice, I'm sure there's nothing more to it than she's concerned about you. We all are. You've suffered an unimaginable loss and... Well, understandably, you're struggling. I think returning to the UK and seeking therapy is a good plan.'

'Will you talk to Tom?' I asked. 'Tell him you're planning on coming back with us?'

'Sure. I expect Tom will appreciate the support. It will be tough for the both of you to return home.'

Frowning, I remembered something from the conversation I had overheard.

'What?' asked Oli.

'Blair works at MGH. I think she's a neurosurgeon there.'

Oli didn't look surprised. 'Barbara said in passing about how great it would be for Tom to work with Blair again. She said they had spent a residency together at one of the hospitals in New York.'

'NewYork-Presbyterian Hospital?' I questioned.

'Ahuh, that's the one.'

I breathed out and shook my head.

They worked together at NewYork-Presbyterian Hospital, Alice... And now they'll be together at Massachusetts General Hospital... Was that why Tom wanted this post in Boston so badly? To be with her? And what about you?

Oli stared at me. His face was etched with concern. He had so quickly reverted back into big brother mode. 'Look, I'll update Tom regarding my plans and double-check that Barbara and William don't mind me staying a few more nights until we fly back to London. All right?'

I didn't reply as I clicked on my phone again.

'Alice, don't!' he warned.

I ignored him as I opened my Instagram account this time, pointedly avoiding the hundreds of notifications waiting for me, and started typing Blair Worthington's name in the search bar.

'Oli!' I spluttered as I stared at her account. 'I've found her.'

'Alice! You're being ridiculous. What do you think you'll discover?' he reasoned.

I made sure not to open her Story; otherwise, it would alert her that I was looking at her account. I stared at the countless posts instead. She looked stunning in the photographs, making me conscious of how terrible I must look. I clicked on the photograph of her and her fiancé. For a moment, I was taken aback by how much he looked like Tom, only an older version. But they looked happy together; I couldn't deny that.

Maybe Oli's right and you are being ridiculous, Alice. You're searching for something that doesn't exist. Perhaps it's a way of avoiding what's happening between you and Tom. Your baby died... The two of you have lost the most precious thing you ever shared. How can you possibly continue together after a loss so unimaginable?

'Alice, stop it! Please?' Oli begged as I continued searching through her posts.

Then, something caught me off guard. I froze, not entirely understanding what I was seeing. It was a post from eighteen months back, shortly before Tom came to the UK. It was a photograph of Blair and Tom together.

Oh God...

Shocked, I stared at them, arms wrapped around one another, on some exotic beach, Blair tanned and stunning in a revealing bikini, with Tom, chiselled, bare-chested and muscle-bound in swimming shorts.

'It doesn't mean anything, Alice,' Oli said as he looked at what I was staring at.

I couldn't find the words to argue with him.

I doom-scrolled further down her posts. Then I found it. Irrefutable evidence that I wasn't going insane. I hadn't imagined the intimacy between them. They were more than friends. Much more...

I let out a wounded sound as I clicked on a photograph of them kissing.

'Oli?' I questioned as I looked up at him.

He looked equally shocked.

I looked back down at the stylised image. They looked like the perfect couple attending some fancy black-tie event.

But it was the words beneath the photograph dated three years ago that threw me:

> Tom Fitzpatrick asked me to marry him tonight at NewYork-Presbyterian Hospital's Annual Gala, and of course, I said yes! We're officially engaged! #Proposal #HappyEverAfter!

'Christ, Alice...' muttered Oli. 'Tom never said anything to you?'

I couldn't breathe as I recalled witnessing them talking yesterday afternoon. It all made perfect sense. Tom had asked Blair why she was being so nice to him after everything he had done to her.

I then thought of the conversation between Barbara and Tom: 'I planned on telling Alice at some point. But not now... Not after...'

This was what Tom hadn't shared with me. The fact he had been engaged to Blair. And I doubted he ever would have told me.

Mother's and son's words, so cryptic at the time, came back to me now with such a force I felt winded:

'She didn't need to know. It would have destroyed her. Alice would only blame herself if she knew.'

'Isn't she to blame?'

'No! Of course, she isn't. Now isn't the time, Mom.'

The reality hit me so hard that I struggled to breathe.

'Alice?' questioned Oli.

'I'm to blame...' I confessed, looking up at him.

'What?'

'Barbara said as much. They'd be married now if it wasn't for me.' I swiped at the tears that had started to fall. If I hated myself before, what I felt now was unbearable. 'They didn't tell me because Tom didn't expect to meet me and for us to fall in love.'

'What are you saying? That Tom was engaged to Blair when he started his residency in London?'

I nodded.

'Christ!' muttered Oli.

'I can't stay here. I want to go home,' I whispered, dropping my phone. 'Oli, I need you to book flights ASAP. Please?'

He nodded. 'Sure. But you need to talk to Tom.'

It was Barbara's words to Tom that made me realise: 'She's still a part of our lives, Tom. You can't just pretend she doesn't exist. What you did was—'

What did you do, Tom, I inwardly questioned. *What exactly did you do to Blair Worthington?*

You know, Alice. You just don't want to admit it. He was still engaged to Blair when he seduced you. Then he pretended Blair didn't exist. He ghosted her and married you.

And as for Barbara, you will always be the one she will blame. Why do you think his parents never came to your wedding? Because they hold you accountable for losing the daughter-in-law they so badly wanted – still want.

11

When Oli left me, I showered, changed and was about to follow his advice and go downstairs to talk to Tom when I heard the doorbell. I immediately recognised Blair's voice. Her presence was like a breath of fresh air throughout the stagnant house:

'Mom and Dad just wanted to come and offer their support. You don't mind, do you, Barbara? They're just following behind me. I brought this over for you all. I know how much William and Tom like it.'

'Oh darling, that is so thoughtful of you,' replied Barbara.

'Well, I made a huge pot of fish chowder for Mom and Dad's return as I knew they would be exhausted. As usual, I made too much. Mom's bringing over some fresh bread I just baked as well.'

I found myself despising Blair. She was perfect daughter-in-law material, unlike me.

'Oh Blair, you really are too kind,' Barbara simpered. 'How was their Mediterranean cruise?'

'You'll hear all about it, I'm sure. They loved it. So much so they said that three weeks wasn't long enough. But, of course, they are devastated that they weren't here when you needed them.'

I then heard other voices. I assumed they were Blair's parents. I waited, hardly daring to breathe, until the front door was closed, and they followed

Barbara down the hallway. I slowly exhaled, relieved I wasn't already downstairs. The thought of having to sit through an awkward conversation with the Worthingtons filled me with horror. I knew I couldn't withhold what I had found out about Tom: the man who was not that long ago going to be the Worthingtons' son-in-law. I had fallen in love with an image of himself he had projected. Or had I projected that image onto him? He was perfect – too perfect. For he had led a duplicitous life. There was a crossover between Tom dating me while he was still engaged to Blair: the photos and posts on her social media accounts were a testament to that. Yet, here they were, the Fitzpatricks and the Worthingtons playing happy families as if I didn't exist. And in a way, I didn't, for I was the one no one wanted to mention, hidden away upstairs.

I tiptoed back to the bedroom to wait until the Worthingtons had left before talking to Tom. Not knowing how long the unexpected guests would stay, I changed into pyjamas, climbed into bed and reached for my phone. I then sabotaged what was left of my sanity and my marriage by searching all of Blair's posts on Facebook, TikTok and X, only to find that the Instagram posts weren't fake or some in-joke. Tom and Blair were once engaged. Blair even shared photographs of their booked wedding venue. She had posted a video with her four bridesmaids toasting with champagne-filled flutes, announcing that she had found 'the most perfect wedding dress' to 'marry the most perfect man'. Ironically, it was the same evening that Tom and I had had our first date. I checked and rechecked the date of the post countless times, unable to accept the undeniable evidence.

I should have felt sorry for Blair. But I was struggling to feel any sympathy for her. She was beautiful, brilliant and now engaged to a groundbreaking neurosurgeon, twelve years her senior. And she looked happy in the photographs with him, so much so that I felt jealous of her – of the woman I had unknowingly usurped at the altar.

I recalled Tom explaining to his mom that he hadn't told me about Blair because I would blame myself. Maybe that was true. I might have felt guilty that I was indirectly responsible for someone else's unhappiness. Or was he fearful that I would have left him? But I knew I would never have left Tom over his failure to disclose Blair. He wasn't the only one with a past filled with secrets. My secret was so dark that I had no right to happiness, which was why Noah was gone. I knew he was taken from me as some form of biblical retribution. I thought of the lines from Deuteronomy 19:21: 'Show no mercy. A life must be paid for a life, an eye for an eye...'

It was a quote I knew by heart because of my mother.

I realised that Tom didn't know me, as much as I had no idea about him. We both had withheld secrets from one another.

I scrolled past the photographs Blair had posted to substantiate the claims of them as cute, freckle-nosed kids in matching white shirts, shorts and sneakers playing tennis or screaming together in delight, running through a water sprinkler in the Worthingtons' picture-perfect New England backyard.

I continued further down and was surprised to see a post on the day of our wedding. I felt sick as I stared at what she had typed:

> Words can't express how devastated I am. I have lost everything. My fiancé, my childhood sweetheart, my best friend. My heart has been ripped out. How could you marry someone else on our special day? #Broken

It was followed by a post a month later, coinciding with the day Tom announced we were pregnant. I knew I shouldn't, and I hated myself for doing it, but I read it anyway:

> The person I love not only cheated on me but married another woman shortly after breaking off our engagement and is now having a baby with her #Destroyed

I reread the post, lingering on the word 'love'. I wondered whether it was a typo or if she was still in love with Tom even then, although he had left her for another woman – not only left her but broken off their engagement to date and then marry me. I couldn't imagine the betrayal she must have felt, let alone the heartbreak.

To my horror, there was a gentle knock at the door. Then another, followed by it creaking open and Blair walking in, balancing a tray in one hand like a waitress. I hurriedly hid my phone under the comforter as she approached. I felt my face flush with shame at the knowledge I had literally just been prying into her life, obsessing over her photographs and posts and comparing myself to her. I still couldn't understand why Tom had fallen for me when he'd had someone as physically stunning and professionally exceptional as Blair. No matter how much I teased and pulled at it, I couldn't come up with an answer.

'Hello, Alice, we haven't been formally introduced. I'm Blair Worthington. I grew up across the road from Tom. I'm sure he's told you what an annoying brat I was as a kid. All I can say is every word is true!' She laughed.

I awkwardly stared at her, unsure of how to respond.

The truth was that Tom had failed to mention her existence to me at all or that he had proposed to her, and she'd accepted.

I couldn't help but notice the sparkling brilliant-cut diamond set in a white gold band with six claws. It could have easily cost two years' worth of my NHS salary, if not more.

'Anyhoo, I've brought you some of my speciality fish chowder. Perfect pick-me-up food,' she said encouragingly as she walked over to me.

She carefully placed the tray down on the bed beside me.

'Tom said you were too tired to eat, but I insisted on bringing you a small bowl to tempt you,' she said, looking concerned.

Shocked by her intrusion, I simply gaped at her, unable to find my voice.

'Tom said that he's managed to book a flight back for the three of you tomorrow evening,' she continued, breezily filling in my silence.

I assumed Oli had told Tom I wanted to go home as soon as possible. I hid my surprise at this news. Instead, I pulled the comforter up towards my chest, feeling underdressed in my pyjamas, compared to her classic cream wool dress, which hugged her figure to perfection.

'I wish we'd met under better circumstances, Alice. If there's anything I can do to help, let me know. Tom has my number. Anything,' she added with that same sympathetic smile.

I wanted to scream at her to take her condescending pity and get out. Instead, I nodded and whispered a barely audible, 'Thanks.'

'This is hard on the Fitzpatricks, especially poor Tom, but I can't imagine what it's doing to you,' she continued as she stared at me, her eyes filled with compassion.

Uncomfortable, I broke away from her worried gaze, wishing she would leave me alone.

'Hey, there you are.'

I looked up to see Tom in the doorway. A flicker of unease crossed his face as his eyes looked from Blair to me, betraying the faux-casual tone of his voice. At that moment, I realised he was terrified that Blair had told me about them.

'I see you've brought Alice some of your famous chowder after all, eh?' he lightly mocked.

Blair turned to him, her long, thick blonde hair luxuriously swishing as she did so.

I briefly caught her perfect white, winning smile framed by her full red lips.

'Yes. I'm in surgery tomorrow, so I won't be around when you guys head off. I couldn't let Alice leave without introducing myself or my chowder!'

She then turned her attention back to me.

'I hope you can manage a little bit,' she said before smiling and heading towards Tom's waiting figure.

She reached the door but looked back to me.

'Remember, Alice, if you need anything – and I mean anything – I'm here,' she softly repeated. 'The Fitzpatricks mean everything to me, and now you're a Fitzpatrick, that includes you.'

I stared at her beautiful face and bluest blue eyes as they gazed at me, filled with sympathy.

Tom didn't say a word to me. He simply nodded in my direction before closing the door behind them.

'That was really thoughtful of you,' I heard him say to her outside. But there was an unmistakable strain to his voice.

'I just wish there was more I could do for her. Oh, Tom, she's... Well... I'm worried for her. You're doing the right thing taking her back to London. She needs to get away from here and all that terrible stuff about her online. It just breaks my heart to see what the two of you are going through—'

Her gentle voice, filled with commiseration, faded away, leaving me feeling stunned and violated.

I knew Blair had every right to hate me. I had unwittingly stolen her dreams of the perfect future with 'the perfect man'. I also knew I had no right to hate her. But hate her, I did. What I hated the most was that she didn't hate Tom. Instead, she cared about him, extending her generosity to the woman who had stolen her place as his wife. Her compassion and ability to forgive was beyond anything I could comprehend. I hated her for her pity, for the way she looked at me as the young, grief-stricken waif whose world had fallen apart around her. I would rather she stared at me with the pure animosity she had conveyed upon me at the funeral.

But something had shifted for her. Whether it was the online hate campaign against me or Eve Truth's comment citing I deserved to die, I couldn't say, but she now looked at me with genuine sympathy and concern.

* * *

The three of us – Tom, Oli and me – were at Boston Logan International Airport, about to leave Barbara and William and head through to Departures. I was the only one who wasn't uncomfortably smiling and pretending that everything was normal.

'Alice, I don't know what to say. I wish you weren't going back so soon,' Barbara said before pulling me into her arms.

It was awkward as she held me for a beat too long, making a show for all to witness that she forgave me for the tragic death of her grandson. For that was how it felt. That she believed I had killed Noah. I sensed it whenever she looked at me with those dark eyes filled with distrust. Even now, there was an indisputable coldness in her embrace.

Not that we had talked about it. The Fitzpatricks were experts at sweeping everything under the rug and acting as if their lives were perfect. There had been no mention of William's mini-stroke or his unblemished forty-year business reputation, now destroyed after he'd allegedly sold out his ex-employees and friends in a takeover that made him substantially wealthier at their expense.

Tom had called the police, just as Oli had said about the disturbing comments on my X account. Still, I suspected it had more to do with his parents being rattled by the fact that Eve Truth suggested the Fitzpatricks had paid off the medical examiner. From their concern, I surmised that there was some truth regarding William Fitzpatrick and his disgruntled ex-employees. As Oli had said, Marblehead was a small place where everyone knew everyone's business.

Oli had told me the police advised Tom to take screenshots in case the offender removed the posts and to report the content to X. There had been three posts in which Eve Truth had tagged me, all alarming and one openly threatening. The police had classed it as a criminal offence by 'malicious communications'. They advised not to interact with the posts. At this point, I followed everyone's advice to close my X account, not check my social media, and wait for Tom or Oli to tell me whether Eve Truth posted anything else. But as of yet, nothing new had appeared. Whether the police would successfully trace the true identity of 'Eve Truth' was doubtful, and I wasn't holding out much hope.

Noah was the other subject no one dared bring up in front of me. It was as if he had never existed. I assumed that the Fitzpatricks' way of dealing with challenging issues was to pretend they had never happened, which explained the disappearance of all Noah's baby items from the second-floor guest bedroom.

Before we left the Fitzpatricks' residence for the airport, Oli had given me Noah's Peter Rabbit. He had asked Tom for it, who had dutifully retrieved it from the attic. Barbara and William had stored all of Noah's belongings there until a time when Tom and I 'felt able to decide what to do with them'. If that time ever came. Not that they had disclosed that to me. It had come second-hand from Oli, who had heard it from my husband. Tom and I still weren't talking, in part down to me. I shut him down whenever he came near me, unable to even look at him. I assumed everyone dismissed my icy behaviour towards Tom as a casualty of grief. Only Oli knew the truth behind me freezing Tom out.

* * *

We flew home in separate aisles, a relief for me. I couldn't bear to be near Tom for long. I knew he was dismissing my silence as depression. I was waiting until we were back home, away from his parents' prying ears, to confront him about his undisclosed 'engagement' to his alleged 'childhood friend'.

Why hadn't he told you he was engaged when you met him, Alice? Why would he hide something so significant?

I looked over at him in the window aisle behind me. He had fallen asleep, oblivious to the fact I knew about his duplicity. I was dismayed he had hidden it from me. But I was also secretly pleased he had fallen so head over heels in love with me to break off his engagement with someone as beautiful and perfect as Blair Worthington.

I watched him as he slept. Tom wasn't the only one with a secret. However, mine was so dark, so terrible, that if he discovered it, he would leave me. He was completely unaware of the significance of Eve Truth's accusation.

The question I couldn't fathom an answer to was who was this Eve Truth, and why was she so fixated on proving that my mother's death wasn't an accident?

What does she know about that night, Alice? And how far is she willing to go to prove it?

12

Oli and I sat on the deck, watching the river Thames gently lap against the shore below. I glanced at the tree-lined bank opposite. Tom and I had spent countless weekends across the river wandering around Richmond or walking the Thames path. Recently, we had proudly pushed Noah in his pram or fought over who would get the glory of carrying him in the baby sling. It felt like a foreign land, part of another life, lost to me now.

It was late morning, and we were exhausted from the overnight flight from Boston. Oli hadn't slept on the flight back either, too preoccupied, I assumed, about what support could be arranged for me back in London. We were waiting for Tom, who wanted some time in the house to move all Noah's items into his nursery. He didn't want me to be reminded of him everywhere I looked. For such a tiny person, Noah had taken up so much space.

I hadn't argued with Tom, too fatigued to care any more. I suspected Barbara had suggested her son clear our home of Noah's paraphernalia to ease my grief. But nothing could lessen the all-consuming anguish inside me. Raw and savage, it consumed all my thoughts. However, I appreciated that Tom was terrified that if I walked back into our home and saw everything that belonged to Noah, I would fall apart – again. I would relive losing him. But Tom couldn't know that I relived that moment of reaching for him beside me on the bed, only to find he was cold, over and over again, and there was nothing I could do. I couldn't wake him, no matter how much I tried, pleaded, begged, frantic that he wouldn't respond.

Tom had been shocked and scared by my meltdown in the hospital when Noah was taken from me. He hadn't expected my pain to be so ugly, so loud, so destructive, so vengeful. I knew I was close to losing it again. I could feel myself teetering on the brink of a precipice that would lead me to insanity.

Ironically, finding out about Blair and Tom had given me a brief respite from my grief. But the disappointment and sadness I felt at the knowledge my husband hadn't confided in me about Blair was nothing compared to the profound, unimaginable loss that overshadowed everything. Noah's death took with it a piece of my heart, a part of my soul. I had returned home not the same person I was when I left; a part of me was missing and always would be.

I sipped from my bottle of water as I lifted my sunglasses from my eyes to fully appreciate the sun's rays sparkling on the tranquil surface of the water. But I was blinded and numbed by a grey prism of sorrow. All I could see about me was death. It had stalked me since the night of my mother's drowning, and now it had finally reached out when I had least expected it and taken from me. I should have been more vigilant. I should have known that something would happen to Noah, that his life was in jeopardy because of what I had done all those years ago. I had grown complacent, fooling myself that there would be no reprisal.

A life for a life...

I put my water bottle down, realising my hand was trembling.

I pushed away her accusatory, cold, dead eyes that relentlessly haunted me these days. I hadn't thought about her or what had happened for years. I had succeeded in compartmentalising and locking her and the memory of that night away in the furthest, darkest recesses of my mind. But Noah's death had somehow released her, and she had come back filled with hatred and vengeance.

I didn't want to be here, so close to the water. Or back at this house. But I had nowhere else to go.

'I'm surprised you choose to live here, Alice,' Oli commented as if reading my mind.

I watched as he turned his deep emerald green eyes – my mother's – and looked up at the impressive three-storey property off Hartington Road that overlooked the Thames.

'Don't get me wrong, Chiswick is lovely, and this property is stunning; I just didn't see you living so close to—' He cut off as he turned back to me, seeing my expression.

'Tom wanted to rent it precisely because of the riverside location. I couldn't find a reason to say no,' I flatly answered.

If only I had known the man I loved, the man I married, who fathered my son, was a liar and a cheat, then—

I stopped myself. I was guilty of a crime so shocking that Tom's failure to disclose his relationship with Blair paled into insignificance.

What will happen when Tom finds out? Because he will, Alice. You can't keep running...

It was getting more difficult to block the dark thoughts that seemed to relentlessly attack me now.

'But the water triggers you. With what happened to—' Oli stopped himself.

I sighed. My brother was right, as always, but I didn't want to admit it. When the weather was terrible, I could hear the river violently swelling, threatening to flood and make its way up to the house and take me. The fear could be so overwhelming that I had to resist the compulsion to run.

I had argued with Tom that a riverside property could be dangerous for our expected baby, but he had dismissed my fears as illogical, as it was a short-term lease, and the plan was to relocate to the States. He knew I was a competent swimmer, paddle-boarder and surfer and had grown up learning how to ride the waves in Croyde Bay from conversations with Oli about our childhood. But Tom didn't know that I hadn't been back in open water since that night. I could still recall her grey, lifeless body as her milky, glazed eyes stared straight through me to my soul, for she knew what I had done – to her.

I would sometimes dream of her. Not that I told anyone, not even Oli – especially not Oli. In the darkest hours, I would hear our mother softly calling for me to come to her. Always the same dream; I would climb out of bed to follow in a trance-like state her siren voice, unable to stop myself from walking through the house, down the garden, past the deck with its outdoor furniture, and through the gate leading out onto the private stretch of shore. I would then feel the sudden rush of icy water enveloping my waist as I was pulled into the waves. Then, I would look down to see her reddish-blonde hair spread like bleached seaweed below the surface. Her bulging eyes stared straight up at me as her mouth opened wide in terror as she screamed and screamed as I—

I would wake up from the dream always at that point, drenched in sweat, with my fringe matted to my forehead and my heart pounding so hard, I expected it to rupture with the terror.

I shuddered, recalling those dead, all-knowing eyes.

'Are you cold? Let's go in. I'm sure Tom must have sorted everything by now,' Oli suggested, scraping his chair back and standing up.

But I still wasn't ready to face going inside. The house would feel so empty without Noah. And it would make it all the more real that he wasn't with us any more. Tom had manipulated my grief and temporary breakdown, and somehow, Noah was left behind in Marblehead, separated from me by thousands of miles and the Atlantic Ocean, interned in some foreign land with unknown ancestors. I could never forgive my husband for that: for separating me from my baby.

I stood up, feeling unsteady, and turned to the house, sensing someone was watching us. I looked up to see Tom staring down from our bedroom window. He didn't smile or acknowledge me. At that moment, I felt a chill run down my spine as simultaneously, the hairs on my neck stood up. There was something about the way he was staring at me that made me feel uneasy.

We hadn't talked as we'd disembarked the American Airlines plane. Nor as we'd passed through customs at Heathrow and then collected our bags. I was acutely aware that all I was bringing back of my baby was his Peter Rabbit soft toy, clutched like a talisman in my hand, and if it hadn't been for Oli, I wouldn't have even had that. Oli had been the one who had made small talk to ease the tension between us. But it had only made me feel even more uncomfortable. The cab journey back to Chiswick had been equally awkward. Tom had spent the entire drive home on his phone. There was an unmistakable edge to him. It was like the last place he wanted to be was in the UK with me. I had resisted the urge to ask him who he was messaging, unsure of whether I could cope with the answer. The thought that he couldn't share everything with me had made me doubt him.

I accepted I had pulled back from him, fearing he would start asking questions about Eve Truth's accusations and the newspaper article. I hadn't only lost my baby, it felt as if I had lost my best friend and lover and the future we had so happily envisioned.

13

'What time is it?' I questioned as I felt Tom climb into bed.

I had been lying awake for hours, unable to sleep.

'Late,' he answered.

'Where's Oli?'

'He went to bed about an hour back,' he replied.

I rolled over and looked at him. I had expected him to sleep on the couch. But here he was next to me, lying with his left arm behind his head, staring blankly at the ceiling. I wondered whether it was because Oli was staying with us that he had decided to join me. Not wanting to make Oli doubt him or his behaviour towards me.

'We need to talk,' he uneasily began.

I didn't answer.

We had spent the day avoiding each other. However, I knew he was watching my every move, terrified I would do something stupid. But I had taken the Xanax as prescribed by the Fitzpatricks' family doctor to temper the darkness inside me.

'Alice?'

I didn't respond. I didn't want to talk. I wanted to sleep and forget my life.

'Alice, please. Don't shut me out,' he softly begged.

It was then that I saw the tears trailing down his cheek to his right ear.

'I'm not shutting you out,' I whispered.

We both knew it was a lie.

'I need to tell you something I should have told you when we first met.'

I waited, barely daring to breathe.

'I was engaged to someone...' he began. He sighed heavily. 'Not someone... To Blair.'

I stared at him.

'I... I didn't tell you when we first met. But I should have done. She and I should never have got engaged. I felt pushed into it by my parents, her parents and by Blair herself. We had grown up together, and I had only ever dated her. We were high-school sweethearts. She followed me to the same college and med school. She wanted to be a surgeon and specialise in neurosurgery like me. But... She... She was—' He broke off. 'I hate myself for it, Alice. More than you can ever realise. I... I feel as if what happened with Blair and the way I cut her out of my life is somehow responsible for us losing Noah.'

I was taken aback by this sudden disclosure. Tom was always so rational, so grounded in logic, and to hear him talking about some form of karmic retribution threw me. Although I understood exactly what he was feeling. I knew only too well how a tragic event could change everything you once believed in.

'She... It was happening too fast, and I had no control. No say. And when I broke it off, she—' He abruptly stopped.

I watched his prominent Adam's apple bob as he attempted to swallow.

I shallowly breathed in and held my breath.

I felt my body stiffen. While we were having our first date in London, his fiancée was in New York with her girlfriends buying her wedding dress. I had repeatedly watched the video on her Instagram account as she beamed ecstatically, telling the world she was the happiest bride-to-be alive. I couldn't imagine the humiliation and pain Blair experienced sharing the video, only hours later, to have her future shattered.

Then it hit me. Why hadn't Blair deleted those posts? If Tom had any posts himself of him and Blair, I had never seen them. They no longer existed.

'Why are you telling me this now?' I heard myself ask.

Tom shakily sighed as he turned his head to face me. 'Because I'm scared of losing you, Alice,' he whispered. 'And with Blair... Well, there's stuff I haven't told you about her. I'm scared of what she's capable of...'

I thought of the photographs and videos of Blair and her fiancé. They looked so perfect together, and she seemed so happy. Evidently, she had moved on and accepted that Tom was with me. She had even defended the Fitzpatricks and me against Eve Truth, putting herself out there to be attacked and vilified by strangers.

'What do you mean? She's engaged again, isn't she? She's moved on.'

'I don't know. Maybe. It's just when I realised that she'd gone up to see you, I just—' He broke off.

'She was lovely, Tom,' I assured him. 'If I'm honest, I was surprised she was so nice to me, considering what happened. I don't know if I would have been so gracious if it had been me.'

Tom was silent for a moment.

I watched as he swallowed.

'I... I should have told you when we first met,' he began, his voice barely a whisper. 'It was just—' He faltered, shook his head. 'I love you, Alice. You know that? Right? More than anything. I would do anything for you. I just wish I had told you. I'm so sorry. All I wanted was to protect you and—' He broke off.

I held his gaze. His eyes were filled with desperate sadness. I realised at that moment he believed he had already lost me. Here he was, confiding in me, sharing something that he feared would tear us apart, and it couldn't have been further from the truth. I didn't deserve him.

'Hey,' I said as I reached out and touched his damp face, overwhelmed with love for him. 'I'm still here.'

'Are you?' he asked, searching my eyes.

'Yes,' I gently assured him.

'The longer I left it, the harder it became to tell you. But I was terrified I would lose you. That Blair would come between us. I had planned on telling you when we were with my parents. I suppose I hoped it would be easier doing it back home. But then... Oh God, Alice,' he whispered in a tremulous voice.

I could feel his silent tears running over my hand as I cupped his cheek.

The anger I had felt at him withholding this from me evaporated as relief took over that he had told me first rather than me forcing his hand.

Neither of us spoke as we stared for what felt like an eternity into one another's eyes, trying to find our way back to each other. His arm reached behind me and pulled my body into him. I didn't resist, wanting desperately to be touched by him. Held by him, to have his body pressed against mine. In the darkness, a primitive urge to physically connect took over, dispelling the grief and anger that had separated us as we pulled each other's clothes off so our bodies could fully intertwine in a desperate, frantic need to find one another again.

I forgot Tom's words at that moment. Words that troubled me. For why would he be fearful of Blair?

14

Stirring, I slowly opened my eyes. The bleak, grey dawn was beginning to break the stranglehold of night. I started to panic, not recognising my surroundings. Then it came to me. I wasn't with the Fitzpatricks. I was finally back home. I reached out for Tom, to touch him, have him hold me as pain ripped through me at the knowledge we'd returned without Noah, only to find his side of the bed empty and the sheet cold.

A wave of relief and elation engulfed me, driving away my panic at his absence. I luxuriated in the memory of Tom pulling me into him. He had held me so hard, loving me as if it were the first time our bodies had ever touched. At that moment, I had never felt more needed or desired by him. He had given me the reassurance I so craved that we would be all right. That nothing could come between us. Together, we could survive what had happened to us – to our baby. The loss of Noah had divided us, and internal recriminations kept us apart, yet during the longest, darkest of hours, we had found each other again.

I threw the duvet back and climbed out of bed. I approached the chair and picked up my slate-grey silk kimono robe. Slipping it around my naked body, I headed out into the hallway and padded along the shadowy corridor, avoiding the silent nursery. I made my way down the stairs and to the living room. As I suspected, Tom was asleep on the couch, his long, athletic body partially covered with a throw.

I could feel a pang in my heart as I longingly stared at his tousled black, unruly hair and chiselled jaw covered in dark stubble. I knew then that I loved him more than life itself. After last night, whatever doubts I had about Tom were gone. I needed him, and I knew that he equally needed me.

On the floor next to him lay documents spread out. I assumed they were work-related. His laptop sat open on the coffee table with his phone beside it. An empty coffee mug and a browning apple core lay discarded.

I had drifted off to sleep in his powerful arms, feeling safe and connected to him for the first time since Noah's death. I assumed that Tom, having woken in the early hours and been unable to sleep, had decided to look at his work schedule. I knew he would have to go back at some point. I just hadn't realised it would be so soon.

I bent down and picked up the documents scattered about the floor to place them neatly on the coffee table.

I froze when I read what I was holding. It was a contract for the post at MGH.

I looked at Tom's sleeping face, oblivious to my discovery.

I had no idea he had even attended the interview in Boston, let alone been offered the post.

When was he going to tell you, Alice?

I recalled him studying me yesterday from the bedroom window when Oli and I were out on the deck. Perhaps that was why he looked so pensive. He was wondering how to tell me.

I let the papers drop from my hand and stood up. The pain of betrayal tore through me. The man who had held me and whispered how much he needed me was the man I had fallen so helplessly in love with. I stared at Tom, questioning what last night was about. Why had he confided in me about Blair? And then why make love to me? Or was it simply an act of sex for him? And the words of devotion and adoration I had so desperately craved that he had uttered to me as our bodies intertwined, were they lies? Last night, he'd suggested he was scared of what Blair was capable of, but she had moved on, proving herself to be the better person after he had cheated on and ghosted her. What kind of man could do that to someone he had known most of his life?

I watched his eyelids twitch as he slept, wondering what he was thinking, doubting I would ever know him. My life had changed in the blink of an eye: my baby was gone, and my husband was a stranger. I glanced at his laptop and phone. I remembered his preoccupation with his phone on the cab journey back from Heathrow Airport. I resisted the compulsion to check for proof that he wasn't the man I had fallen in love with, for I already had enough evidence against him. I didn't want to be that kind of wife scrolling through my husband's phone and emails to prove that he was cheating. But I was the one he had been cheating with – I was the other woman.

But what did it matter now? Tom couldn't even bear to lie in bed with me, too obsessed with his plans for the future – ambitions that he didn't even decide to discuss with me. The question that I couldn't stop asking myself was whether I was included in his plans. Did he intend for me to relocate to Boston with him? Or was he going to cut me from his life like he had cut out Blair?

Oh God, Alice...

I could feel the terror coursing through me, making it difficult to breathe. I turned and ran out of the room before Tom sensed I was there.

I went to the large, bespoke kitchen with its Italian marble worktops and grand island. Glancing at the kettle, I considered making some chamomile tea to help me sleep rather than taking more sedatives to numb the relentless, overwhelming pain. I had already lost my baby and knew I couldn't survive losing Tom as well.

I looked over at the French doors that led out to the garden, hearing the water lapping against the shore. I resisted the compulsion to walk barefoot through the grass to the river. Shivering at the treacherous thought going through my head, I broke the spell and turned away.

I walked over to the Belfast sink and poured myself a glass of water. I picked up my bag from the kitchen chair where I had left it and rummaged around for the bottle of Xanax that I had brought back with me from the States. I took the bottle and the water and returned upstairs to the bedroom, averting my eyes from the door with Noah's colourful name on it.

Climbing into bed, I opened the bottle and took two tablets, swallowing them with a mouthful of water. I then picked up Noah's Peter Rabbit from the bedside cabinet. Holding the soft toy to my chest, I pulled the duvet over me and closed my eyes against the world. It was one I no longer recognised or cared to know.

What happened to you, Alice? You had it all until you dared, like Icarus, to reach for more. You should have known that the past would eventually catch up with you. You should have realised that you didn't deserve to be happy. You know what happened to Noah was because of what you did all those years ago. And now, Tom's going to leave you as well. Everyone leaves you eventually. Why haven't you figured that out yet?

15

'Alice? Alice?'

I ignored him. I didn't want to talk.

I felt the mattress sink down on the opposite side of me.

I inwardly sighed.

'Go to work, Tom,' I muttered. 'I'm fine.'

'Alice, someone here wants to talk to you,' Tom gently explained.

I felt my body stiffen, rattled by the intrusion.

'I told you I don't want to see anyone,' I hissed, protectively pulling the duvet around my shoulders.

'You've refused to see anyone since Oli left.'

I didn't respond.

I was devastated when Oli had said he had to return to the States. He had stayed with me for twelve days, allowing Tom to return to work. But he had upcoming competitions to train for and needed to return to California. Oli was on the British surfing team, and the International Surfing Association Championship Series was in May. He was focused on being part of the best European team to qualify for the World Surfing Games. I had taken up five years of his young life when he should have been surfing professionally and not having to work an exhausting and demoralising minimum-wage job to support me. I didn't want a repeat scenario, adding to the guilt that already burdened me. So, I'd promised him I would be fine and that I would engage with the therapy my GP had referred me to and continue to take the prescribed medication for the depression and anxiety I was suffering. But it was all lies to ensure Oli would get his life and hard-fought career back on track. Therapy couldn't dispel the miasma of grief that clung to me. And as far as I could tell, the medication wasn't elevating my depression. If anything, it was getting worse.

'Alice? Did you hear me?'

I could hear the desperation and fear in his voice. No matter how much he had begged and pleaded with me, I wouldn't let him in. But it wasn't just Tom; I refused to speak to Oli, too exhausted to pretend everything was all right.

'I told you I don't want to see anyone,' I muttered through clenched teeth.

I felt embarrassed and humiliated. I didn't want 'our friends' – in reality, Tom's friends – seeing me like this. I didn't have any close friends. Nor did I want any. I had intentionally kept people at a distance; my distrust formed in childhood. When I was at school, I was teased relentlessly and cruelly about my father's sudden disappearance. The old nursery rhyme 'Sticks and stones may break my bones, but words will never hurt me' had always struck me as untrue, as my peers' vicious taunts had cut me to the core. My mother falling apart, overmedicating on prescription tranquilisers and Sauvignon Blanc, had only singled me out further. Seen as a freak, abandoned by my father, and rejected by my mother, I was an easy target. Even my best friend since nursery, Phoebe McDonald, had ostracised me for fear of suffering the same fate by association.

After my mother's death, the name-calling notched up a level. Vicious messages were scrawled all over the toilets and on my locker, accusing me of being a killer. I would find myself shoved, kicked, and my hair pulled by anonymous perpetrators, always with Zara Anderson, the worst bully of them all, laughing at my misery in the background. I would imagine escaping my life and reinventing myself in a city where no one knew me.

Loneliness didn't bother me when I left Oli and Croyde behind for London. I couldn't wait to escape the confines of the tragedy that had defined my childhood and how people saw me: the adults through a prism of pity and my peers through a hatred driven out of boredom and the fact I was different.

In the course of the two weeks since Oli had returned to the States, Tom had arranged for various mutual friends to visit in an attempt to help me with my loss. But I didn't want to see anyone. All I wanted was Noah. I could feel Tom's embarrassment when I refused to get out of bed to see whoever had called in with their condolences, or worse when one of our friends would dare to venture into the bedroom to talk to me, only for me to pretend to be asleep. I hadn't washed or showered since Oli's departure and fought Tom's attempts to get me to do so. Even my physical effort to clean my teeth had become too much.

Since Oli had left, Tom would return from work to find me lying on the nursery floor by Noah's empty cot, clutching his Peter Rabbit to my cheek. I had no idea how long I had lain there or whether I was hungry or cold; all I knew was that my body ached to be close to Noah. I would beg Tom to leave me, but he would always carry me back to bed, heat up some soup and spoon-feed me a few mouthfuls until I refused to take any more.

'Alice,' a woman's voice began. 'I'm Dr Samuels. I'm a consultant psychiatrist.'

The knot in my stomach tightened. I hadn't expected this, nor did I want it.

'Your husband's concerned about you,' she continued, filling my silence.

Go away, I thought as I pulled my knees up, tucking my body into a foetal position.

'I'm not here to hurt you, Alice. I'm here to help,' she soothingly stated.

'I don't want your help,' I muttered.

'What we want and need are two different issues,' she replied.

'I'm fine,' I argued.

'Do you remember what you did last night?'

I stared at the wall ahead. I could sense her watching me.

'No,' I fearfully whispered.

'Tom woke up to find you missing. He searched your home and couldn't find you. He went out looking for you in the garden, and luckily, he was just in time to see you fall into the river from the decking.'

I inwardly gasped. I had no recollection of leaving the house. But I did remember hitting the water and being pulled under. I recalled the relief I finally felt at letting my body go. It had felt like a dream.

'If Tom hadn't dived in and managed to get you out, then—'

She didn't continue.

There was no need. I understood perfectly why she was here.

'Alice, I'm what is called an Approved Mental Health Professional. I'm here with two other AMHPs. They're waiting in the living room. Isla Benfield is a social worker, and Dr Patterson is a psychiatrist.'

I squeezed my eyes shut against her words.

I felt Tom's hand rest on my shoulder but recoiled away from his touch. He had betrayed me.

'The three of us are here to assess your mental health, Alice.'

I didn't respond.

'Tom has explained to me about Noah. I can only imagine how his sudden loss has impacted you. That's why I'm here, to try to help you process your grief.'

'Please, just go away. I'm fine.'

'I will after you've answered some questions. Okay? Could you join my colleagues in the living room, or shall I invite them in here?'

I didn't answer her. All I wanted was for them to leave me alone.

'Alice?' Tom questioned.

'It's fine,' stated Dr Samuels. 'I'll ask them to join us in here.'

* * *

Following questions I refused to answer, the two psychiatrists and social worker left the bedroom to privately confer. I had kept my eyes squeezed shut against them, not wanting to see them or acknowledge what was going on.

Tom tried talking to me to explain why this was happening, but I ignored him.

'Hello, Alice,' Dr Samuels softly greeted when she returned.

I refused to turn to look at her and continued lying on my side with my back to her and Tom.

'We've discussed your current situation, and we are all in agreement that it would be better for you to spend some time in hospital,' she began.

I could feel my body trembling as her words fell around me.

'Your husband has asked if you can go in voluntarily as he's worried about travelling abroad. The Equality Act protects you from discrimination in the UK, but this does not apply when you travel overseas. It would mean you would have to check with the embassy of the country you are planning to visit whether they will ask for details regarding your mental health, and if you have been detained under the Mental Health Act of 1983, they can refuse your entry.'

I shut my eyes, not believing what I was hearing. Why was Tom doing this to me? But then I realised that this was about getting rid of me. He wanted to accept the post at Massachusetts General Hospital. Who knew how long I would be in a secure psychiatric unit? Long enough for Tom to relocate to the States and start a new life. He could tell himself and others that he had done everything possible to help his wife, but she'd had a severe mental health breakdown and never recovered. It was genetic, as her mother had suffered from mental health issues and drowned in suspicious circumstances.

I questioned whether Oli knew anything about this. I doubted he was aware of what Tom had initiated. I knew Oli would never sanction it and would be on the first flight back here if he knew.

'Alice, you need to understand that you will be sectioned if you don't agree to go in voluntarily. This means that you would be placed in a secure psychiatric unit for twenty-eight days, after which you will be assessed again to see whether you can be discharged home. If you go in voluntarily, you will have the right to leave at any time. But I must warn you that if you discharge yourself after a few days, we will have no choice but to section you, under the circumstances.'

I heard myself give out a tremulous sigh.

'Alice? Do you understand what I have just told you?'

'Yes,' I whispered.

'Do you wish to go in voluntarily?'

NO! NO! NO!

I ignored the rage inside me. I knew I would lose my liberty if I didn't go in voluntarily. I needed to be clever and not get emotive. I was going into hospital whether I wanted to or not. Better I do it under my own volition.

'Yes,' I quietly replied.

'Sorry? I didn't hear you.'

'Yes, I wish to be admitted voluntarily.'

I heard Tom breathe out a low sigh of relief.

'That's good, Alice. Well, since your husband wants you admitted to The Woodlands, which is a private psychiatric hospital, there's no need to wait for a bed to become available within the NHS. We can have you admitted today.'

I clutched at Noah's Peter Rabbit. I felt as if I was losing myself, piece by piece. I had completely lost control of my life. It was in Tom's hands and the hands of these strangers who had come into my home and judged me a threat to myself.

And others? Yes, Alice. You know you are a danger to others: the past is a good predictor of future behaviour.

'What about my medication?' I asked.

'You'll continue taking it until I have assessed you. Then I might make some changes to it.'

'And if I'm pregnant?' I whispered.

'Pregnant?' Tom echoed.

'Do you think you're pregnant?' Dr Samuels asked.

'I did a pregnancy test yesterday. I had an unopened one left from when I became pregnant with Noah. It showed a positive reading,' I quietly answered.

I knew that pregnancy tests could give a false negative reading too early in the pregnancy; however, they never gave a false positive. I knew I was pregnant again. I could feel it, and it terrified me. So much so that I had—

I stopped myself, not wanting to acknowledge what I had attempted to do.

'Pregnant…' muttered Tom again. 'Oh, Alice…'

I could hear the disbelief in his voice. We had only made love once, the first night we had returned here. What were the odds? But I knew our chances of pregnancy had exponentially increased because of the cabergoline I had been prescribed to dry up my breast milk.

'Alice,' Tom softly said, touching my shoulder and leaning over me. 'Oh my God… You're pregnant—' His voice cut off, the emotion in his words choking him.

But all I felt was fear. Fear that this baby, too, would be taken from me.

16

I gazed at the well-maintained landscaped grounds of the sprawling eighteenth-century manor, once known as Woodland Manor House, hidden in the beautiful Hertfordshire countryside. I had gleaned that it had originally belonged to the Cornell family, whose intricate and proud crest dominated the building's stonework, original fittings and furnishings and stained-glass windows. A staff member explained that after falling into financial strife and unable to maintain their ancestral home, the Cornells had had no choice but to sell to an American investor in the late nineties. And so it became The Woodlands, with its glossy brochure showcasing its luxurious five-star hotel-style accommodation, absent of the stresses and strains of the modern world. There were no distracting computers, iPads or TV streaming apps here. Clients had to relinquish their phones at check-in and would receive them at check-out – whenever that might be. The premise of such a totalitarian communication blackout was to remove the anxiety caused by modern-day society and its addiction to immediate access to news and social media in an attempt to offer respite and recovery from the maelstrom of afflictions affecting the guests.

I questioned how Tom knew about this place or whether Barbara had had a hand in my stay. The American company also had exclusive private hospitals for those who could afford the tranquillity and peace in Europe and the United States.

Dense woods lined the perimeter, and beyond, high stone walls and an electronic gated entrance secured the property from intruders or errant guests.

'Alice?' a gentle voice interrupted.

I turned away from the garden and the skeletal, huddling trees beyond, hiding us from the outside world, to see a young nurse standing in my bedroom doorway.

'Your husband is here to see you,' the young woman said warmly.

I didn't move from the plush window seat by the large sash window. Instead, I pulled my knees tighter into my chest as I returned my attention to the empty grounds.

'Alice?'

'I don't want to see him,' I replied.

'Dr Samuels has recommended that you see him.'

I chewed my bottom lip as I considered Dr Samuels' request. Tom had travelled here on five occasions to no avail, and I had refused to see him every time. Soon, his visits would surely become less frequent until, eventually, they would fizzle out altogether. He had a new life awaiting him in Boston with his ex-fiancée, Blair Worthington, who also worked there. I didn't need his pity or guilt. I needed him to let me go, for us to pretend the other had never existed. Maybe then I could learn to live with the loss of Noah.

Then I remembered. My hand instinctively touched my flat, but fecund stomach. Dr Samuels had arranged for a blood test when I was first admitted three weeks ago, which substantiated the positive pregnancy test. I imagined that Tom had more invested in me and our relationship than I had formerly anticipated now that I was carrying our child – his child. Not that I wanted to be pregnant. I was too terrified of the prospect of the future and what that held for me. I knew if I couldn't keep Noah safe, then—

'Alice?'

I sighed with irritation.

I didn't want to see anyone.

'You don't have to spend long with him, Alice. Seeing him might help you.'

* * *

I was taken aback to note that Tom looked exhausted. He was clean-shaven, and his clothes were typically immaculate and stylish, but his tired, red-rimmed, bloodshot eyes betrayed him.

'Are you sleeping?' I asked.

'Shouldn't I be asking you that question?' Tom said with a half-hearted laugh.

I watched as he fidgeted with his light blue shirt cuff. He was struggling to look at me. I was surprised. He had always seemed so confident and self-assured. Yet, sat in the Queen Anne chair opposite me, clearly wishing he was anywhere else.

I noted, like me, he hadn't touched his Earl Grey tea or the tray of delicate sandwiches and cakes.

Perhaps it was my silence that made him so uneasy.

He finally brought his eyes up to meet my gaze.

He cleared his throat. 'You're looking better than I anticipated.'

'I wouldn't know. The highly polished sheet metal, a substitute for a glass mirror in my bathroom, doesn't give a clear reflection,' I retorted, unable to hide my anger at him for being here.

'Alice, please… Don't,' he muttered.

I could see the hurt ripple across his dark brown eyes.

'Don't what? Be angry that you put me here? That I was subject to suicide watch for the first five days. Do you know what that entails? Do you?' I demanded.

He didn't answer.

'It's twenty-four-hour surveillance. A nurse was always with me, even when I needed to use the bathroom,' I stated. 'Do you know how humiliating that is?'

Again, he remained silent.

'I suppose you can't tell me when I'm free to go?'

Tom looked uneasy.

'You can leave any time, Alice. You know that,' he quietly answered.

'Can I? So, they won't section me under the Mental Health Act if I walk out of here? Or have you forgotten that part of the deal you made with Dr Samuels? I can't leave under my own volition, and you know that!'

'Dr Samuels reports that you're improving day by day. I can see a difference in you, Alice,' he softly stated, bringing his hurt eyes up to meet mine.

'It's good to know that you're getting such positive daily updates on me,' I caustically replied. 'What else do they report to you?'

'I did what I thought was best—'

'For who? You? You never asked me! You arranged all of this without my knowledge or consent!' I raged as I swung my arm for effect, gesturing around the room.

I watched as he uncomfortably looked around the ground-floor room reserved for visitors. It was my first time here, as aside from my husband, I had no other callers. For all I knew, no one else was aware of my confinement.

I followed Tom's uneasy gaze as he appraised the imposing, stately room with its high ceilings, original ornate ceiling rose and cornice. It was beautiful and presented to impress or perhaps ease loved ones' feelings of guilt. The furnishings, strategically placed around the room, included comfortable sofas adorned with plump cushions and throws, small tables and chairs with chess and checker boards set up ready to play, and high-backed, sumptuous leather armchairs. There was even an impressive bookcase that lined one wall. The open fire added to the luxurious and relaxed ambience. Our table, with exquisite afternoon tea and armchairs, was in front of the imposing sandstone mantle fire surround so we could fully appreciate the burning logs.

The mid-December afternoon was heavily overcast, and the glowing lamps around the room added to the warmth. Yet, it did little to thaw the iciness between us. We were the only ones in here, but I was aware of the surveillance camera in the corner of the room. Someone was watching us – or, to be exact, watching me. The opulent surroundings and tranquillity came at a high price – my freedom.

I hadn't socialised with anyone, preferring to remain in my room. I didn't have the energy to become absorbed in other people's problems, and it was evident that I wasn't the only patient struggling in here. I knew there were various mindfulness classes that guests were encouraged to participate in.

However, no amount of yoga, Pilates, Tai Chi and meditation sessions would help me escape myself. Nor could I escape the grounds monitored by twenty-four-hour surveillance cameras. The place deceptively gave off an air of serenity, but behind locked doors, I knew another reality.

I followed Tom's focus to the French doors onto the grounds.

'Would you rather we took a walk outside? Dr Samuels said we could go for a stroll through the woodland if you would like?' he suggested, looking at me.

I shook my head.

'Can I ask about...' Tom hesitated, unsure.

'The pregnancy?'

He nervously nodded.

'The medication I'm on doesn't affect the—' I broke off, unable to say the word.

'The baby?'

I nodded.

He slowly breathed out.

I could feel the tension radiating from him.

'Alice, I... I've been wanting to talk to you,' Tom began.

'You could have visited me when I was first admitted. But you didn't. Do you know how scared and out of control I felt? I thought you had abandoned me, Tom! You don't get to leave me here, not knowing if I would ever see you again!'

Tom shook his head. 'It's not like that, Alice. If you recall, Dr Samuels advised that there should be no visitors for the first nine days to help you acclimatise and she monitored your medication. I didn't like it, but I had no choice but to accept it. She is your clinician, after all. But I have visited you several times these past two weeks, and you've refused to see me. Until now.'

I snatched my hand off the table as he reached across to touch it.

'I understand you're upset with me,' he sympathised.

'Just tell me why you are here. To tell me you're leaving me? That you accepted the post with MGH?'

Tom sighed. 'No, Alice. We've had this conversation before,' he gently reminded me. 'They offered me the post, but we agreed I wouldn't accept it. That we would wait until you felt well enough to relocate.'

We did? When? When did you agree to that, Alice? You hated it there. So why would you say you would go back – to live no less?

I felt a familiar fear returning. I had no idea what Tom was talking about. But I conceded that I couldn't recall most of the weeks after Noah's death. Whether we did have that conversation, I couldn't say. I doubted Tom would lie to me.

Are you sure about that, Alice? What about Blair Worthington?

I accepted that Tom hadn't lied to me about her. Instead, he had withheld the fact he had been engaged to her when he met me.

'I'm sorry that you're here. But I had no option. I couldn't take care of you, and your behaviour was becoming unpredictable. I was... I was scared, Alice. Scared I'd lose you. That night you fell into the river...' He turned his head away from me, his strong jaw clenched.

Tom had spent the darkest hours before dawn watching over me after he had dived into the water to pull me out. Dr Samuels had reasoned with me that Tom's decision to have me psychiatrically evaluated was out of love and desperation and not because he wanted out of our marriage and out of the UK.

'We've got a second chance, Alice. Do you know how lucky we are? It's... It's nothing less than a miracle,' he softly said.

He turned back to me, his eyes glistening.

I could only stare at him, at the joy and hope that radiated in his beautiful dark brown eyes, which so cruelly reminded me of Noah.

'I love you, Alice. And I would do anything for you,' he continued.

I didn't reply.

'Alice? Please believe me. I love you more than life itself. I'm barely coping without you. I stay at work to avoid going home, knowing you won't be there. I'm just trying to do what's best for you. Don't you think it kills me that you're in here? Christ! I would give anything for you to be able to come home with me.'

I watched as, shakily breathing out, he dropped his head into his hands. It took him a few moments to look up at me again. I was taken aback by the vulnerability and sincerity in his eyes. I hadn't considered how what had happened to me would have affected him; too caught up in my anger and resentment at him for being forced to be here.

'All I want you to do is promise to stay here and get better,' he quietly said. 'You need to get better for... For—' He shook his head. 'I don't want to jinx it. I didn't think that we could ever be happy again after what happened to Noah. But there's a chance that we could be, Alice.'

I pulled my baggy white sweatshirt sleeves over my hands and pressed my nails into my palms as I fought the compulsion to scream at him.

I didn't want to risk having another baby to go through the excruciating pain of losing Noah all over again. I had been so in love, so ecstatically happy for it all to abruptly end. I didn't deserve happiness. I couldn't outrun my past.

My skin broke out in goosebumps as a familiar coldness descended upon me. I could feel the pain resurfacing. Dr Samuels had managed to alter my medication successfully, so the overwhelming sense of hopelessness and finality dissipated. And now Tom had disrupted everything. He had dared to suggest I could be happy. That we could experience joy together again, when I knew that would never be an option for me.

'Oli? Does he know where I am?' I abruptly asked.

Tom nodded. 'Of course. He wanted to fly back, but I told him to focus on his training. That you would be fine. I'm in touch with him nearly every day. He's desperate to talk to you. Do you want me to pass a message to him?'

I couldn't bring myself to talk to Oli. Not yet. I didn't want him to see me like this. I had already disrupted his life enough without him coming to my rescue again.

'Alice?' Tom questioned.

I shook my head.

'If you're sure,' he replied.

'Have you talked to Blair?'

'What?' he questioned, thrown.

'You heard me.'

'No. Why would I have any contact with her?'

I shrugged. 'Maybe because she works at MGH as well.'

'Alice, no... Look, she's not at MGH. She's relocated to New York with her new husband.'

'How do you—'

'Mom updated me,' Tom cut in. 'Blair invited Mom and Dad to the wedding in New York a few weekends back.'

'Oh,' I uttered, remembering the closeness between Barbara and Blair. 'But you said you were scared of her. Of what she was capable of,' I continued.

'Did I?' asked Tom. His brow furrowed as if he was trying to recall saying such a thing. He shrugged it off. 'She's moved on, Alice. I hate myself for what I did to her, but she's finally found happiness.'

'And Eve Truth? Did the police ever find out who was behind the fake account?'

'No,' Tom answered.

I heard myself let out a low, irritated sigh.

I had driven myself to the brink of insanity, desperate to figure out Eve Truth's identity. Before being checked into The Woodlands, I had scoured through Oli's followers and Tom's and Blair's, searching for her. But she didn't exist. However, Zara Anderson – someone I hated and feared from my childhood – did. For some reason, she was following my brother on Instagram. Zara had been the most popular and envied girl in my year at school and bullied me relentlessly. She had twisted the news about my mother's death into something monstrous, starting the rumours with my peers that I might be responsible.

I had cut ties with Croyde when I was eighteen, relieved to escape her malign taunts. When I searched for her on Instagram, I was surprised that her life hadn't turned out as she had envisioned as a teenager. Now she was obsessively liking and commenting on Oli's posts. The timeframe jarred with me as she had started following Oli days after Noah's death. Her heartfelt condolences about him on one of my brother's posts made me question her. She had always hated me, so why act any different now?

I had suggested that Zara Anderson could be Eve Truth to Oli, but he'd discredited the idea as paranoia, claiming the timing of her following him was simply a coincidence. Unlike me, he still had a lot of close friends in Croyde, including Zara's older cousin, Matt, who was a surfer. I hadn't pushed my suspicions any further, out of fear that Zara's deep animosity towards me when we were children could be driven by something she may have witnessed me commit. But why now? Why bring it up again after all these years?

'Look, it's over with, Alice. That account has been shut down. It was just some stranger who got a kick out of hurting people already in a lot of pain,' Tom pointed out in response to my silence.

'People?' I asked, confused.

'You, me, and my parents,' Tom explained. 'We need to focus on the future, not the past. We have this second chance, and I promise you nothing or no one will take this away from us.'

I stared at Tom. I so wanted to believe him, to be able to buy into the 'happy ever after' scenario. But I had done that once before and—

I stopped myself, hearing Dr Samuels' words in my head. If I engaged with the therapy here and continued with the medication, there was a chance that I would be all right.

Maybe you'll be okay, Alice... Tom wants to be with you... Hasn't he proven that? Perhaps you can trust him? Maybe the two of you can have a second chance?

But what about your past? You still haven't told him. Or Dr Samuels...

Tom reached out again and took hold of my hand. 'I can't imagine my life without you. I'll never hide anything from you again, Alice. I promise. Please believe me,' he begged.

'Okay,' I whispered, aware that what I was withholding would make him recoil in horror if he knew the truth.

17

TWO MONTHS LATER

'Dr Sharma feels you aren't fully opening up with him,' Dr Samuels began.

I sighed.

'Alice, please? Humour me,' she quietly said. 'You've made such great strides in these past couple of months. I'm pleased that the course of new medication appears to be helping manage your clinical depression and anxiety disorder. Also, you are now sleeping better. But what does concern me and Dr Sharma is that you have a problem talking about your past—'

I broke away from her penetrating gaze.

'I'm sorry this makes you so uncomfortable. But to move forward, you need to face the trauma that led you to be admitted here,' she suggested quietly.

I didn't respond. I couldn't face talking about my past and was fighting the compulsion to jump up and run out of the room. But I knew that would only extend my stay here at The Woodlands. I wasn't sure I was ready to go home, but I didn't want to continue indefinitely here. As far as Tom was concerned, I was residing in a luxury hotel with spa facilities offering complementary therapies such as yoga. He saw all the glossy brochure benefits and not what was behind the tranquil façade. He never questioned the electronic gates or knew guests were constantly monitored and prohibited from walking freely throughout The Woodlands' premises and its extensive grounds.

However, I couldn't complain about my treatment by the clinicians and staff members. The other guests, as they were referred to, didn't bother me either. But I kept myself to myself, not wanting to socialise or get pulled into someone else's misery or drama. For guests did resist, rebel or openly rage at their imposed confinement. The Woodlands wasn't comparable to the psychiatric hospital in Ken Kesey's harrowing novel, *One Flew Over the Cuckoo's Nest*. But it was still a psychiatric hospital, and I wasn't at liberty to discharge myself without consequences. My primary struggle was with the loss of my freedom and the claustrophobia of being locked in and waiting for staff members to buzz me from one secure area to another. I was also under constant surveillance, and everything I did or said was analysed to the nth degree. I was careful to keep whatever disillusionment I felt to myself. I could ask to walk out at any time, but the threat of being sectioned hung over me like the sword of Damocles. I knew to play the long game and pretend everything was fine when it couldn't be further from the truth.

I had been summoned to Dr Samuels' office for an impromptu session because I had slipped up. My recent therapy appointment with Dr Sharma, a consultant clinical psychologist, hadn't gone too well. I had refused to cooperate with him when he'd tried EMDR (Eye Movement Desensitisation and Reprocessing) therapy, after CBT (Cognitive Behaviour Therapy) had proved futile. My intrusive memories of waking up to the realisation that something was wrong with Noah, assaulting me at any time, were too overwhelming and emotionally distressing for me to challenge them through CBT. So Dr Sharma had decided to deploy EMDR psychotherapy to help me process and move on from my past traumatic experiences involving side-to-side eye movements combined with talk therapy. Effectively, EMDR requires the patient to relive their trauma to process it properly. In an ideal outcome, EMDR leads to a rapid decrease in negative emotions and flashbacks or relived disturbing images of the traumatic events in question. For EMDR to be effective, the patient has to be willing to talk about the trauma that had caused their issues.

And therein lay the rub, as I wasn't willing to talk about the traumas that had caused my breakdown.

I distracted myself from Dr Samuels' suggestion that we discuss what had led to me voluntarily admitting myself to a psychiatric hospital by looking around her office. It was a large, comfortable room on the first floor. I couldn't help but notice the exquisite wallpaper with its intricate design of mint blue peacocks with finely crafted feathers interwoven against a neutral cream backdrop. Her mahogany desk was by the large bay window overlooking the extensive grounds and woodland at the front of the manor. I could feel her eyes discreetly studying me as we sat opposite one another in comfortable armchairs. I glanced at the two empty glasses, the jug of water and the elaborate lilac bouquet in a vase on the low table between us, wishing I was anywhere but here. My mouth was dry, but I didn't trust myself not to spill the water if I poured myself a glass. I could feel the nerves building up in me, fearful that Dr Samuels wouldn't end the session until I had given up something about my childhood.

'Alice?' she prompted.

I reluctantly dragged my head up to meet her dark blue eyes. There was a warmth in them. She wore her sandy blonde hair tied back in a no-nonsense French plait, which hung down her back. Her sophisticated light marl grey woollen dress and knee-high, low-heeled black boots made me feel underdressed in my go-to white jogging bottoms and white hoodie with pale blue old-school Vans. I suspected she was in her mid-forties. I felt young and awkward in comparison. And vulnerable. I pulled the cuffs of my hoodie over my fingertips, wondering what she made of me.

'I know this is unimaginably difficult for you,' she said.

I pressed my nails into my clenched hands, wishing she would stop.

'To find yourself unexpectedly pregnant so soon after the loss of your baby must have come as a shock,' she softly continued.

I blinked back, threatening tears, not wanting her to say any more.

'Alice, we need to talk about this. You need to talk about this,' she said.

I shook my head.

'You need to process what happened to Noah to be able to accept this pregnancy. If you want to continue with the pregnancy, of course?'

I blinked again, startled by her question. I was now three months pregnant, and no one had asked me if it was what I wanted – not Tom, not Dr Sharma, not even Dr Samuels – until now.

'If you want a termination, you have time,' she continued, filling my silence. 'And, of course, Dr Sharma and I will support you if that's what you want.'

'I... I...' I stuttered. I had done nothing but compulsively think about a termination, but I knew I couldn't go through with it. Tom was right: it was a miracle that I was pregnant. But after Noah, I was unsure I could keep this baby safe. Ironically, when I was pregnant with Noah, I couldn't wait to give birth and hold my baby, but now, the thought of holding this new baby filled me with terror.

I shook my head. 'I couldn't do that to Tom.'

'And what about you, Alice? What do you want?'

I shrugged. 'Not to feel this way any more.'

'How do you feel?'

'Scared,' I answered. In truth, I was terrified.

She leaned forward, clasping her hands together. 'Okay. Can you talk about why you are so scared?' she softly asked.

'Because I killed him,' I whispered, swiping at an escaped tear with the cuff of my hoodie.

'Alice, you know that's not true.'

'It is,' I replied. 'If I hadn't fallen asleep breastfeeding him, he might still be alive. If I was a better mother, I would never have fallen asleep with him in bed with me.'

'From what I gather, you were an excellent mother. Noah was exceptionally well looked after. Alice, you did nothing wrong.'

'No. He died because of me. Because I didn't put him back in his Moses basket. Because I—'

'I read the medical examiner's report,' Dr Samuels interrupted.

I understood why she cut me off. I could hear the hysteria building in my voice.

'No matter what you did, you wouldn't have been able to prevent Noah's death.'

'No,' I hollowly whispered. 'It was my fault. If I—'

'Alice, your baby died from sudden infant death syndrome,' Dr Samuels soothingly stated. 'We don't know why it happens, but it does, and there is nothing you could have done differently to change the outcome.'

'That's not true,' I argued.

I had gone over it again and again in my head. If only I hadn't fallen asleep. If only I hadn't left him in the bed next to me. But I had on both counts.

'It is, Alice.'

'He must have overheated lying next to me, or I smothered him without realising,' I argued.

Dr Samuels sighed. 'You know that didn't happen. You've read the findings into Noah's death. Two hundred babies die a year in the UK from SIDS, Alice. All healthy babies with no underlying medical conditions and all well-cared for, but it happens, and sadly, it happened to Noah. To you. It's cruel and unfair, Alice. But you weren't responsible for his death.'

'It happened to him because of something I did wrong,' I asserted. 'I didn't deserve him. I was jet-lagged and exhausted. His screams were driving me to distraction. All I wanted was for him to stop. To stop screaming... To just stop!'

I stared at her in horror, realising what I had confessed. I was surprised that she didn't look shocked. Instead, she looked at me with compassion.

'That's perfectly understandable. You must have been exhausted. But you didn't act on your feelings?' she asked.

'No... No... Of course not. I finally got him to settle and latch on for some milk. And then... Then, when I woke up, he... He was cold—' I stopped.

'Alice, you suffered a terrible tragedy. But that doesn't mean it will happen again. You need to learn to accept that what happened to Noah was arbitrary. You were in no way responsible—'

'I can't have this baby,' I blurted out.

'Why?' Dr Samuels asked.

'If I couldn't keep Noah safe, then how could I—'

'Alice,' gently cut in Dr Samuels. 'You need to accept that you are not responsible for his death,' she repeated with a firmness to her voice.

'I can't. And I can't risk it happening again.'

'Everything you're feeling is understandable. But it won't happen again.'

'You're wrong. I... I'm scared I will do something to hurt this baby. I... I'm terrified I will—' I stopped, pressing my fingernails deeper into my palm.

'Is it because of the positive pregnancy test that you went into the river, Alice?' she suddenly asked.

I stared at her. It was a question she had never asked me. Nor had Dr Sharma.

'I fell,' I corrected her.

I could see from her expression that she didn't believe that what had happened was an accident.

I shuddered as I thought back to the night when I discovered I was pregnant. Had I jumped in? Perhaps. I couldn't remember. All I recalled was being overwhelmed with desperation when I read the word 'PREGNANT' on the pregnancy test stick. No matter how much I tried to hide from the truth, I was accountable for Noah's death. I couldn't outrun my past and the consequences of my actions. I knew I didn't deserve happiness and that it would always be taken away from me if I found it. After all, I was responsible for my mother's death.

18

'Your mother,' Dr Samuels began on a new topic. 'What was your relationship like with her?'

'My mother?' I muttered, confused by the sudden change in conversation.

Dr Samuels nodded.

'I... I... hated her,' I blurted out, surprising myself.

'Why?'

'Because she hated me. She made my life a misery.'

'Do you know why?'

'Yes,' I said in a low voice. 'My father left us when I was ten. He relocated to Australia. He said I would be joining him when he was settled into his new job and had found us a house. At least, that's what he said in the letter he left for me, which I found when I came home from school. But I never heard from him again.'

'Do you know what happened to him?'

'I didn't until recently. Oli and I had a huge falling out over it. He'd withheld it from me for all these years. I idealised my father. And I lived in hope every day of receiving a letter from him or a phone call. But nothing ever arrived, not even a birthday or a Christmas card. It was as if he had died the day he left.'

'I can only imagine the pain and confusion his sudden abandonment caused you,' she said.

I stared at her. I hadn't considered him or what he had done to me – to us. Or how that had destroyed me. It had set me up to distrust everyone who came into my life, always waiting for them to leave me.

Tom? Yes, you know he'll leave you.

He left Blair, his childhood sweetheart and fiancée, for you. Who will he leave you for, Alice? You were, after all, just a whirlwind romance that went tragically wrong.

I slowly breathed in to break the whispers attacking me. But they came at me again.

Maybe he's already found someone while you've been inside this psychiatric hospital. There was a reason Tom chose The Woodlands, which is in the middle of the Hertfordshire countryside and not somewhere in London. Maybe that would be too close to home for him. Think about why his visits have dwindled to once a week, Alice. Why is he always so tired and agitated when you see him? Is it connected to long hours at work and concern over your health and the pregnancy, as he says? Or is it that he's met someone else?

'Alice?' Dr Samuels said, interrupting my spiralling thoughts. 'It's understandable you would have been traumatised by your father's sudden disappearance. You said your mother made your life a misery?'

I gave a half-nod, the burgeoning pain of Tom's anticipated betrayal stirring within me.

'Can you tell me how?'

'She... She couldn't stand to look at me after my father left. I reminded her of him. I have his dark grey eyes and straight dark brown hair, whereas Oli, my brother, took after my mother.'

I reached out and picked up the jug of water. I gestured to Dr Samuels, who shook her head. Despite my trembling hands, I managed to pour myself a glass without spilling any.

'Is it simply that you inherited his physical traits?' Dr Samuels asked after I had taken a few mouthfuls of water.

'No...' I hesitated, wondering how she knew there was more to my mother's rejection of me. 'I... I thought, in some way, she was responsible. I adored my father, and it was mutual. At least, I thought it was—' I stopped and took another sip of water to try to rid myself of the dryness that plagued my mouth.

I looked back up at Dr Samuels.

'You said you believed your mother was in some way responsible for your father leaving?' she questioned.

I nodded. 'I would hear them arguing all the time. It was always her who I would hear screaming at him. At times, she would be so angry, she would throw whatever was close at hand at him. Once it was a crystal vase filled with flowers that he had just bought her.'

'What would your father do when your mother was angry with him?'

'He would leave,' I flatly answered, trying to suppress the disruptive feeling of anxiety it elicited.

'Would he take you and your brother with him?'

I shook my head as I remembered one such occasion. I had begged him not to go, holding his hand and pulling him back. But he had pushed me away and walked out the door, slamming it, leaving me behind crying.

'You blamed your mother for driving your father away?' Dr Samuels asked me.

I focused back on her. I nodded.

'And she blamed you for...?'

'For blaming her. I hated her. My father was the only good part of my childhood. He would bring home these lavish gifts and make us all laugh. He defined happiness and security for me. Then, one day, it was all gone.'

'I imagine you lived in fear of him walking out and never coming back for a long time before it actually happened,' Dr Samuels suggested.

I frowned, surprised by her observation. 'I suppose you're right. I never thought about it like that.'

'You said your brother recently told you why your father left,' she continued.

'Yes. My father had been cheating with a colleague for over a year. That was why my mother would have these terrible arguments with him. She suspected his infidelity but had no evidence. He would tell her it was all in her imagination. Effectively gaslighting her. He and this colleague started a new life together in Australia. They had spent months planning it. She had family out there, so they cut ties with the UK and left.'

'And where is he now?'

I shrugged. 'I don't know, and I don't care.'

'Has he tried to reach out?'

'After my mother's death. But Oli withheld that from me. He didn't think I could cope with the truth. Dad had a new life. He had a baby girl, and his partner was pregnant again with twins.'

'Did he contact your brother to make arrangements to take care of you now your mother had died?'

'No,' I whispered. It hurt to admit it.

'Why did he make contact then?'

I wanted to scream at her to stop, to say I didn't want to think about it. But I didn't. For some reason, I felt compelled to continue: 'Because of the family home,' I admitted, feeling the shame of his abandonment overwhelm me all these years later.

I took another sip of water to steady myself. My clammy skin felt prickly, and I could feel my fringe sticking to the beads of sweat on my forehead.

Dr Samuels sat back and waited.

'It was his now. Our house,' I finally resumed. 'My parents hadn't divorced. My mother had no idea of his whereabouts. I presume someone from the village contacted him about my mother's death, or he saw something on Facebook. I don't know how he knew, but he didn't waste any time claiming what was legally his.'

'Oh, Alice,' Dr Samuels sympathised.

I shook my head, not wanting her pity. 'Oli had to put surfing professionally on hold and take a full-time job for a mortgage to keep our home. Our mother had left some money for us in a will, and Oli used it as a deposit to secure the mortgage. He persuaded my father to sell it to him rather than selling it on the market. I had no idea. I assumed Oli had inherited it from our mother. Maybe if he hadn't kept all of this from me, then our mother wouldn't have died.'

'What do you mean?' Dr Samuels suddenly asked.

I looked at her, realising I had said too much.

'She drowned in the sea, didn't she?' pushed Dr Samuels.

I felt my neck flush and the sudden infusion of blood creeping up to my cheeks.

'What happened that night, Alice?'

I shook my head as I chewed my bottom lip.

'Whatever you say is confidential. It's between us. No one else.'

'What about Tom?' I demanded. For I knew she gave him weekly updates on my progress.

'No, not even Tom,' she assured me.

'You promise?'

'Yes.'

I stared at her, unsure of whether I should say it.

'Alice, if you want to fully recover, you must be honest about your feelings. No matter how abhorrent or frightening they are to you. Once you acknowledge them, you can move on from your past. You clearly had a challenging childhood. Your father walked out on you. And your mother was unable to care for you because of her own complex issues. She, too, rejected you when you needed her most. So it's understandable that your feelings towards your mother and what happened the night she drowned will be complicated, to say the least,' she gently assured me.

'I wanted her dead,' I whispered. 'I'm to blame for her drowning—'

19

A flicker of surprise momentarily crossed Dr Samuels' dark blue eyes at my candid admission. She hadn't expected me to say that. I hadn't expected to say it.

'I had no idea what she was suffering,' I hurriedly garbled to detract from admitting I was responsible for my mother's death.

I looked at Dr Samuels, trying to read her expression. But whatever surprise she had felt at my disclosure had been replaced with her typically calm, reassuring countenance.

She nodded as if what I was saying was perfectly natural. 'Go on, Alice. You're doing well,' she encouraged.

I breathed out, mentally counting to six before continuing: 'All I knew was that she hated me for still loving my father and waiting and wishing that he would send for me to join him—' I faltered, not wanting to continue.

'And she never said anything to challenge your belief he would come back for you? Or even that it wasn't her fault he left?' Dr Samuels asked.

Startled, I looked back up at her. 'No. She never told me the truth. Until... Until the night she drowned,' I whispered. 'That night, she told me something terrible... Something that made me—'

'What happened that night, Alice?'

I dropped my gaze to the glass I was holding. I couldn't bear to see the compassionate expression on Dr Samuels' face. I didn't deserve her pity.

'I hated her for what she said about him,' I defensively continued. 'I screamed at her that I wished she would die. That it was no wonder he left her. That she was a drunk addicted to sedatives. That she was a terrible mother who was better off dead.'

I realised I was gripping the glass of water so tight I was scared it would break. With trembling hands, I placed it down on the table.

'And?' Dr Samuels softly prompted.

I shook my head, not wanting to remember.

'Alice, you need to do this,' she insisted.

I sighed. 'It was late at night, and she was drunk as usual,' I reluctantly continued, 'but this time, she was different. I suppose her anger had more to do with what she had just discovered than because of me. But at the time, I didn't realise that.'

'What had she found out?'

'She told me she found out that he... That he had a new family in Australia. He had a baby daughter. That he didn't want me. That he was never coming back for me. And so, I ran out of the house. Realising what she had said, she ran after me. Oli was at some friend's party and had no idea what was happening. I headed along the cliff path down to the beach. When I saw her following me, I pulled off my pyjamas and ran into the water to escape her. But she followed me, ripping off her clothes, shouting out to me to be careful. That the tide was coming in, and I was dangerously close to the rip current.'

I squeezed my eyes shut as the memory assaulted me. I could feel the white, frothy sea spray hitting my face and the stinging salty air in my nostrils. I sensed the shock of the cold water against my skin as I submerged my body, diving headfirst into an oncoming wave.

'I plunged into the water to get away from her,' I recounted. 'But when I surfaced, she was behind me. She was trying to tell me she was angry with him, not me. But I didn't want to hear it. I hated her so much for what she had said and for what she had become. She had abandoned me. Just like my father. The only difference was, she hadn't physically left.'

Opening my eyes, I shakily breathed out.

Dr Samuels silently waited for me to continue.

'She was a strong swimmer. But she was drunk and had taken diazepam, as well as some barbiturate—'

'She'd also taken a sleeping pill?'

I nodded. 'It came up in the toxicology report. I didn't know, otherwise, I wouldn't have left her alone in the water.'

'Alice, you were still a child. You were only thirteen. You need to remember that,' Dr Samuels pointed out.

'No… No, I should have known…'

I paused as I recalled her grabbing my wrist and pulling me around. I shook my head, not wanting to remember.

'Alice?'

'She was trying to get my attention. To tell me she was sorry for what she had said,' I admitted. 'But the waves were getting higher and more forceful, and I was starting to get scared. She was frightening me, hurting my wrist as she held onto it too tightly. I was scared we would both get thrown under the water by one of the waves. I managed to break free and pushed her away. A wave unbalanced her and I took my chance and somehow managed to swim back to the shore. I didn't want to hear any more of her lies. But it wasn't until recently that I found out she was telling the truth about my father. About his new family and his baby daughter. That's why I fought with Oli. I was mad at him. I was angry that he let me believe my mother was the problem. He thought he was protecting me from the truth about Dad. But the harsh reality was my father didn't want me. It was unfair and spiteful after all Oli had done for me. He cared for me when my father wanted nothing to do with me. And yet, I wanted to wound Oli so badly to try to release the pain I felt at being abandoned. So, I told him how much I hated our mother and how I had wished her dead. Worse, I revealed that I was there that night and did nothing when she—' I faltered, recalling the horror in Oli's eyes when I had thrown that at him. For in that moment, he knew I was responsible for our mother's death.

I tried to swallow. Failed.

Dr Samuels waited.

'I heard her shouting for me when I reached the shore. Frantically yelling my name over and over above the sound of the waves. But I was so furious with her for what she had said, for how she had failed me since my father had left, checking out of life, my life, that I wished she would drown—' I abruptly stopped. 'It was a split-second thought, but it was there all the same. I've repeatedly gone over that scene, wishing I could change it. Thinking if only I hadn't wished she would die. Because I didn't know it would really happen...'

I could feel the tears stinging my eyes as the horror of that night filled my mind. But the medication Dr Samuels had prescribed left me too numb to cry. My eyes would begin smarting with the pre-warning sensation of tears, but that was it; no tears came. It was the odd, dissatisfying feeling that one has with the anticipation of a sneeze for it not to come to fruition.

I was aware of Dr Samuels' silence. But still, I couldn't look her in the eye, too ashamed. The only other person who knew all of this was Oli, and if it hadn't been for Noah's death, I doubted we would ever have reconnected. The truth of that night was too dark and horrific for Oli to accept. But he knew he was culpable. His lies to protect me from our father's deception had only served to fuel my destructive hatred of our mother.

'Is that when she drowned?' Dr Samuels asked.

Thrown off guard by her question, I looked up at her. I nodded. 'All I could hear was the roar of the waves crashing against the shore as the sea suddenly became even more volatile. That's when I realised that I couldn't hear her calling my name any more. I couldn't see her when I turned back,' I continued. 'It was dark and—'

I looked at Dr Samuels, fearful of her reaction. But her eyes were filled with empathy.

'I expected that a wave had taken her out but that she would surface. But she didn't. There was no sign of her. I ran back into the sea, but I couldn't find her. She was... She was gone.'

'Oh Alice, I am so sorry,' Dr Samuels sympathised.

I shook my head. 'It was my fault. I shouldn't have run into the sea to get away from her. I didn't plan for her to follow me. Or for her to—' I faltered, unable to say it.

'Of course, you didn't know, Alice, you were just a child.'

'I was thirteen,' I argued. 'I wasn't a child. I was thirteen. And I... I wished her dead... And that was what happened. I led her to her death. And when she was yelling out for me, I ignored her, not realising she was in trouble. Until it was too late...'

I slowly breathed out as I recalled running back up to the house, calling Oli at his friend's house, and lying to protect myself. Telling him that our mother was drunk and behaving oddly. That she had said something about our father and then headed down to the beach. He'd immediately driven home. It had given me enough time to dry my hair and get changed. We had both searched for her, and Oli had called the coastguard when we found her discarded clothes on the sand. And still, I didn't tell Oli, the coastguard, the police or the paramedics, who came when they found her body, what had happened: that I had lured my mother to her death.

You killed her, Alice...

Eve Truth's X post suddenly came to mind, suggesting that my mother's drowning wasn't an accident. Had someone seen me on the beach with her after all? Had they witnessed her following me into the sea? Her struggling with me and me pushing her away?

'Alice, you're not responsible for your mother's death. It was a tragic, unfortunate accident. But talking about it means you can process the trauma you experienced and hopefully be able to move on,' Dr Samuels gently said, attempting to comfort me.

I knew I was responsible for her drowning, regardless of what Dr Samuels said. And evidently, so did someone else.

20

SIX MONTHS LATER

Exhausted, I lay back against the pillows.

'Alice, he's perfect,' cooed Tom, staring adoringly at the tiny bundle wrapped in a blue wool blanket protectively cradled in his powerful arms.

I weakly smiled at him, trying to pretend I shared his exhilaration.

'Here, you take him,' Tom offered as he sat on the hospital bed next to me. 'You haven't held him yet. I've been selfishly keeping him all to myself.'

I shook my head. 'Later, after I've rested,' I suggested.

'Of course. You must be tired,' Tom conceded.

But there was no mistaking the look of hurt and doubt in his eyes.

He quickly shook off any disquiet as he gazed back down at our son. Tom's dark brown eyes gleamed with such happiness that I found it painful to observe. I strangled back a sob, hating myself for not sharing in his euphoria. This should have been one of the most joyous moments of my life – our lives.

I heard myself moan as I tried to move my body into a more comfortable position.

'Are you in much pain?' Tom asked, his gentle eyes filled with concern as he looked back at me.

'No, the morphine is doing its job,' I answered, glancing at my right hand with the intravenous cannula inserted in it. 'I'm just worn out. It was a long labour and then... the shock of everything.'

My labour had failed to progress as hoped, and then the baby's heartbeat had started to become irregular before suddenly dropping. It was at that point I was rushed to the operating theatre for an emergency caesarean section. The anaesthetist had been able to give me an epidural so I could be awake during the delivery of our second son, Elijah Oliver Fitzpatrick.

'Of course. You've had quite an ordeal,' Tom agreed. He then looked back down at Eli. 'Hey little buddy, you hear that? You've wiped your poor mom out already, and you're not even two hours old,' Tom whispered to him, grinning. 'I can see I'm going to have to keep an eye on you, young man.' Tom glanced at me. 'Eli says to tell you he's sorry for making such a big entrance to the world and causing such a fuss.'

I smiled at Eli, held snugly in his father's arms. He was wearing the oatmeal beanie hat I had crocheted towards the end of my pregnancy.

'I hate to say this, but the nurse did suggest you try to latch Eli on for some milk,' Tom reminded me.

I didn't respond.

'He's opening his mouth and turning his head to the side for milk, Alice,' Tom added.

Tom knew, of course, that this wasn't necessarily hunger. Eli wasn't controlling his movement; it was an innate response. The rooting reflex to locate the breast evidenced that his brain and nervous system were functioning healthily. I accepted it was a ploy to get me to connect with our son. But that was the one thing I didn't want to do. I couldn't do it. I was too terrified of what would happen to him if I dared to breastfeed him. I had been there before with Noah and—

I cut the thought off. Dr Samuels came to mind. She had relentlessly forced me to question these compulsive thoughts. The tormenting, taunting terrors that tore through me, telling me I deserved to die for what I had done to my mother. To Noah. I had failed them both. It was because of me they were both dead. Regardless of how often Dr Samuels challenged that belief, I knew I was a bad person who didn't deserve happiness.

I had remained a resident within The Woodlands for two further months while Dr Samuels worked with me to process the formative events in my childhood that convinced me I was dangerous. That my intrusive thoughts were powerful. Powerful enough to cause harm – or even kill. She had explained that my mother's drowning and Noah's sudden death were cruel, arbitrary events, unconnected to one another. I was finally coming to terms with the fact that even though I had desired my mother would drown, I wasn't guilty of matricide. My mother had tragically died and I was in no way responsible. In as much as I wasn't culpable for Noah's death, despite desperately wishing he would stop crying so I could get some sleep. I had held onto both desires coming true as empirical evidence that I was a bad person. But now, I could accept that both events were beyond my control, a journey that was made possible with the support and guidance of Dr Samuels and the therapy sessions.

I had even managed to come to some form of acceptance over my mother's death and my father's rejection of me. This process of self-acceptance wasn't easy, but I persevered. Nothing was wrong with me, and I wasn't responsible for their actions. I was a child who had lost both parents through no fault of my own.

I was finally discharged from The Woodlands when I was just over five months pregnant, but I continued weekly therapy sessions with Dr Samuels as an outpatient. She had been invaluable in helping me process the childhood events that had led to my obsessive thoughts and informed her diagnosis: obsessive-compulsive disorder or OCD.

'Alice?' Tom questioned, interrupting my ruminations. 'Are you going to try feeding him?'

'No,' I quietly replied.

'No?' repeated Tom, surprised.

'Maybe we should bottle-feed,' I tentatively suggested.

'Why? You breastfed—' Tom stopped himself.

After all, we miraculously now had a beautiful 8 lb baby boy. We had a second chance.

When the doctor had held Eli up for Tom and me to see above the green cloth screen partition covering my abdomen, it felt as if my heart had stopped. He startlingly resembled Noah, with his long, black eyelashes and black hair. The pain of remembering Noah had blighted the moment as I'd stared at our newborn baby. It had taken a few moments to realise there was no fuzzy black peach hair across his cheeks and forehead, his tiny button nose was slightly flatter, and his lips more pronounced than Noah's. However, the real discernible difference was his eyes; they were dark grey, like mine, whereas Noah had the blackest of black eyes when he was born.

'Alice, you can't seriously be thinking of using formula? You know the positives of breastfeeding. Your milk—'

'It's colostrum. The milk won't come in for a few days yet,' I interrupted, failing to hide my irritation.

He looked at me. There was a flicker of concern in his eyes as if evaluating what was really behind my comment. 'Isn't that even more reason to breastfeed him? Your colostrum is nutrient-rich, which will significantly boost Eli's immune system. These next few days are crucial, Alice. And it will help you to—' He faltered, not wanting to say it out loud for fear, I imagined, of making it real.

I could see the desperation in his eyes for me to bond with our new son.

I shook my head, unable to give him the reassurance he needed. 'I don't want to take the risk of breastfeeding while taking so much medication,' I lied.

I had hoped beyond hope that I wouldn't feel this way, that I would be high on oxytocin, seducing me into falling in love with my baby. I questioned whether the emergency C-section had interrupted the oxytocin effect.

But I knew the truth had nothing to do with my oxytocin levels. I didn't want to hold Eli, to have him pressed against my skin, to linger over his beautiful face, taking in every perfect detail, losing myself in his dark grey inquisitive eyes because I was terrified that I would somehow hurt him. That we would lose him the way we lost Noah. And that I would be to blame.

I recalled a saying I had once heard: Past behaviour is a good predictor of future behaviour. If exhausted and burned out, I might wish Eli would stop crying in a moment of desperation. Would history repeat itself?

Maybe, Alice...

I knew I was empowering this intrusive thought, but ultimately, I couldn't risk it happening again.

Tom shot me a confused look. 'Dr Samuels said that you would be able to breastfeed. Remember? You raised your concerns about your medication and whether you would be able to feed Eli, and she assured us that you would be fine. That the medication wouldn't affect him.'

I shook my head. 'I can't take that risk. I just can't.'

'He's hungry, Alice. He needs you,' Tom pleaded.

'No...' I objected.

'Alice, please? You don't need me to tell you that breastfeeding can help protect him from bacterial meningitis, respiratory infections and sudden infant—' Tom abruptly faltered.

A coldness coursed through my body. I stared at him, resisting the compulsion to scream at him that I had breastfed Noah, and he still died.

Tom looked at me, his eyes filled with regret. But it was too late. 'I... I'm sorry,' he said, standing up.

I squeezed my eyes shut, shakily exhaling. I was angry with myself, not Tom. I wanted so badly to be happy. I wanted to hold my baby and feel nothing but joy. Instead, I was blinded by some unspoken, paralysing terror that something bad was going to happen to my new baby, and I would be responsible. I was terrified of the dark thoughts hurtling through my mind. I managed to control them by diminishing their power, as Dr Samuels had taught me. Yet, now they seemed more dominant than ever. I realised that perhaps Eli's birth was the trigger. I hadn't expected him to look so much like Noah.

When I opened my eyes, I saw Tom delicately laying Eli down in the plastic hospital cot by the side of my bed.

'Oh honey,' he whispered, turning to me. 'You're exhausted. I'll go home and bring back those things you requested, yes? You'll feel better once you've rested. I promise. On my way out, I'll ask Eli to be moved to the nursery so you can get some sleep. All right? I'll tell them if he's hungry to give him some formula. I'm sure one bottle won't make any difference.'

'Thank you.'

He leaned over and softly kissed my forehead. 'You were amazing. You know that? I love you, Alice Fitzpatrick. I always will.'

I stared up at him and smiled. 'I love you. And I do love Eli... I'm just... Just tired.'

'I know you do. That goes without saying.'

If Tom could hear the voices in my head, telling me that I was a bad person and that I was responsible for—

'Alice, why are you crying?' Tom suddenly asked as he pulled back from me.

With trembling fingers, I touched my cheek and was surprised to find tears trailing down my face.

I could hear the fear in his voice. After all, Dr Samuels had forewarned us that 'baby blues' or postpartum depression could be a possibility. But that typically occurred a day to four days after birth, not within hours of delivery, unlike postpartum psychosis.

Oh God, Alice...

I dismissed the notion out of hand as ridiculous. It was a rare and extreme form of postpartum depression which could take effect directly after delivery and could continue for months.

'I'm just overwhelmed. Let me sleep, yes? You go home, get showered and eat something. I'll be right as rain by the time you return,' I assured him.

I was quietly hoping that would be the case. That after some sleep, I would feel differently.

'You sure?' he questioned.

I nodded.

Tom then headed to the door of the private room.

He hesitated, as if unsure whether to leave. He turned back, and there was no mistaking the flicker of unease that crossed his eyes as he glanced from me to Eli.

At that moment, I knew he didn't trust me on my own with our newborn baby.

21

FIVE WEEKS LATER

I realised my hands were trembling. I stared at the untouched cup of peppermint tea I was holding. I couldn't quell the unease in the pit of my stomach or shake off the feeling of dread that clung to me most days. I always feared that something terrible was going to happen. I shook my head, trying to refocus.

'Alice?'

'Sorry?' I questioned.

'I think he may be stirring,' Dr Samuels pointed out.

I looked at the baby monitor on the coffee table, surprised to see the blue lights arcing as Eli started to let out tiny, punctuated whimpers.

'Florence will get him,' I assured her.

'The nanny?' she questioned.

I noted the briefest flicker of concern cross her eyes, and then it was gone.

'Yes. She's in her room upstairs and has the other baby monitor, so she'll know he's starting to wake up. It's worked out well having Florence here with Tom having to leave the country so suddenly,' I enthused, aware I was perhaps sounding too upbeat.

I didn't add that my husband didn't want me to be left alone with Eli, not that Tom had said as much, but the insinuation was there. He had wrapped it up as concern for my physical welfare. After all, I was recovering from major abdominal surgery. He had left out any fears he had regarding my mental health, but I knew Tom was worried, which was why he had insisted I kept this session with Dr Samuels. I couldn't legally drive for a further week, so Tom had arranged for Dr Samuels to come to our house in Chiswick.

'Florence is lovely, and she just adores Eli,' I added, realising I sounded defensive.

Eli's grumblings suddenly notched up a level.

'I'm all for you having support, Alice. But remember we talked about this? You need to start looking after him yourself,' Dr Samuels insisted.

Startled by the atypical firmness in her tone, I looked at her, wishing I hadn't listened to Tom and had postponed the appointment. It felt intrusive having her here. I placed my cup down, reached over and switched the volume on the monitor off.

'Alice?' Dr Samuels questioned.

I looked at her. She seemed surprised I had muted Eli's cries.

'I'm fine,' I breezily assured her, wishing she would stop looking at me in a way which suggested I was anything but. 'And I do interact with Eli,' I continued. 'I feed, change, bathe and put him down to sleep. Tom instructed Florence that I wasn't to be disturbed this afternoon. That I had a visitor. She'll get to Eli in a moment.'

I remembered my odd conversation with Florence this morning in the kitchen. When I'd told her about my appointment this afternoon, she had already known as Tom had informed her. I had asked her when she had talked to him, and she awkwardly admitted, after much persistence on my part, that Tom had been calling for an update every evening. When I'd demanded to know more, she became unnerved and flustered, stuttering that it was only about Eli. Not that I believed her. I suspected Tom was asking for daily reports on me.

Why? I wondered.

Because he doesn't trust you, Alice. Not after Noah...

'Are you, Alice? Fine?' Dr Samuels asked.

'Of course I am,' I replied.

'I talked to Tom yesterday evening,' she said.

'You talked to Tom?' I hollowly repeated, feeling sick.

He hadn't told me he had talked to my psychiatrist when we spoke late last night. Nor had he told me he was in the habit of calling our twenty-one-year-old nanny.

'Yes. He's worried about you,' she explained.

'That's guilt talking,' I quickly replied. Perhaps too quickly.

She leaned forward on the couch opposite. I noted her clasping her hands as she waited for an explanation.

I dropped my gaze to the baby monitor. Panic coursed through me when I saw the arc of blue lights still frantically flashing. I stared at it, blankly watching the blinking dots, unable to move.

Why isn't Florence picking him up? Alice, you need to do something before Dr Samuels thinks—

'He's still crying,' Dr Samuels said as if reading my mind.

'I can hear him upstairs,' she explained in response to my confusion.

'Oh,' I muttered. I could hear Eli now. Faint howls of indignation and anger.

I realised he must be hungry after his afternoon nap. Again, my eyes drifted back to the monitor in front of me and the accusatory flashing blue lights as I waited for them to stop – for him to stop.

'Why don't you go up and bring him down? I would love to see him. How old is he now?'

'Five weeks,' I replied, dragging my eyes away from the silenced monitor to meet Dr Samuels' concerned gaze.

She quickly adjusted her composure and warmly beamed at me. 'Gosh, five weeks old. It doesn't seem like five minutes since he was just days old.'

I recalled her unexpected visit to the maternity hospital. Tom had arranged an impromptu psychiatric session. For that was what it was, a mental health assessment. He had been troubled by my resistance to breast-feeding Eli. Or holding him. I had used my C-section wounds to rationalise my inability to pick him up. But as Tom had challenged, that didn't excuse my capacity to hold him in my arms when offered to me. Then there was the fact that I couldn't stop crying.

Dr Samuels had suggested that this was to be anticipated, considering the traumatic circumstances of Eli's birth. I had also confided to her that when I'd first laid eyes on Eli, the resemblance to Noah was so startling it had thrown me. She had then questioned me about my feelings towards Eli and asked if I was worried about whether I was going to hurt him. But I had lied, not wanting to admit to the torturous whispers in my head that told me I was a bad person and because of that, terrible things would happen to those close to me. I didn't want to be separated from Eli. Nor did I want to be admitted back to The Woodlands. All I wanted was some time to adjust.

Dr Samuels had increased my medication, booked me in for a follow-up session a few days later and advised Tom to give me time. She had assured him that not all mothers felt an innate bond or rush of inexplicable love for their newborn. But with time and understanding, it would happen. She'd also suggested the expectation that I breastfeed was exacerbating my anxiety and to respect my wishes on the subject. Consequently, Tom had accepted Dr Samuels' advice and dutifully backed off.

My eyes automatically returned to the baby monitor. I slowly exhaled, seeing that the lights had stopped their frenetic strobing. I looked at Dr Samuels and tried to give her a confident, relaxed smile. 'Florence has picked him up.'

Dr Samuels returned the smile, but it felt forced. 'Okay. Well, maybe I'll get a chance to see him before I leave?'

'Of course,' I replied, knowing that it wasn't Eli she necessarily wanted to check up on. It was how I interacted with him that was her concern.

'How have you found it without Tom this past week?' she asked.

I nodded. 'Fine.'

'Fine?' she questioned.

'Yes,' I replied. 'He said he's hoping to fly back next week.'

'And his father?'

'The stroke hasn't caused as much damage as first suspected,' I explained. 'But, of course, Tom is understandably concerned. His father, William, had a mini-stroke last year, and he was on medication and had taken the right precautions, but—' I shrugged.

I broke away from her and nervously cast my eye around the living room. It was tidy. Too tidy. That was when I realised something that Dr Samuels would have picked up on immediately. Aside from the baby monitor, there was no other evidence of a baby in the house. I had tidied everything away before Dr Samuels had arrived, worried in case she perceived me as not coping. But looking around, I could see that perhaps I had gone too far. I had scrubbed and cleaned the entire house until the early hours, so it would be acceptable, fearful that if my psychiatrist saw something, anything, that she would deem dangerous or neglectful, she would suspect I wasn't coping.

It was clear why she was here: to check up on me because of Tom. He had concerns about my ability to cope. Why else would he have employed a live-in nanny? He had claimed we had agreed to a nanny after his paternity leave ended because of his, at times, long, unsociable hours at work. Not that I could recall the conversation. I had stayed at the private maternity hospital that Tom had insisted we use for two weeks after Eli's birth to help my recovery after the C-section. In truth, it was also to support me as a new mother again. When I'd returned home, I'd discovered he had already employed a live-in nanny without my knowledge or consent. Florence had been his first choice from the handful the agency had suggested would be a perfect match. He insisted that he didn't want to burden me with any more unnecessary stress and had made the unilateral decision for my benefit. I had accepted Florence's unwelcome arrival, too exhausted to fight him. Not only did I have Tom scrutinising my every move, but there was also a nanny, eight years younger than me, living in my house and watching me. Ironically, instead of easing my intrusive thoughts, it exacerbated them. If Tom didn't trust me on my own with our baby, it meant there was some merit in my fears that Eli could come to harm.

I could feel slick moisture rolling down my back as Dr Samuels appraised me.

I had showered, washed my hair and chosen a long, flowing floral printed summer dress, despite it being late September, hoping the bright colours would suggest to her that I was coping. I didn't know why I felt so on edge with her here. It shouldn't have made a difference whether I saw her at her office or in my home. But it did. I could feel her judging everything about me and how I lived, from the choice of expressive artwork on the subtle, mute sage walls to the immaculate cream rugs and the neatly arranged light beige plump cushions on the two matching four-seater sofas. Nothing was out of place. And perhaps that was the problem. It appeared staged. Too staged.

'Alice, are you feeling all right?' Dr Samuels questioned.

Her voice startled me.

'I was asking whether Tom is an only child.'

'Yes,' I hurriedly replied.

'That must be quite a strain for him,' she said.

I stiffly nodded, clasping my hands together on my lap. I didn't want to talk about Tom and his parents. We'd had a blazing row before he'd left. I wondered whether Dr Samuels was aware of it. Tom had made it clear that we would need to relocate back to Marblehead to support his mother, now his father had suffered a stroke. Sooner rather than later. But I had opposed the plan, terrified to take Eli there after what had happened to Noah. I suspected this was the real reason for Tom's insistence that I see Dr Samuels, for her to persuade me that my fears were unfounded and I had to work through them.

I noticed her gaze drop to my lap.

'Your hands look sore again, Alice,' Dr Samuels calmly stated.

I dropped my head and stared at them. I was surprised to see that my skin was so red and inflamed.

'Your OCD, how is it?'

I dragged my gaze up to hers. 'It's... It's under control. I'm washing my hands more because of Eli and ensuring everything is clean. I don't want to pass any germs onto him.'

I could feel an itchy, burning sensation creeping over the raw, broken skin as if on cue. I clenched my hands, digging my nails into my palms, angry that I had slipped up.

I shakily breathed out, feeling out of control.

'Alice, we've discussed your OCD at length and your feelings of over-responsibility for causing harm. Your hands suggest it's becoming dominant again, and you're over-vigilant, fearing your germs will hurt Eli.'

I didn't respond.

'I'm concerned that avoiding interacting with Eli reinforces these thoughts. You have to challenge them.'

I stared at her, wishing she would just stop. That she would leave me alone.

'I know you think you're dangerous and that, ultimately, you're unacceptable at your core. That you're a horrible person and that there is something wrong with you. But you're not,' she gently insisted. 'I think you are a kind and caring person, but I can see you can't hold the thought right now.'

I tried to swallow the lump at the back of my throat. I could feel my skin prickling all over as her kind words stung.

'Alice, I know you're trying to keep Eli safe from you. But I assure you that you would never harm him, regardless of what your thoughts are telling you. The over-importance on thoughts gives them power.'

I dutifully nodded.

'Remember, theory A is that you're a horrible person. The problem is that you worry that you're a bad person. But you're not. The question is, how do we build your belief in theory B that you aren't dangerous? That you're not going to harm anyone? That you are a good person? You're obviously trying to control the worry, exemplified by over washing your hands or not picking up Eli,' she observed.

I wanted to challenge her that she had misconstrued the situation. Tom had orchestrated this scenario so she wouldn't see me with Eli. That he had insisted that Florence keep Eli out of the way.

But why, Alice? It makes no sense. Why would Tom do that?

My attention was suddenly drawn to the white smart speaker. It was on the antique sideboard cabinet behind Dr Samuels. Tom had installed it before I came home from the hospital. I found myself questioning whether Tom was watching our session. A coldness crept up my spine at the fact that he had bought a smart device for our bedroom and the nursery. I had thought them harmless, but not now. It meant he could check up on me whenever he felt the need. I now questioned whether Tom had had other cameras installed while I was still in the maternity hospital with Eli, hidden around the property.

Why would he need to check up on you, Alice?

But I knew why. He didn't believe that Eli was safe with me.

'Do you remember what I told you to repeat?' Dr Samuels softly questioned.

I stared at her blankly.

'Alice? Do you remember?' she again asked me when I didn't reply.

I dragged my attention back to her and nodded.

'Thoughts aren't facts,' I whispered, wishing so dearly I could believe that.

But it was lies. All of it.

My thoughts were telling me that Tom didn't trust me. He suspected that I was dangerous and that I couldn't be left on my own with our baby. Why else would he have asked Dr Samuels to come to our home? And why employ a live-in nanny who, to all intents and purposes, had taken over my role? My thoughts didn't lie. I had the empirical evidence to prove I wasn't paranoid or insane.

Why are you trying to make me think I'm too dangerous to be on my own with our son, Tom? I have worked so hard to get better and to be able to accept the past. Crucially, what are you saying to our nanny and my psychiatrist about me? Are you sowing seeds of doubt in their minds about me, Tom? And if so, what are you planning? Especially now I've opposed your proposal for us to return to Marblehead to live.

22

TWO WEEKS LATER

'How's Tom doing?'

I considered Oli's question as I anxiously stared out of the guest bedroom window overlooking the front of the property. Florence had taken Eli out in his pram for fresh air. But that had been a couple of hours ago.

I swapped my mobile phone to my other ear. 'It's hard to say. You know how Tom hides his feelings,' I answered.

'How long has he been back for?'

'Over a week. He went to work the same day he returned,' I stated. 'I've hardly seen him, Oli. If I was paranoid, I'd say he was avoiding me.'

'I'm sure that's not the case. Tom will have a ridiculous amount of work to catch up on,' he suggested.

Relief coursed through me when I saw Florence finally returning with Eli. I suspiciously narrowed my eyes as a woman approached her. If she was a neighbour, I didn't recognise her. Then again, I had kept myself to myself after returning from the States last year. I didn't want to have to explain to anyone what had happened to my baby or the significant period I had spent in hospital in Hertfordshire. It now struck me why Tom had insisted The Woodlands would be the best place for my recovery, perhaps because it was far enough away from London and our neighbours and friends for him to keep my mental health breakdown discreet.

'You've got to agree that Tom's had a lot of time off work. It's not a surprise he's having to put the hours in now,' continued Oli when I didn't answer him.

'Mm...' I muttered, not feeling reassured. 'I'm just... Just lonely, I suppose,' I admitted. I didn't add that I felt as if I had no purpose. That neither my baby nor my husband needed me. Now that Florence lived with us, I felt like a stranger in my home, and I found myself hiding in my bedroom more and more. More so with Tom now working all hours to catch up after his compassionate leave. Or was it that he was tying things up before relocating back to the States? I couldn't ignore the feeling that he was acting oddly around me, as if hiding something. I would try talking when he got back from the hospital, desperate for reassurance that he was okay – we were okay – but he would make some excuse about needing to make calls or catching up on patient files and retreat to the study.

'You know Eli would love to see his favourite uncle.'

'Only uncle,' pointed out Oli, laughing.

'I know, but even if he had a hundred uncles, you'd still be his favourite,' I countered before adding: 'And I could do with having you around for a bit if I'm honest.'

'Alice, you know if I could, I would come and stay. But I've got things to tie up back home before the winter season kicks off.'

'Oh,' I quietly said, unable to disguise my disappointment.

Neither of us had ever revisited our huge blow-up when I was five months pregnant with Noah. We both had said terrible things and revealed cruel truths that could never be untold. But the loss of Noah had reunited us, and the arrival of Eli had given us a second chance at being a family. Oli had flown over from California as soon as he'd heard the news that I had gone into labour. He had arrived the morning following Eli's birth, armed with the most elaborate and beautiful bouquet and a giant plush Winnie the Pooh with blue metallic coloured balloons attached to it for his baby nephew. He had stayed for ten days at our home, visiting me every day in the maternity hospital before flying back. I had relished the time with him and had adored watching him hold and talk to Eli. But Oli was also there for me and understood my struggles after losing Noah. Perhaps better than Tom as we still hadn't talked about what had happened to our baby – to us as a couple. Not really. The unexpected pregnancy and my mental health issues took precedence, and then, before we knew it, Eli arrived. I had Dr Samuels to help process what had happened, but I had no idea who Tom talked to – if anyone.

'Home as in Croyde Bay?' I questioned.

Oli still owned the property we grew up in, unable to cut ties with the place despite residing most of the year at his beach home in La Jolla, San Diego.

'Yes, Croyde,' he uncomfortably answered. 'If I could make time, I would, but my schedule's really rigid, Alice. Sorry.'

Even speaking the name of my childhood village triggered me. I thought back to the post on X that had suggested there was more to my mother's death than an accidental drowning. I still had no idea who Eve Truth was and whether she was someone from my childhood who had seen me on Croyde Beach that fateful night. I hadn't reopened my account after being trolled. Tom had persuaded me it was better that way. He had reasoned that if I reactivated it, this Eve Truth would target me again. Neither the police nor X had ever traced their real identity, and I realised after all this time they never would.

And if it was Zara Anderson, she had gone quiet. She rarely liked or commented on Oli's Instagram account now. So whether she had simply seized an opportunity to bully me again using Noah's tragic death to hurt me anonymously via social media, an adult version of the school playground, I couldn't conclusively say.

I shivered, feeling a sudden coolness touch the back of my neck as the woman talking to Florence turned and looked up at the window, catching sight of me. I quickly stepped backwards, not wanting to be caught spying on my nanny. Curious, I peeked out from behind the curtains at her. I realised the woman, whose face I couldn't see because of her sunglasses, was heavily pregnant. I watched Florence chatting, with such ease, to the long, dark-haired woman who now had her back to me. Florence then lifted Eli out from his elegant Silver Cross Balmoral pram. A pang of envy cut through me as I watched her protectively holding him. It was clear that she really cared for Eli. Ironically, I should have felt reassured by this fact, but instead, it filled me with unease.

Again, the feeling that I was redundant in my baby's life struck me. Every time I went to do something for Eli, Florence was always one step ahead of me. It was as if she didn't want me around him. She was always so insistent that it was her job to look after him. I was relegated to sterilising his bottles or laundering his baby clothes. Whenever I challenged her, she would hover in the background, watching me as if fearful I would do something wrong. Her scrutiny made me so uncomfortable and paranoid that I found myself stepping back. Also, my insistence, encouraged by Dr Samuels, that she let me do more with my son had caused friction between Tom and me. Florence had privately complained to him when he'd returned that she felt I didn't trust her and didn't want her around. I had argued with Tom that the converse was true, but he had backed her, telling me that he paid Florence to look after Eli so I could relax and focus on recovering. When I'd suggested that I had recovered and was perfectly fit and able to look after Eli by myself, Tom had looked at me as if my statement couldn't have been further from the truth. It had started me doubting myself again, believing that perhaps I couldn't be trusted around Eli alone, despite Dr Samuels' reassurance that I was perfectly competent.

'So, what will you do about relocating to the States?' Oli asked, filling in the awkward silence between us.

'I don't know. We're at a stalemate just now. Tom is adamant he wants to return to Marblehead. He's worried about his father.'

'Didn't you say William was doing well?' he asked.

'I thought that was the case, but he's taken a turn for the worse.'

'Oh dear,' muttered Oli.

'Tom wants us to move out there as soon as possible. He doesn't see any point in delaying. He's worried that Eli will never meet his grandfather if we leave it too late.'

'Christ, Alice. That's a difficult one,' Oli stated.

I nervously gnawed at my bottom lip as I watched Florence and the long, dark-haired woman laughing about something. It struck me that I should be the one out there making small talk to my pregnant neighbour while she fussed over my baby, not my twenty-one-year-old nanny. I could feel the jealousy burning through my body.

'How soon are we talking?'

I didn't answer as I watched Florence hand my baby over to the woman. I heard myself gasp in horror.

'Alice? Are you still there?' Oli questioned.

'Oh God...' I cried, terrified.

What is Florence thinking? That woman could be anyone, Alice. She could take him. Do something before it's too late!

I was about to furiously bang on the window and scream at Florence to get Eli away from her, but the woman carefully handed him back. I watched as a wave of panic came over me at my overreaction.

What were you thinking? If you had banged on the window, screaming at Florence to grab your baby, what would they have thought? Worse, what would Tom think? For Florence would tell him. Of course, she would...

Horrified at what I had nearly done, I watched the woman coo over Eli, smiling at him as she stroked his soft, chubby cheek.

'Alice!' Oli repeated.

'Sorry, yes,' I distractedly answered. 'I'm here.'

'I was asking when Tom's thinking of you guys moving out there?'

'I'm not sure. He won't talk to me about it,' I admitted.

'What do you mean he won't talk to you? This isn't just buying a car; this is moving from one country to another, Alice.'

I sighed. 'I know. Maybe it's because—' I faltered as I watched the pregnant woman rummage in her bag for something. She then took out her phone and keyed in the number Florence was reading from her mobile. It then struck me that she might be interested in hiring Florence for the baby she was expecting. I felt a knot of panic in my stomach at the realisation I would be solely responsible for Eli if Florence were to leave. Yet, paradoxically, I hoped she would move out so I could be alone with my baby. It was as if Florence was watching my every move, making me doubt myself and my ability to keep Eli safe.

'Alice? Are you all right?'

'Yes. Sorry, just a bit tired,' I apologised. 'Maybe Tom doesn't want to talk about it because he knows I'm so against it,' I confessed.

I didn't add that Tom had taken to sleeping on the couch since he had returned from seeing his parents. Or what had precipitated this action. I questioned whether it was the call from Barbara as soon as he'd returned. She had said she was at the hospital and wanted Tom to talk to the consultant in charge of his father's care. When Tom had ended the call, there was something different about him. A coldness that I hadn't witnessed before. He'd simply stated that we had no choice but to move to the States to support his mother. He had said that he should have relocated last year but had continuously put it on hold for me. That he had been transparent from the day I'd met him about his temporary stay in the UK. And now, I needed to step up and support him for a change, rather than making his life even more difficult.

His words had cut me to the core. Whatever Barbara had said to guilt-trip her son had worked. When I'd asked him what would happen if I didn't want to go, he didn't answer. But there was a look in his eyes which suggested he would go anyway, with or without me.

'Look, maybe it won't be that bad, Alice. I mean, Tom clearly must be feeling conflicted. And from what he's told me, his plan was always to return home,' he gently stated.

'I know,' I agreed. 'It's just that with what happened to—' I shook my head, unable to continue.

'Look, I get why you're scared. But you can't let the fear of what happened to Noah destroy your marriage. You can make this work. For Eli's sake.'

I didn't reply. I couldn't.

'What has your psychiatrist said about this?' Oli asked.

'That I need to face my fear. That I shouldn't give my thoughts power. They're only thoughts, nothing more.'

'You were excited about moving to Marblehead—'

'That was before,' I cut in.

'I know. But what I'm trying to say is that maybe you need to push through this fear, Alice. You could be happy there. I spend over half the year in the States, so I can visit you more. And you'll have Barbara there to help with Eli. It might be the change you need to—' Oli abruptly stopped.

'To what?' I demanded.

'Nothing. Forget I said anything,' Oli quietly replied.

'Have you been talking to Tom?' I cynically questioned.

I heard Oli give out a low sigh. 'He called me the other day,' he reluctantly admitted.

'Why?' I heard myself asking.

'He's... He's worried about you,' Oli ventured.

'About me? Why?'

Oli didn't answer.

My skin suddenly felt hot and prickly.

'Oli!'

'Tom said that you don't seem to be coping, Alice. That he's worried that you might be... becoming unwell again.'

'Why would he think that? I'm fine! Even Dr Samuels said that at my last session.'

'Tom said you missed your appointment with her on Tuesday.'

I swallowed. He was right. That was two days ago.

I felt numb. I now understood why Oli had called me. It wasn't for a catch-up, as he had intimated. Tom had asked him to check up on me.

'I... I'm fine!' I repeated. 'Eli had a temperature, Oli. That's why I cancelled. Ask Dr Samuels. I rang her secretary and explained why I couldn't make it. I rescheduled for next Thursday. I'm her first appointment that morning if you must know. Why would Tom tell you I intentionally missed it?'

'I don't know, Alice. It's just what he said,' Oli uncomfortably explained.

I shakily breathed out. 'What else has Tom said to you?'

Oli was silent.

'Oli?' I demanded.

He sighed heavily before reluctantly answering. 'He said that he's worried about your relationship with Eli. That you don't seem that interested in him.'

'I am!' I spluttered. 'Tom's never here to see me with Eli!' I argued. 'He's been away for over two weeks and is working all hours at the hospital. He's never home, Oli! And when he is, he locks himself away in the study. He's the one who has nothing to do with Eli, not me. I'm a good mother, I am!' I insisted. But I could hear the pitched hysteria in my voice.

Why is Tom saying this about you, Alice? And if he's telling these lies to your brother, who else is he telling them to? Our nanny? Dr Samuels?

23

FOUR DAYS LATER

'Tom?' I repeated.

'Not now. I'm exhausted.'

He walked past me and out of the bathroom.

'When are we going to talk?' I asked.

He stopped and ran a hand through his black, wet, tousled hair as he spun round to face me. He had a large bath towel wrapped around his waist. I felt a pang as I stared at his bare chest and the defined pecs and muscular arms, a testament to how hard he trained when not at work. All I wanted was for him to hold me, to tell me that he still loved me. I desperately needed his reassurance that we would get past this.

'Alice, I need to get some sleep. Okay?' he replied, exasperated. 'I plan to be at work early to review some notes before my appointments. I have the prospect of a twelve-hour surgery on Wednesday, if not longer. I don't need this right now!'

'Why are you home so late? You know we need to talk about—' I suddenly stopped, hating myself for sounding so accusatory – so desperate.

Tom sighed. Irritation flashed across his face. 'It's called work, Alice. As I've said, I have a complicated surgery on Wednesday, and I was prepping for it.'

'Have you had a chance to eat? I can make you something,' I quickly offered. 'Maybe we could talk about—'

'I grabbed something before I came home,' he interrupted.

I tried to hide the disappointment I felt.

'Look, Alice. This isn't the time. I've cleared my diary for Thursday morning. I can take you to see Dr Samuels. After your appointment, maybe the three of us can talk then. Yeah? Given the circumstances, it would be better if she was present.'

'But—' I preferred to talk privately with him. I didn't want Dr Samuels acting as a mediator. Thursday was—

I could feel the tears threatening to fall as intrusive memories started to blindside me.

Tom watched me and sighed again. 'Alice, I'm concerned about you.'

'I'm fine,' I retaliated, angrily swiping at my eyes with the cuffs of my sleeves. 'I'm just—'

Tom cut me off before I could finish. 'You're not taking care of yourself. You're not eating properly—'

'I am!' I interrupted. 'I haven't had dinner because I was waiting for you to come home so we could eat together. Remember we used to snuggle up on the couch on Monday evenings, watch something on Netflix and eat together? I was hoping we could start doing that again.'

He shook his head. 'Alice, look at yourself. You've lost an unhealthy amount of weight. You need to start eating regularly.'

It was as if he hadn't heard me. It was as if I was invisible. I glanced at my reflection in the bathroom mirror opposite me. I was shocked to see how pronounced my clavicle was and how gaunt and tired I looked.

A wave of embarrassment hit me. I looked dreadful. I questioned when I had last properly looked at myself in the mirror, other than a fleeting glance as I cleaned my teeth. I couldn't recall when I had last worn make-up or taken time to do something with my hair other than pull it back into a sloppy ponytail.

'What do you expect me to look like?' I lashed out, feeling humiliated. 'I'm not some celebrity yummy mummy. I'm the reality of what happens when you have a baby!' I defiantly answered, feeling the heat rise on my cheeks.

'This has nothing to do with Eli. You barely sleep and never leave the house, Alice,' Tom pointed out. 'It's like before when you started to become unwell.'

I noted that he had now lowered his voice.

'It's not! I'm fine! And I do go out,' I objected.

'Only to see Dr Samuels. Tell me the last time you took Eli out for a walk.'

I stared at Tom, unable to understand why he was attacking me.

'See? You can't even answer me,' he quietly pointed out.

There was an unmistakable sadness in his voice.

'Tom? I... I will. I'll do it tomorrow,' I assured him. 'I'll take him out. Florence can have the morning off.'

The look in his eyes told me he didn't believe me. He turned away and walked down the hallway towards our room.

As if on cue, Florence opened her door and stepped out as he passed her bedroom.

'Hey, Tom,' she chirpily said, beaming. 'Sorry, I thought I heard Eli.'

At that moment, I couldn't have hated her more.

'I checked on him before my shower,' answered Tom. 'He's fast asleep.'

'Oh, okay,' she breezily replied.

She waited, as if expecting Tom to say something else.

Tom awkwardly stood, dragging his hand back through his wet hair again.

I watched, unsure of what I was witnessing. A knot of unease unfurled in my stomach as something seemed to pass between the pair. I couldn't help but note that Florence wore skimpy pyjama shorts and a revealing vest top. I suddenly felt embarrassed in my frumpy, light grey loungewear pants and long-sleeved top. I looked down at myself, noting the sour-smelling stain where Eli had kindly vomited some of his milk on my top.

As if remembering I was there, Tom broke away from the spell Florence held over him and continued down the hallway.

I stared at our nanny, caught off guard as she seemed to covetously watch my husband walk away.

As if sensing me, Florence suddenly looked over her shoulder. Seeing me, her cheeks flushed crimson. 'Oh, I... I... I didn't see you there,' she stuttered.

I didn't respond.

'Night,' she said before quickly retreating back into her room.

I was angry at what I had just seen and followed Tom into our bedroom.

Tom ignored me as he continued pulling on a pair of pyjama bottoms. I noted he had started wearing them when Florence had moved in.

'Is there something you need to tell me?' I demanded, crossing my arms.

'What?' Tom questioned as he turned to me.

'You heard me,' I replied.

'Alice, I am serious. I haven't got time for your paranoid games. I'm exhausted,' he muttered through clenched teeth. 'I'm going to get some water and my laptop. I need to double-check something for tomorrow.'

'You're coming back to bed though?' I asked, unable to hide the vulnerability in my voice.

'Of course,' he replied. 'Why don't you take some temazepam to help you sleep? You look exhausted.'

I turned away so he couldn't see the hurt in my glistening eyes.

'Hey,' he whispered, coming over and embracing me and cradling my head against his chest. 'I'm not going anywhere. Okay? I'm just caught up with work. I'll make it up to you at the weekend.'

I didn't reply.

'I promise we'll do something special,' he assured. 'Everything will seem different in the morning after you get some rest.'

I let out a low, tremulous sigh as relief coursed through me as I allowed my body to relax into his embrace. Perhaps I was overthinking everything, and Tom was right – all I needed was a good night's sleep.

'I'll be gone before you wake up. But it doesn't mean I don't love you. Okay?'

Without waiting for a response, he bent down and kissed my forehead, then gently guided me out of the way of the doorway and walked out of the bedroom. There was a finality in this action, which scared me.

I climbed into bed and picked up my phone from the bedside cabinet, hoping Oli might have replied to the video clip of Eli I had sent him on WhatsApp, but he hadn't even opened it. I was shocked to see it was nearly 11 p.m. I did as Tom suggested, took out the blister pack of temazepam, popped one in my mouth and washed it down with a mouthful of water from the glass next to me. Maybe he was right, and I was acting paranoid. I thought back to when I had nearly banged on the window to scream at Florence to get my baby back from the pregnant woman she had been talking to. Not that I had questioned Florence about the woman. Too embarrassed that she would suspect me of spying on her.

I switched the bedside lamps off and lay down. Tom had again taken the baby monitor in case Eli woke up; between him and Florence, I felt I didn't have a chance to look after my baby. I needed to prove Tom wrong and take Eli out in the morning. I would insist Florence take the time off. I could do it. Couldn't I?

But the doubts started creeping back in. I lay in the darkness, questioning myself. Was I too dangerous to be trusted with Eli? Why else wouldn't Tom let me get up during the night if Eli cried? And as for Florence, she seemed to get in between my baby and me at every opportunity. But was it just my baby she wanted to take from me? Or was it also my husband? I knew Tom was a catch: he was tall, dark-haired, ruggedly good-looking, athletic, and a neurosurgeon to boot. And his interaction with Eli made him exceptionally attractive; he adored his son and would do anything to care for him – to protect him.

From who, Alice? You?

* * *

One Day Later

I yawned, leisurely stretching my arms and legs as I woke up. I slowly opened my eyes. The room was still dark. I reached across the mattress, hoping against hope that Tom would be there. His side of the bed was empty, and the sheets were cold. I pushed myself up onto my elbows. The pillows were still plumped up and arranged neatly against the headboard. I heavily exhaled as unease coursed through me.

Why didn't you come to bed, Tom? I wondered. I tried to ignore the thoughts racing through my mind.

I picked up my mobile to check the time: 6.31 a.m. I realised Tom would have already left for work as he wanted an early start to prepare for his surgery tomorrow. I had slept for over seven hours straight without stirring, which surprised me, considering how agitated I was when I came to bed. But then I remembered I had taken temazepam on Tom's recommendation. And it worked.

But why did Tom want you to take a sleeping pill, Alice? Why didn't he want you to wake up during the night?

I dismissed the cruel scenarios hurtling through my mind of Tom and our nanny. I was due to see Dr Samuels on Thursday morning, and the appointment couldn't come sooner. I was concerned that maybe Tom was right and I was suffering from paranoia.

I thought back to the other day when I witnessed Florence talking to the heavily pregnant woman, who I now suspected must be a neighbour. I had seen her again yesterday in a black BMW SUV, pulling into the grounds of the neighbouring detached property. I had been watching Florence out of the guest bedroom window as she took Eli for his afternoon walk in his pram. The neighbour had braked before the turn into her driveway and buzzed down the window to chat with my nanny. Then she had stepped closer to the driver's window and said something conspiratorially, gesturing back towards my house. I couldn't help but note that Florence's expression changed from relaxed and carefree to pensive. As if she was worried about something or someone. Me perhaps? I had felt my throat constrict at the thought of what she was saying to this stranger about me.

I had stepped back out of view as the long, dark-haired woman, again wearing sunglasses, looked up in my direction. She had stared for what felt like an eternity at the window – it was as if she knew I was there. She had then turned back to Florence. I was surprised to see her stretch her hand out the car window, gently touching Florence's arm and nodding as if concerned about something my nanny had just told her.

My phone buzzed, snapping me back to the present.

It could only be my brother or husband. My world had frighteningly shrunk. I had lost touch with my colleagues from the hospital where I had once worked and met Tom. I didn't see our friends any more either. The trauma of Noah's death and the effect upon me afterwards had been too much for people to deal with, unsure of what to say or what to do to help. In reality, there was nothing they could say or do to ease my suffering. Not that I had wanted to see anyone anyway.

I looked at my phone, surprised to see a message from an unknown mobile number. I expected it to be a spam SMS text, but I couldn't have been more wrong. I felt the room suddenly close in on me as I struggled to breathe as I read the words.

> You should know your husband is cheating on you with your nanny

24

Shocked, I stared at the words. It felt as if poisonous darts were embedding themselves in my flesh, causing searing heat to spread through my body and my heart to begin to flutter erratically. I couldn't move, unable to process what I had just read. Perhaps they had keyed in the wrong digits?

Tom wouldn't do that to me, surely?

No. No, it's not possible.

My phone buzzed. It was another text. I felt my stomach plummet.

I have evidence, Alice

Startled that they knew my name, I threw my phone across the bed.

My body felt numb as if it didn't belong to me. I pulled the duvet over my head and lay there, barely breathing, too terrified to know what to do. Tortured thoughts of Tom with Florence flashed through my mind. The problem was that he had form. He had cheated on his ex with me. But Blair Worthington wasn't just his ex; she was his childhood sweetheart, whom he had promised to marry. Then he'd met me and ghosted her. But we were married with a baby, so how could he be cheating on me? And more so, how could he possibly be unfaithful to me with our nanny? It didn't make sense. Or did it?

I felt what little there was in my stomach curdle as I thought of Florence and how she had looked at Tom last night. And the way he had awkwardly stared at her when she came out of her bedroom wearing those little pyjama shorts and see-through vest top. She was only eight years younger than me. But we couldn't physically be more different: her nubile body was perfect and pert, whereas mine was far from flawless with stretchmarks, saggy skin and an angry, raised C-section scar that hadn't yet disappeared. It was as if someone had swapped my perky, beautiful body for one I didn't recognise, nor care for. I wanted my old body back, the one I had once thought imperfect until I knew what imperfection looked and felt like.

My phone buzzed again.

NO! NO! Please, God... NO! Don't let this be happening to me...

I tried to swallow but couldn't. It was as if my mouth was filled with sand. I peeked out from the duvet and looked at my phone. I questioned whether to pick it up. I knew if I did, my world would further implode. But still, with a trembling hand, I reached out and snatched it up. I opened the new text. It was a video clip. I knew I shouldn't watch it, but something compelled me to click play.

I let out a shocked gasp as I viewed with sickening clarity two people having sex. But they weren't any two people.

Oh God... OH GOD! NO!!! TOM?

I felt bile rise to the back of my throat. I let go of my phone, not wanting to see any more evidence that my husband was sleeping with our nanny, but still, the groans and grunts of ecstasy tormented me as the video clip continued playing.

I threw the duvet back and jumped up out of bed. With my hand covering my mouth, I stumbled down the hallway to the family bathroom. I shakily locked the door behind me and then knelt down by the toilet bowl and retched. Even when there was nothing left in my stomach, I couldn't stop the convulsions. Finally, panting with exhaustion, I sat up and rested my head against the cool wall.

I squeezed my eyes shut, trying to block out the lurid, torturous images I had seen from replaying in my head. There was no mistaking it was them. I had no choice but to accept that I hadn't imagined the frisson between my husband and our nanny the night before. Nor was I paranoid, as Tom had claimed. I questioned whether he had chosen Florence out of the other applicants for the nanny post because she was his type. She reminded me of Blair: Scandinavian-looking with intense blue eyes, thick, shoulder-length blonde hair and long, athletic legs. I acknowledged that was one of the reasons I disliked Florence; she reminded me of what I lacked and what Tom had once so desired.

I forced myself up from the marble-tiled floor and yanked off the grey bottoms I hadn't bothered to change out of last night. I then peeled off the long-sleeved loungewear top with baby vomit on it, threw it on the floor and shakily stepped into the shower cubicle. I turned the water on full, bowing my head, and rested my hands against the tiles to steady myself. The furious, scalding water pummelled my skin as I sobbed and sobbed. Eventually, with no more tears left, I turned the water off. The shock, hurt and betrayal that had consumed me were now replaced with anger.

How could you have been so stupid, Alice? It was happening right under your nose. Yet, Tom was making out that you were going mad.

It then struck me. Who had sent the video clip, and how did they get it?

I wrapped myself in my bathrobe hanging on the back of the bathroom door and crept back to my bedroom. The house was quiet. I didn't expect Eli to stir for another hour. Lately, he had started waking up just after 7.30 a.m. The thought of seeing Florence made my flesh crawl. Her workday began at 8 a.m. and typically ended at 8 p.m. It took all my willpower not to bang on her bedroom door and drag her out of bed. First, I needed to establish the identity of the unknown texter and how they came to have this incriminating evidence.

I pulled on some clothes, took my meds and then allowed myself to pick up my phone. I decided to call the number. I listened as it rang and rang. It then cut to an automated voicemail. I hung up and texted:

Who are you?

They immediately texted back:

A concerned friend

I nervously chewed my bottom lip. I had no friends to speak of, unless it was someone who knew Tom and me. But then, how would they have this footage?

I sent another text:

How do you have the video of them?

They quickly messaged:

Florence shared it. She filmed them together

I felt winded. How could a twenty-one-year-old be so conniving? And why had she filmed them having sex? As leverage? For what?

I sent another text:

Why are you telling me this?

My phone buzzed.

I feel sorry for you, Alice

I stared at the reply. I didn't want their pity. I wanted to know their connection to me.

Do I know you?

It felt like an eternity before they responded.

All you need to know is that Tom plans to get rid of you

I gasped out loud as I read the text. It took me a moment to steady myself before I replied.

You're lying.

I watched tiny blue bubbles bob up and down as they typed their reply. I then stared in disbelief at the response.

Am I? Check Tom's emails. He thinks you're dangerous and wants you locked up. For good this time

Fingers trembling, I typed back:

How do you know all this?

I waited for a reply. Nothing happened.

I sent another message:

Please. Tell me how you know this?

I stared at my phone, waiting for a response. Nothing.

I looked at the white smart speaker on the bedside cabinet. I shuddered as I wondered whether Tom was watching me from his office at work. I knew my face was blotchy and puffy from crying. Then again, I doubted that would make him suspicious. I wanted to scream into the camera that I knew about him and Florence. I had the evidence of him having sex with her on my phone. Instead, I shakily breathed out. I had to focus. I needed to see whether this 'concerned friend' was right.

Gripping my mobile, I walked past the smart device, left the bedroom and tiptoed downstairs to the study. I needed to make the most of the time before Eli woke up. Or Florence.

I closed the door behind me and sat down at Tom's desk. Steeling myself, I clicked the mouse. The screensaver came to life. It was a photograph of Tom, Eli and me. It was a striking, beautiful image of the three of us. I heard myself emit a choking sob and willed myself not to cry again. I had to stay in the moment. I couldn't let myself get lost down the rabbit hole of regrets, 'what ifs', and the question of how Tom could so callously and casually destroy what was left of my heart after losing—

Stop! Stop! STOP IT, ALICE!

I closed my eyes, pushing all paralysing thoughts of Noah away, and focused on my breathing: four in, eight out. Then again, and again.

Centred, I logged in with Tom's password, which he had no reason to hide – until now.

I stared at the brightly coloured icons on the computer screen. Finding what I wanted, I clicked on my husband's Gmail account. I slowly breathed, ignoring the voice warning me not to cross this line. The lurid image of the video clip that I had watched of Tom having sex with our nanny quickly silenced it. For that was a monumental breach of trust. I stared, slack-jawed, at the most recent email sent to Tom this morning at 6.51 a.m. It was the email's headline that filled me with terror: Mental Health Assessment: Alice Fitzpatrick.

All I could hear was the blood pummelling in my ears. I suddenly felt light-headed as the words on the screen screamed at me. Psyching myself up, I clicked on the unopened email. I didn't care if Tom knew I had looked at his Gmail account. Not now.

I scanned over the contents, my hand instinctively covering my mouth to stifle the gasp that threatened to escape. The words in the email seemed to mock me, daring me to believe them. But there they were, in black and white, a cruel reality I couldn't deny.

Oh, Alice... How? How could Tom do this to you?

But I knew how and why. My husband had found my replacement – our nanny. She was physically stunning, young and malleable, and she epitomised motherhood in her unwavering devotion to Eli. Unlike me, there was no question she would follow Tom to the ends of the earth if he asked her.

I stared long and hard at the words signed off by a psychiatrist I was unfamiliar with affiliated with The Woodlands, a place I knew well – too well.

I reread Dr Adam Keyes' email, struggling to absorb the pertinent facts that I, Alice Fitzpatrick, would be subject to a Mental Health Assessment under the Mental Health Act of 1984 on Thursday 24 October, between 8 and 9 a.m.

Two days away, Alice... Thursday morning! That is why Tom has cleared his diary, not because of your appointment with Dr Samuels but because he has arranged to have you sectioned.

I skipped over the details explaining that if sectioned, I would be detained for four weeks in a private, secure unit at The Woodlands psychiatric hospital. But there was no 'if' here. I knew it was a certainty. Hadn't Tom already sowed the seeds of doubt in everyone's minds? My brother, our nanny and Dr Samuels.

And after the four weeks? Then what happens, Alice? Will they release you?

I could feel the sheer panic coursing through my body as one terrifying question threw me.

What will happen to Eli if you get locked up, Alice? Who will care for him?

But I already knew the answer:

Florence.

25

Then I noticed an email from Blair Worthington ping into Tom's Gmail account.

What the—?

Confused, I stared at it. Why would Blair be emailing him? I was certain Tom said he had no contact with her. He even went as far as to tell me that he'd deleted and blocked her number soon after breaking off their engagement. He had never elaborated why he had effectively ghosted her.

Is that what he is going to do to you, Alice? Cut you out of his life.

But you have Eli together. He can't do that. Can he?

I thought back to the conversation I had witnessed between Blair and Tom at his parents' home on the day of Noah's funeral. I recalled how she had touched his face so tenderly. It was clear she still had feelings for him. It occurred to me that they might have met up when Tom had spent some time there because of his father's stroke. I looked at my phone lying on the desk next to me. The video clip of Tom and Florence evidenced that I couldn't trust him.

The email subject line simply read: Hi.

I hesitated, my finger hovering over the mouse. What did I have to lose? I was going to be subject to a mental health assessment two days from now, which could result in me being hospitalised. I thought of how Tom talked to me last night, suggesting I was becoming unwell again. That I wasn't eating or sleeping properly and that I had become socially withdrawn, not wanting to leave the house or interact with our baby.

How much of it is true, Alice? And how much of it is hyperbole?

I shook my head. He was lying. I did look after Eli. Why was he implying – saying – that I wasn't?

Because he has an agenda. He wants it to fit a narrative. One where you are too unwell to cope and need to be held in a secure unit for your own well-being and that of your baby. And so, what happens to Eli while you're gone, Alice? Think about it...

Before I could talk myself out of it, I opened the email. My eyes quickly scanned the content, and I could feel my cortisol levels rising as I did.

> Hi Tom, know it's late on my end. Just finished at work and thought I'd email as promised. It was great seeing you. I wish it could have been longer. Like I said, you need anything for your dad and mom, and I'm there.
>
> Your mom told me the news – congrats! Finally! MGH is a great place. They're lucky to have you. Sorry about Alice. Can't imagine how difficult it must be for you. Your mom said you have done everything possible to help her, but she's too unwell. You know this stuff is hereditary, and with what happened to her mom, it's sad but no surprise. You need to do what's right for you and your son. Protecting him is the priority – more so after Noah. At least you have your nanny to help keep him safe when you're not around. Great that she's agreed to come to Marblehead with you as well so you can focus on making your name at MGH. Your mom said she's counting down the days to when she gets to hold her grandson. Next week can't come soon enough for her! And for me, of course. See you soon, B xx

Stunned, I sank back in the chair. I struggled to make sense of what I had just read.

Tom has accepted a position at Massachusetts General Hospital, Alice! That's what.

And he's going without you. He's taking your baby with him and the nanny, who he just so happens to be sleeping with...

The pain that ripped through me was so intense that I clenched my hands into fists to stop myself from screaming. For a moment, all I felt was panic and dread. I couldn't lose Eli. He was my baby – mine. I had already lost Noah. How could Tom do this to me? He knew it would destroy me. That there would be no coming back from this. I was only now beginning to bond with my son, but Florence's constant taking over repeatedly sabotaged it. And now? Whatever time I believed I had with Eli to build our connection would be taken from me.

I sat for what felt like an eternity, but, in reality, was just minutes, rereading those three damning lines: You need to do what's right for you and your son. Protecting him is the priority – more so after Noah. At least you have your nanny to help keep him safe when you're not around.

I shakily blew out. It was there on the screen in black and white: Thursday morning was about removing me from Eli's life. I questioned what Dr Samuels had told Tom and what lies he gave in return. The two people I trusted, my psychiatrist and my husband, had conspired to separate me from my baby. I had noted Dr Samuels was referenced in Dr Keyes' email not by name but simply as my clinician, writing that my psychiatrist agreed that I was a threat to myself and others.

My mind was in chaos, veering off in different directions. Vacillating between calling Tom at work and telling him I knew all about his plans to have me readmitted, this time against my will, or—

Or what, Alice? What are you going to do?

I had no idea.

Then it occurred to me: how long would Tom pay the fees for a luxury, private psychiatric hospital for a wife he no longer wanted? Where would I end up?

I thought back to my sessions with Dr Samuels when we worked on my OCD and fear of something terrible happening to those close to me because of the formative traumatic experience of my mother's death. And my terror that I had somehow hurt Noah, that he had died because of me. Dr Samuels had reasoned that these were intrusive thoughts and not reality. But had she shared these terrible thoughts of mine with Tom? Wouldn't that be a breach of patient confidentiality? Unless my psychiatrist had genuine concerns that I could hurt Eli.

There was a reason that Tom had insisted that I went in voluntarily to a secure psychiatric unit after the emergency mental health assessment last year. That reason was not wanting my travel to the States or other countries potentially restricted. But the email I had just read made it clear that he was pushing for me to be sectioned this time. Not only would I lose my liberty, I would lose my baby and perhaps my freedom to travel abroad. If Tom intended to have me hospitalised Thursday and return to the States next week with Eli and Florence, then I would never be able to get my baby back.

I stared at the computer screen as I contemplated what to do. I had already lost Noah. I couldn't bear to lose Eli as well. Oli came to mind. I was confident he had no idea about Tom's plans for me. I suddenly thought of photographing both emails as evidence. If I had sent the emails to myself, it could have been suggested that I had somehow altered them before forwarding them to Oli. I took photographs of both emails, making sure I captured everything.

It occurred to me that Eli didn't have a passport. I recalled Tom taking Noah to get a passport. At the time, I had signed the official documents from the Embassy instead of attending with him, too busy trying to organise everything else that we had left to the last minute for our trip to the States. It suddenly struck me that Tom could have taken Eli to the American Embassy to get his passport without my knowledge or consent. He could have forged whatever signatures he needed from me. Who would know?

I yanked open Tom's desk drawers, frantically rummaging around for our passports. I couldn't find them. I looked at the small safe on top of the filing cabinet, remembering Tom saying he was worried about the house being burgled. I stood up and went over to the safe. It was a lock combination. I tried our first-ever date. It didn't open. I then tried our wedding day. Again, it didn't unlock. I realised my fingers were trembling. I flexed them a couple of times, trying to calm myself down. But I knew time was running out.

What are you planning to do, Alice? Tick-tock...

I wanted to scream at the voice in my head to shut up. That I needed to concentrate. I then tried Eli's birthday. Still, it didn't budge. Then Noah's. Again, it remained locked. Then I thought about the date Noah died. Surely, Tom wouldn't have used those numbers? I had been trying not to think about the date, fearful that it would destroy me, but now I had no choice. We lost

Noah a year ago this coming Thursday, and still, we hadn't talked about how we were going to commemorate him. I had tried, even last night, but Tom had pushed me away, suggesting we talk after my appointment with Dr Samuels. But I now knew it was all lies. After reading Blair's email, I suspected Tom had plans to attend Marblehead cemetery. After all, Blair had stated he would be there sometime next week. It tore me apart to think his timing wasn't a coincidence. Did that explain, in part, why he had arranged for a mental health assessment for me on Thursday morning?

I shuddered. It felt as if hundreds of black spiders were scuttling all over my flesh.

I forced myself to key in the numbers. I stared in disbelief when the safe unlocked. Aware I was running out of time, I opened the door and looked inside. There were three passports: two American and one British. I grabbed the two American passports. I opened the first one and was shocked to see Eli's baby face.

The passport was issued on Friday. I could only assume that Tom had forged my signature on whatever documents I was supposed to sign – unless he had given me the paperwork, and I couldn't recall?

Did I sign some official-looking document last week? Perhaps...

I recalled Tom taking Friday morning off to take Eli out. I hadn't questioned it. I couldn't even remember where he had said he was taking him. I hadn't slept at all the night before, and Tom had insisted I take a sleeping pill and go back to bed, resulting in me not waking up until the early afternoon. I then remembered Tom had come in as I was drifting off and asked me to sign something, which I did without giving it much thought. When I awoke, Tom had left for work, and Florence was with Eli. I asked her where Tom had taken Eli earlier, but she'd said she didn't know. I hadn't thought anything was odd about it – until now.

I tried calling Oli. I desperately needed to talk to him, to tell him what was happening, and to get him here to stop the assessment on Thursday.

The call immediately cut to voicemail.

Damn it, Oli!

'Call me as soon as you get this!' I instructed before hanging up.

I stared at the three passports, not knowing what to do.

You need to take your baby and run, Alice. Run before they separate you. Once Eli's in the States, you'll never get him back. You'll have lost him forever.

Hands shaking, I threw Tom's passport back in the safe, locked it and shoved mine and Eli's in my jeans back pocket to put in my handbag.

I looked at my phone, willing Oli to call me back. Nothing.

I texted him.

Call me asap

I waited. A terrifying silence ensued. My mind was in freefall. I considered sending Oli the photos of the emails I had taken, but I was worried he might then talk to Tom. I needed to speak with Oli first. So, I could explain about the texts and video clip of my husband and nanny from this 'concerned friend' and the mental health assessment arranged for me Thursday morning.

Agitated, I looked at my mobile again, willing it to ring. I realised that Oli might already be on the beach as October was the best time for surfing in North Devon. The sea would be at its warmest after the months of summer sun, and at this time of year, the swells would be picking up nicely. If he did go in the water, he could be out for most of the day. By the time Oli checked his phone, it could be too late.

I needed to leave the house before Tom realised I knew his plans for me and my baby. There was only one place I could think of that Tom would never dream I would return to – Croyde. He knew I hated the place. I had left at eighteen and had vowed never to return – until now. I needed to get to Oli. I needed his help to hide us. For there was no way I was leaving without my baby.

26

Relief coursed through me as I looked at the incoming call on the Audi's wireless Apple interface. I had spent the past hour analysing everything I had discovered earlier, agonising over the disturbing details in my head as I tried to figure out how I could have missed the signs. I felt as if I was going insane, and I needed Oli to reassure me that I hadn't lost my grip on reality.

I reached over and pressed accept on the screen.

'Sorry it's taken me so long to get back to you,' Oli apologised. 'What's up?'

I had called Oli multiple times while driving, only to become increasingly frustrated and panicked when it repeatedly cut to voicemail.

I had woken Eli, fed and changed him, stuck a note on the fridge door for Florence to buy myself time and left. All I could think about was getting out of the house before anyone could stop me.

'Oli...' I began in a tremulous voice. 'Oh... Oli...'

I was trying not to cry. Oli was the only person I had left, and without him, I didn't know what I would do or where I would go. I was in a motorway service car park with my eight-week-old baby, miles from home, terrified of the consequences of my actions. I had spent the entire drive since leaving West London looking in the rear-view mirror, expecting to be pulled over by the police.

'Hey, what's wrong?' he quickly asked, his voice filled with concern. 'Is Eli all right?'

'Ahuh,' I answered, glancing at the display monitor secured on the dashboard. The baby car camera was attached to the backseat headrest, facing Eli, so I could see him while driving. He was contentedly gurgling to himself as he stared at the spiral of brightly coloured safari toys hanging above him from the car seat handle. A sharp pang of sadness hit me because he had no idea what was happening.

'Alice, you're scaring me. What's wrong?'

'Give me a second. I need to text you something. It will make more sense if you read what I send you,' I explained as I opened up my phone. I was surprised to see the battery had drained so quickly; it was on less than 10 per cent. I plugged it into the charger.

I noted nothing further from the 'concerned friend'. Crucially, there was no word from Tom, which I suspected meant he had no idea I had taken Eli. I brought up the texts and the video clip and then forwarded them to Oli.

'Where are you?' Oli asked as a car alarm suddenly started screeching close by.

'I'm at Reading Motorway Services,' I distractedly replied.

'Is Tom with you?' Oli asked.

I hesitated.

'Alice?'

'No. It's just me... and Eli,' I uneasily admitted.

'Alice, what's going on?'

I could hear the fear in Oli's voice.

'I've just sent you texts I received earlier with a video clip and photos of two emails.'

'Alice—'

'Look at what I've sent you!' I insisted, cutting him off.

I waited, staring at Eli's face on the mirror monitor. No matter how scared I was, I knew I was doing the right thing. I couldn't bear to lose him.

The silence on the other end of the line lasted for over a minute.

'Oh... Alice...' Oli finally muttered. 'I... I don't know what to say. I mean, Tom? He adores you. At least, I thought he did. When you were in hospital, he was in a terrible state. But you know Tom. He was adamant he was okay. That it was you that we should focus on, not him.'

I didn't respond; the betrayal I felt was choking me, for I, too, had foolishly believed in Tom's love for me.

'This... This is just so out of character...' Oli commented, the incredulity in his voice audible. 'The video, how could it be possible? Are you sure it's real?' he questioned.

'It's real, Oli. It's definitely Tom with our nanny,' I answered.

Oli heavily exhaled. 'I would never have thought Tom capable of something like this.'

'Maybe we shouldn't be so surprised,' I suggested.

'Meaning?' asked Oli.

'Blair Worthington.'

'I thought Tom had explained that to you.'

I didn't reply.

'Didn't you say he had struggled with what he did to her?'

'It's just that he has form for cheating, Oli,' I argued.

'I still can't see it. Tom and your nanny,' Oli muttered. 'He's thirty-nine and she's only a kid.'

'I can promise you, she's not a kid. She's twenty-one, Oli and I know it's not very feminist of me, but I can guarantee she knows what she's doing.' I recalled the skimpy PJ shorts and see-through vest top she had been wearing, which enticingly revealed her perfectly pert body.

'This anonymous texter states that Florence videoed herself with Tom and then shared it with them. Why would Florence film it? Never mind share it with someone.'

'I don't know, Oli!' I snapped.

He was silent for a moment.

'And what about the texter? Do you have any idea who they are?'

'No, not a clue,' I admitted. 'I did ask them, but they ignored the question.'

Oli again remained quiet.

'And the emails, what about them?' I challenged.

'Honestly, I'm at a loss. I can't believe he's arranged an assessment for you without discussing it.'

'Whether he discussed it with me or not is a moot point! I don't need an assessment. I'm fine! I've been coping well. It's Tom. He's been trying to gaslight me,' I agitatedly pointed out.

The shame I felt at not being able to cope when Eli was first born was always with me. No doubt, it always would be. I had struggled to hold him because of my fear that something would happen to him. But Tom had used this against me. How could he not see how hard I had worked to challenge those fears and rationally process what had happened to Noah? To accept, as Dr Samuels had explained, that it was cruel and arbitrary, but it hadn't happened because of something I had done in my past.

'The email from Blair, do you think something is going on between her and Tom?' Oli suddenly asked, interrupting my thoughts.

'No,' I flatly answered.

'How can you be certain?'

I sighed, reluctant to admit to stalking my husband's ex-fiancée. 'I initially had the same suspicion, so I started scrolling through Blair's Instagram account while parked here. She seems happy. I mean, living-the-dream happy. She married another surgeon. They both work in New York City and have the most out-of-this-world apartment overlooking Central Park. Her life looks amazing, Oli. They look so in love. I mean, if I'm honest, I'm jealous. She's got it all. I reckon she had a lucky escape when Tom bailed on her.'

'Oh, Alice, hey, you've got a lot as well,' he assured me.

I automatically looked at the mirror monitor and breathed out. Eli's smiling face was enough of a reminder that I had everything I could ever desire. But for how long?

'Would you think about going back home? I'll call Tom and talk to him. Find out what's going on—'

'What's going on?' I furiously interrupted. 'He's sleeping with our nanny, and without my knowledge or consent, he's arranged a mental health assessment for me with some psychiatrist that I've never met. And then, while I'm locked up in a secure unit for four weeks, my husband plans on taking my baby and our nanny to the States to start his new position at MGH. That's what's going on!' I exploded.

'All right. I just think this isn't like Tom—'

'There's no disputing the video of Tom having sex with our nanny,' I fired back.

'No,' Oli quietly agreed, his voice hollow. 'I'm just at a loss for words.'

Neither of us spoke for what felt like an eternity.

'Oli, I'm scared,' I admitted, breaking the heavy silence.

'I know. I am so sorry, Alice. I'll kill him for this, I swear. I can't believe he would do this after what you went through. Who the hell does he think he is, planning on having you put back into hospital on Thursday of all days? When was he going to tell me?'

I had never heard my brother talk like this. He rarely, if ever, got angry and would always be impartial and try to mediate. But now, he could see Tom for the man he was, and I was grateful to have him on my side. Without Oli, I didn't know what I would have done.

I checked the time on the car dashboard: 9.35 a.m.

'Look, we can talk about this when I get to yours. I want to make a move before Eli gets restless. I reckon I should make it by 1 p.m.'

'Oh, Christ! I should have realised where you were heading.'

I could hear the horror in his voice.

I suddenly felt light-headed. The world around me froze as icy fingernails trailed down my spine. I squeezed my eyes shut, trying to stop myself from spiralling. 'You're not in Croyde, are you?' I whispered, fearing the answer. I knew it was a rhetorical question.

'I left on Sunday. I've spent the past couple of days travelling. I didn't arrive until late last night. I was going to let you know today.'

'Where are you?' I heard myself ask, terrified of the answer.

'Nazaré.'

'Oh...' I heard myself mumble. I should have known. The biggest waves in the world were ridden at Nazaré, breaking at 80 feet during the peak season, which was now.

I shakily exhaled, feeling queasy as the iced coffee I had just drunk started to curdle in my stomach. I had no idea what I would do now. Where could I go?

Oh my God, Alice... You're on the run with your eight-week-old baby. What will happen when Tom finds out you've taken him?

Dread consumed every particle of my body. I had played into my husband's hands. He wanted me committed, and I had just given him cause.

27

'Oli? What do I do? You need to help me,' I begged. 'Where do I go? I can't go back. Not with what I now know. I'm not safe.'

'No… Of course, you can't. Give me a minute to think this through,' Oli suggested.

I waited as terror gripped me. I needed Oli to talk to Tom, to reason with him that I didn't need a mental health intervention, that I was coping. However, I could see that my actions didn't substantiate my claim. I had literally grabbed my baby and ran.

'I take it that Tom is at work, and he doesn't know you've gone?'

'Yes, he's at work. He won't worry about me for the next couple of hours, as I promised him last night that I would take Eli out by myself. He was…' I faltered, struggling to say it. 'He was saying I was becoming unwell again. Like I said, Oli, he's been gaslighting me.'

'And Florence?'

'I left before eight, which is when she starts. I stuck a note on the fridge telling her I was taking Eli out for a few hours. That Tom had suggested it was a good idea, and she could have the morning off.'

'Okay,' muttered Oli. 'That's good. So, no one suspects anything?'

'No… At least, not yet.'

'Tom's emails? How long will it take before he realises you've opened them?'

I blew out as I considered the question. 'Tom checks his work emails regularly, but his Gmail account, not so much. Unless, of course, he's expecting something.' I immediately thought about the email from Dr Keyes, which I assumed he would be anticipating.

'Florence is expecting you back this afternoon. You could call her and make some excuse to buy you time. But when Tom returns from work, he'll realise something's wrong and—' Oli stopped himself from saying it.

'And call the police,' I filled in. I shook my head as my eyes started to tear up with frustration. I had no idea what to do.

'Okay, you head back home—'

'What?' I cried out. 'Why would I go back? Have you listened to anything I've just said?'

'Our old home,' Oli calmly replied. 'My neighbours, Helen and Ben, have keys. They've got Clifftop. Remember that place? They bought it a few years back and have transformed it. I'll call them now and tell them to expect you.'

'I'm not sure it's a good idea without you there.'

'Look, you need to take Eli somewhere. You can't just sit in a motorway service station with him. I'll book a flight from Lisbon and head back to the UK. Give me a second while I check the flights.'

I stared out of the car window at the people walking in and out of the service station. I noticed a couple holding hands while the husband carried a baby in a sling. It reminded me of Tom and I with Noah. We would walk for miles along the banks of the river Thames hand in hand. We were happy then and so in love. I would have trusted him with my life – I did. The memory, bittersweet, felt so far removed from my world now. How could so much change in a year?

'Okay, I might be able to get a flight from Lisbon at fifteen fifty. It lands in Bristol at nineteen twenty-five. There isn't a direct flight to Exeter, so Bristol is the closest airport. I'll hire a car and be with you late evening.'

'Oli, would you really do that?'

'Of course, I would,' he assured me. 'I... I regret that I wasn't there when you were in hospital after—'

I could hear the choked emotion in his voice. 'Hey, there was nothing much you could have done even if you were there,' I interrupted. 'I didn't want to see anyone, Oli. It took me forever to see Tom; even then, I didn't want to talk. What matters is that I need you now, and you're here for me.'

'Of course I am. I would do anything for you and Eli. You're my little sister, always will be.'

'Thanks, Oli,' I whispered, feeling overcome with gratitude.

Neither of us spoke for a moment.

'But, if there's a problem, I might not be able to get a flight back to Bristol until tomorrow,' Oli warned.

'But then what? You'll need to return to Nazaré for the rest of the season,' I pointed out.

'We can discuss that when I'm back. What's important is that I'm there with you before Tom or the police show up,' Oli explained.

I didn't reply.

Come on, Alice... You're running out of time...

I glanced at my handbag on the passenger seat. It suddenly came to me that I had the answer. 'Oli, how did you travel to Nazaré? You must have travelled by ferry because you'll have taken all your gear and boards if you've gone for the season.'

'Yeah, I took the Transporter to Plymouth, got the ferry to Santander, and then drove through Spain to Portugal. Why?'

'I'll do that,' I said decidedly.

'How? You'll need passports.'

'I know,' I answered, reaching for my bag. I opened it and took out our passports that I had taken without thinking. 'I panicked and grabbed them before I left.'

'Them? Does Eli have a passport? I thought you weren't planning on taking him travelling yet.'

'I wasn't. I had no idea Tom had one issued for Eli. I found it in the safe this morning.'

'Oh, Christ! Of course, the email from Blair. He really intended to take him to the States then,' Oli muttered.

'I need to get to you. How do I do that?'

Oli hesitated before replying: 'Are you sure about this?'

'I'm not letting Tom take my baby from me, Oli. And I'm not going to let him have me forcibly hospitalised, which will be a definite now.'

'You don't know that,' Oli tried to reassure me. But even he didn't sound convinced.

'I'm sitting in my car in Reading Motorway Services with an eight-week-old baby, Oli. All I have with me are some ready-made formula bottles and a few items of spare clothing for him because I didn't plan any of this. I just grabbed his changing backpack and ran. Tom will push my action as symptomatic of postpartum psychosis. I am currently on medication for anxiety, OCD and postnatal depression. I have a psychiatrist I see weekly, and I spent four months in a private, secure psychiatric hospital. What do you think my chances are of convincing two psychiatrists and a social worker in an emergency assessment that I'm compos mentis?'

'But travelling to Europe with Eli, that's notching it up to another level, Alice,' Oli stated.

'I know. But I'd prefer to be in Portugal with you than run the risk of staying here,' I answered. 'Tom won't even think I'd travel abroad with Eli. It won't cross his mind. Not after the trip to the States with—' I stopped myself.

'All right, if you're sure this is what you want,' Oli conceded. 'The ferry from Plymouth to Santander is a twenty-hour-and-thirty-minute crossing. It only leaves for Santander on Sundays and Wednesdays.'

'Wednesday?' I cried out. 'That's tomorrow!'

'Alice, you must fill out an API to travel on the ferry to Spain. It has to be filled out at least twenty-four hours before. You won't be allowed to board without it,' Oli explained.

'An API,' I repeated, flummoxed.

'Advanced Person Information. It's about border control and security.'

'So, what do I do?' I questioned, panicking.

'You're not going to like what I'm going to say, but I think you should drive back home and act as if everything is normal. You get together everything you need without raising suspicion. You leave in the morning once Tom's left for work and then drive to Plymouth to board the ferry.'

'What about if I leave from Portsmouth? That's closer to London.'

'Only problem is you can't get on today's Portsmouth ferry because you need the API completed—'

'I know… I know, at least twenty-four hours in advance,' I interrupted.

'And the next ferry from Portsmouth leaves on Thursday. The earliest you can go is tomorrow from Plymouth.'

'Oh God, Oli…' I muttered, terrified at the prospect of returning home and having to act normal around my nanny and husband, knowing what I did about them.

'I'll catch a flight from Lisbon to Santander on Thursday morning. I'll land at twelve forty-five, get a taxi and be at the port shortly after the ferry docks at thirteen fifteen. It took an hour before we could disembark after arriving yesterday, so I expect it will be the same. I'll meet you and we'll drive to where I'm staying in Nazaré. Fortunately, I've rented a two-bedroom apartment, or I'd be sleeping on the couch. I managed to get a property on Rua Das Dunas, located on a cliff overlooking the North Atlantic Ocean. You'll like it.'

'Thanks, Oli,' I quietly replied, relieved. I was acutely aware of how much I was imposing on him. But I had no one else to turn to and nowhere else to go. 'I don't know what I would do without you,' I added.

I was starting to feel as if everything would turn out okay. The fact that the ferry only left on Sundays and Wednesdays had to be a sign. I would go home and wait until tomorrow.

'When does the ferry leave tomorrow?'

'Fifteen forty-five,' he replied.

'Okay.'

'You've got plenty of time now to book and fill out the API form,' Oli assured me. 'It also gives you time to really consider what you're doing. When Tom discovers you're gone, he'll check to see if the passports are missing. He'll inform the police, who will issue a border alert to stop you from taking Eli out of the country. You know that, right?'

'Oh God…' I whispered, feeling a wave of panic come over me again.

'Alice, you don't have time to panic. If you're doing this, you need to act now.'

'Yes…' I reluctantly agreed. 'Tomorrow. I'm definitely leaving tomorrow.'

'And Tom, he's definitely at work tomorrow?'

'Yes, thankfully, he has this complicated surgery. I suspect he'll be in theatre for twelve hours. That gives me plenty of time to get on the ferry and be in international waters before he realises I've taken Eli and left him.'

'You'll need travel insurance, car insurance and a UK sticker for driving over here.'

I heard myself sigh. It was filled with trepidation.

'You can do this,' Oli encouraged. 'As long as you're one hundred per cent, this is what you want to do.'

'Do I have any other choice?'

'You could go to the police,' Oli suggested.

'And say what?'

'Show them the evidence you showed me. Tell them Tom's planning to take Eli to the States without your consent.'

'He'll counteract any claims I make by saying I'm unwell. That I have a history of mental health illness. He will also get Florence and Dr Samuels to substantiate him.'

I heard Oli slowly breathe out. 'Look, if you want to do this, I'll support you. But you must book your ticket with the ferry company now. Make sure you fill out the API as well. It should be included in your booking procedure. Call me when you leave tomorrow. Promise you'll let me know if there are any issues tonight with Tom.'

'Okay,' I heard myself mumble as reality started to kick in.

'It's better this way. You need to leave prepared. Especially with Eli.'

Oli was right. I should have spent more time thinking it through.

'Oli, if Tom happens to call or message you, don't tell him you're out of the country. When he realises I've taken our passports, it won't take him long to put two and two together.'

'Alice, I promise you I have no intention of talking to Tom right now. Not until I know you and Eli are safe with me. All right?'

I nodded despite the fact he couldn't see me. 'Thanks.'

'Talk soon,' Oli said before disconnecting.

I was terrified of what I was about to do. But the prospect of a life without my baby was even more terrifying.

What choice do you have, Alice? You need to go home and act as if everything is perfectly normal. You can cope for one more night. What's the worst that could happen?

I realised I was trembling. It was the thought of something happening between now and tomorrow.

What if Tom discovers what you're planning to do? What if he can access your emails and finds the ferry booking?

I then thought of Noah and our trip to the States.

Oh God, Alice...

That familiar fear was back with a vengeance, hungry and hostile. I was terrified I was putting Eli in jeopardy. Perhaps he was safer with Tom? Maybe I should let Tom take him to the States to start a new life with our nanny? What if what happened to Noah happens again?

I pushed the horrific thoughts away. I was prepared to do anything, absolutely anything, to stop Tom from taking my baby.

28

I returned home to find Florence had company in the lounge. She came running out of the room looking flustered, apologising as I stepped in through the vestibule. Florence pulled the living-room door behind her before explaining that she hadn't expected me back so soon and she had a friend over. I forced myself to act nonchalant, telling her it wasn't a problem. I added that this was her home as much as mine, and she was welcome to make herself feel as comfortable as possible, which I said through a strained smile, the irony making my skin crawl.

Unable to continue the pretence, I excused myself, saying I would feed Eli and put him down for his nap. Florence attempted to take him, still in his car seat, but I held onto it, telling her he was perfectly fine with me. She looked visibly shocked at my refusal to hand him over but acquiesced and returned to the living room. I called out after her retreating figure that I'd be in my bedroom and would listen out for him. I didn't bother asking who was in the living room. I wondered whether it was the heavily pregnant neighbour from next door. Not that I was interested. I intended to keep as much distance between myself and the nanny as possible.

I gently cradled Eli in my arm, mesmerised by his soulful, searching grey eyes as he slowly sucked his bottle of infant formula as he stared up at me. It was as if he knew something was wrong.

'Oh, Eli...' I whispered, feeling my heart overflow with love for him.

I bit my lip to stop myself from crying. I would do anything for him – *anything*.

The irony wasn't lost on me that now, as I was starting to feel a real connection with my son, Tom wanted to separate me from him.

Your baby, Alice... He wants to take your baby away from you – forever.

'Mummy will protect you, Eli... I promise...' I murmured as I bent down and brushed my lips against his soft cheek.

I nuzzled my nose into his skin, inhaling his scent as the fear of losing him threatened to consume me.

After settling Eli in his cot for his afternoon nap, I retreated to my bedroom. Realising I couldn't find my laptop, I returned downstairs to search for it. I had heard the front door closing about ten minutes earlier while I was changing Eli's nappy and assumed Florence's visitor had left. Not finding my laptop in the kitchen, I went into the empty living room to find it lying on the wooden chest. Assuming I had left it there last night, I picked it up, returned to my bedroom and checked my ferry booking.

I had done as Oli instructed and gone online as soon as our call had ended. I had been relieved that there were no issues securing one of the luxury twin cabin rooms with a fridge, coffee and tea-making facilities and a window on the top deck, guaranteeing me more space for Eli's pram. Booking the car wasn't a problem either. I had then filled out all the necessary online forms for travelling to Spain, including the API. The passports were in my handbag for tomorrow as I doubted Tom would have any reason to go into the safe in his study in the meantime.

I spent an anxious afternoon and evening trying to act as normally as possible despite wanting to confront the pair. I had no idea how I survived without alerting my husband and nanny to my knowledge of them or my intentions to leave. But I somehow kept it together and focused on the bigger picture – getting on the ferry in Plymouth with Eli.

I retired to bed early, not that Tom noticed, as he was too preoccupied with work and the following day's procedure. I gave Eli his 10.30 p.m. bottle, then set my alarm for 5.30 a.m. and lay in bed, restless for the dawn but paradoxically terrified. I must have fallen asleep around 2.00 a.m., waiting for Tom to come to bed. I had lain there panicking that he would log into his

Gmail account and realise I had opened the emails from the psychiatrist and his ex-fiancée. But the plump, undisturbed pillows on his side of the mattress suggested he hadn't come to bed, and I could safely assume he was none the wiser.

* * *

Hearing the front door close, soon followed by the crunch of gravel as Tom's Range Rover pulled out of the drive, I unplugged the smart speaker, in case Tom was watching me, before pulling out a large weekend bag from the walk-in wardrobe. I had been waiting for him to leave before packing. I knew I was acting paranoid about the camera in the smart device, but for all I knew, Tom had pulled out of the drive and parked nearby to spy on me on his phone. The man I had fallen in love with and married was a stranger to me, someone I didn't trust and had no idea how far he would go to get rid of me. If Tom suspected what I was doing, I was under no illusions he would make sure I never saw our baby again.

I started throwing in everything I thought I would need in Portugal. I pushed to the back of my mind my fears concerning looking after Eli on my own. I rationalised that I coped perfectly yesterday without help. I had googled the drive to Plymouth, and if I followed the M4 and M5, it was roughly over 220 miles. I factored in a break to change Oli, feed him and buy a coffee and a sandwich. I would be fine. He would be fine. Dr Samuels had said as much in our sessions. Unless she was lying...

I grabbed the multiple blister packs of pills from the bedside drawer and shoved them into a large travel toiletry bag. I then dashed to the bathroom cabinet for my unopened prescription medication boxes. I gathered my toiletries and other paraphernalia before focusing on everything I would require for Eli.

I tiptoed down the stairs with my bags, straining for any signs of stirring from Eli or Florence. Everything was miraculously going to plan. All I had to do was gather what I needed and load it into the car, which I had left until now, to avoid Tom or Florence becoming suspicious.

I noted that Tom had left the baby monitor on the wooden chest in the living room. I hadn't heard him come to bed for a reason. The throws left abandoned on the couch suggested he had spent the night there – again. Or had he? Was this just a ruse? I didn't want to think of the alternative, which involved him sneaking into our nanny's room. I was trying to hold it together and not get blindsided by emotions. But still, waves of betrayal kept hitting me, taking my breath away. I repeatedly pushed back the questioning thoughts that relentlessly tumbled through my mind, unable to comprehend how the man I loved could have so cataclysmically betrayed me. He had plans that didn't involve me back in the States. He was effectively removing me from his life and our baby's.

Come on, Alice! You need to keep moving before it's too late.

Steeling myself, I went into the kitchen. I started packing organic cans of baby formula, a couple of infant milk starter packs with sterilised bottles for the journey, the portable double bottle warmer and steriliser unit and anything else I could think of for when I was at Oli's rental apartment in Nazaré. I threw Eli's nappy-changing backpack over my shoulder, grabbed the bulging bag, walked out to the hallway and picked up my travel toiletry bag and weekend bag, waiting beside Eli's car seat. I opened the vestibule door, fumbled as I tried to unlock the front door and headed to the metallic grey Audi Q4 e-tron in the drive. I raised the boot and stacked the bags inside, with the collapsed Silver Cross pram wheels for the car seat, which clipped onto it.

I stopped for a moment and looked around. I could feel the hairs on the back of my neck standing up. It felt as if someone was watching me. The light from the front door porch and the hallway spilt out onto the drive, illuminating me. But I couldn't see anyone. I looked down the long driveway and tried to see past the trees and hedges. No one was there. I stared at the yellowish haze of cars zipping by on Hartington Road. I turned to the neighbouring property where the pregnant woman resided. But from what I could see, the house was in total darkness.

I shook my head. It was no wonder I was feeling jumpy, all things considered. I was about to abscond with our baby in the knowledge that my husband didn't believe he was safe in my care. I then turned and looked at the doorbell camera. For all I knew, Tom was watching me right now. He would realise what I was intending to do. I checked my watch: 6.33 a.m.

Oh God, Alice... You're taking too long!

I realised Eli might wake up soon, which might, in turn, wake Florence. I ran back up the steps, collected Eli's baby carrier from the coat rack, his padded honey-coloured onesie, and my long, North Face coat, returned to the car and threw them on the passenger seat. I had placed my handbag across my body, terrified I would forget it. Our passports, my wallet, cash, cards and driver's licence were safely stowed inside. I took it off and threw it on the passenger seat too. I locked the car before dashing to the kitchen and pulled out the drawers, looking for black duct tape. I tore a piece off and headed back to the front door to stick it over the doorbell camera. I hoped Tom hadn't seen me. If he had, I anticipated he would have immediately rung Florence and instructed her not to let me near Eli as he drove back home at breakneck speed. It suddenly occurred to me that he might even call the police.

I pushed the paralysing thought away. I needed to keep moving. If I gave in to doubt, then I would lose my baby. I felt for my phone in my back trouser pocket for reassurance. The ticket for the ferry and other documents were on there. When I reached Santander, Oli would vindicate my actions to the police, if needs be. He would defend me and prove that Tom's intention to have me hospitalised had nothing to do with concern for my welfare. We had the evidence, but I had to get to Oli first.

Breathing in, I prepared myself for what was about to follow.

I stealthily made my way up the stairs with a holdall. I opened Eli's door and crept into the nursery. I instinctively went over to his cot. He was still sleeping. I watched as my heart swelled with such an intense feeling of love and awe, mesmerised as his eyelids twitched and his lips opened and closed. He was perfect. And he was mine. I couldn't let Tom take him from me.

I turned and noted the smart speaker on the white chest of drawers. I walked over and unplugged it. I then gently pulled open the drawers and the wardrobe, grabbing baby vests, sleepsuits, hats, muslin cloths and other items. I planned to take the Moses basket, so I grabbed bedding, a sleeping bag and his blue baby blanket. I knew I had too much, but I didn't know when I would return.

Eli let out a tiny whimper, forewarning me he was starting to awaken.

I tiptoed out of the room, not daring to breathe and crept downstairs to the drive. I put the overpacked holdall on the back seat of the car. Again, I was filled with disquiet, as if someone was watching me. I scanned the drive and garden once more, but I still couldn't see anyone. I turned and looked at the covered doorbell camera. I knew Tom couldn't see me. Nevertheless, it didn't silence the feeling someone was following my every move. I made a mental note to myself to remove the black duct tape as soon as I had Eli secure in the car. I didn't want to make Florence suspicious if she noticed it.

I shivered, locked the Audi and ran back into the house. I needed to get Eli up and get away – now. I couldn't shake the fear that something or someone was going to stop me from escaping with my baby.

29

'Alice? Alice? Where are you going with Eli?'

Damn it, I inwardly cursed. I had hoped to be gone before Florence made an appearance. I had left a detailed note propped up against the vase of flowers on the kitchen island telling her I was taking Eli to his eight-week health check, and then I was meeting my brother, who was unexpectedly in London. Eli and I would spend the day with him and would be back tonight. I also added that Tom had an anticipated twelve-hour surgery and wouldn't be home until late evening. When Florence started to panic about Eli and me not returning, we would have left the UK and be well on our way to Santander.

'I know... I know. I'm just making sure you're safe, buddy,' I soothed a disgruntled Eli as I ignored her and continued securing the car seat into the back of the Audi.

I placed his teddy bear on his lap and softly stroked his cheek before closing the car door and turning to the nanny.

I gripped the Audi key fob in the palm of my right hand as I forced myself to smile at her startled figure, resisting with all my strength the compulsion to scream at her, to drag her by her long, Nordic blonde hair and hold my phone to her face as I played the video clip of her groaning in ecstasy with my husband. I had managed to keep it together for the past twenty-four hours, but now I was at breaking point.

'What's going on? Where are you taking Eli?' she nervously repeated.

'I'm taking Eli for his eight-week check with the health visitor,' I calmly answered, despite feeling the converse. 'I left you a note in the kitchen. I didn't want to knock on your bedroom door and disturb you. I thought you might still be asleep.'

I watched as she frowned, confused.

'Didn't you see the appointment card for Eli on the fridge door?'

She shook her head. 'No... I—'

'No matter. It's in my bag anyway, so I have it when I check in at the doctor's surgery. Look, I need to get going before I miss our appointment. Traffic's crazy at this hour,' I stated, cutting her off.

I opened the driver's door.

'Wait! I'll grab my shoes and jacket and come with you.'

I looked at her, resisting the urge to yell that I wanted her nowhere near me.

'Why?' I asked, trying to keep my voice level.

'I... I just thought you could do with the help,' she suggested uneasily. 'I can sit in the back with Eli to try to settle him. He doesn't sound very happy.'

'I think I'll cope,' I replied. 'And he'll be fine once the car's moving.'

'But Tom—'

I could feel the rage dangerously building in me at the mention of my husband's name on her lips. 'Tom knows. I spoke to him before he left for work this morning.'

'You did?' she questioned, surprised.

I nodded at her, forcing myself to remain calm. 'Yes. Oh, and Oli, my brother, is arriving in London later this morning for a few days. So, Eli and I will be meeting him to go for brunch somewhere. So, you can have the day off. It's all in the note I left you.'

'Oh...' she muttered, uncertain. 'But I had yesterday morning off.'

I smiled at her. 'Well, you can do something special for yourself today,' I suggested. 'Maybe meet up with the friend you had over yesterday?'

I watched as she turned to the detached property next door. It was as if she was expecting the neighbour to materialise to help her. She then nervously shifted her gaze to the mobile phone in her left hand.

'Remember Tom is in surgery today? He's not expected back until late evening,' I stated, in case she considered calling him.

She hesitated before dragging her eyes up to meet mine.

'Tom will be prepping now, if not already in theatre. He won't pick up any calls until postoperative. You can leave a message with his secretary, but it won't be delivered until he's finished. Tom's been preoccupied with this awake craniotomy for days now, Florence. His only focus will be on the malignant tumour he's trying to extricate.'

I was now confident Tom had no idea of what was happening. Otherwise, he would have warned Florence. He would eventually find out that I had opened the emails from the psychiatrist and his ex-fiancée and that I had disappeared with Eli. But, by then, I would be in international waters heading to Oli.

I wondered how long it would take Florence to notice that some of Eli's things were missing. What would she do? I suspected she would leave countless messages for Tom. I suddenly considered if Florence would call the police. But what could she tell them? The woman she works for has taken her baby for a check-up appointment at the baby clinic and then plans to spend the day with her brother.

'Alice, why do you have Eli's snowsuit with you? And your winter coat?' she asked, staring at the passenger seat through the car windscreen.

I casually shrugged despite the fact I felt anything but calm. My palms had started to sweat, and my heart was racing. 'I'm hoping to take Eli for a stroll later with Oli. You can't be too sure with the weather.'

She surprised me by stepping forward to get a closer look.

'And the holdall in the back next to the car seat? Are you taking Eli somewhere?' she asked, turning to me.

I attempted to give her a reassuring smile. 'I told you I'm taking Eli to spend the day with my brother.'

'Alice...' she began, unsure. 'I... I think you should speak to Tom,' she nervously suggested.

I could see the panic starting to build in her.

'As I said, no one can reach him until he's out of surgery,' I stated, hearing the edge in my voice.

She stared at me. Her eyes filled with doubt. 'I'm not comfortable about this. Tom told me—'

'Don't!' I snapped. 'Don't you dare!'

I didn't wait for her to say anything else. I pulled my phone out from my back pocket, threw it on the passenger seat, climbed into the car and started the engine.

She looked horrified as if I was stealing her baby. For all she knew, Eli was in danger. However, that couldn't be further from the truth. No matter how agitated and scared I felt, the prospect of losing my baby forever pushed me through. It was Tom and his constant insinuations that I wasn't coping and was showing signs I was starting to become unwell again that had made me doubt myself.

I glanced up to see Florence turn and look at the doorbell camera. I suspected she planned on using the recording as evidence to Tom that she tried to stop me. I watched her expression crumple when she saw the black duct tape still covering it. It took her a moment to make the connection. She looked back at me.

'Alice! STOP!'

She lunged around the car to get to Eli.

I locked the doors just in time as she started yanking at the back door handle.

Picking up my phone, I found the video clip ready to send to Florence.

Do you really want to do this, Alice?

I jumped, startled, as Florence started pounding on my window.

'Alice? What are you doing? Please, you're scaring me!' she pleaded through the glass.

I turned and looked at her as I clicked send.

It was spiteful and vengeful. I accepted that. But I wanted to disarm Florence. I heard her phone instantly ping. Whether she thought it might be Tom, I didn't know. But she immediately stepped back from the car to check it. She lifted her eyes to me, her brow knotted, not understanding why I had sent her a video. She then clicked on it. Watching, she brought a quivering hand up to her open mouth and covered it as the blood drained from her face.

She brought her eyes up to meet mine again. They glistened with tears.

For a moment, I was surprised she looked so upset.

She shook her head as she stared at me. 'How? How did you—'

I buzzed my window down. 'Someone sent it to me, Florence,' I threw at her. 'They wanted me to know. You can explain to Tom tonight that you filmed the two of you together. Think yourself lucky I haven't posted it on social media!'

I put the car in gear and hit the accelerator, forcing the wheels to kick up gravel. Reaching the end of the drive, I slammed on the brakes and waited for a gap in the traffic.

I looked back. Florence was running barefoot towards the car with tears streaming down her cheeks, yelling: 'Alice? Please? Alice? WAIT!'

I snapped my attention back to the road.

'Come on... Come on...' I muttered, drumming my fingers on the steering wheel as I craned my neck for an opportunity to pull out. Seeing a chance, I took it, tyres screeching as I did so. Someone aggressively beeped behind me. I didn't care.

My phone started to ring through the car's Bluetooth. I looked at the screen. It was Florence. Without thinking, I clicked accept.

'Alice... Oh, Alice... I... I... I'm sorry...' She stammered between hysterical sobs. 'I... I...'

I hung up. I had nothing to say to her.

I looked in the rear-view mirror to see the black BMW SUV pulling out of the neighbour's property. I watched the driver brake and exit the car, running over to a hysterical Florence. Not that I cared. I had more pressing concerns – getting Eli and myself as far away from here as possible.

30

THREE HOURS LATER

I pulled into Taunton Deane Motorway Services and immediately checked my phone. I was terrified there would be a message from Tom alerting me that he knew I had taken off with our baby and had reported me to the authorities. But, thankfully, there was nothing from him. Instead, I had received countless calls from Florence, which I had declined. I now listened to the three frantic voice messages she had left, pleading with me to call her back. However, I had no intention of doing so. I didn't want to hear her pathetic, snivelling excuses. There was no way she could lie her way out of the video clip of her cheating with my husband. It was incontrovertible proof. How did she possibly think she could absolve herself? Thankfully, she hadn't mentioned calling the police. I suspected that she was too shocked that I had a video of her having sex with Tom to question the fact I had taken Eli and left.

I was so close to getting away that it terrified me. I wanted to stay on the motorway and put as much distance between us and London, but when I had noticed Eli had woken up, it forced me to turn off. I knew he would be hungry soon and due a nappy change. I heated his milk in the portable bottle warmer, then fed him. I then forced myself to walk into the service station, carrying Eli in the baby sling, to change him in the toilets and buy some provisions. The place was typically busy, and luckily, no one looked twice at me, too preoccupied with their own journeys to bother about some woman with a baby. Yet, I couldn't shake the disquieting feeling that someone was following me. I furtively glanced around, expecting to find someone watching my every move. But I couldn't see anyone. I shook off the unease, accepting I was justifiably feeling paranoid.

The next eighty-four miles following the satnav's directions to the ferry terminal in Plymouth passed in a tense, white-knuckled blur. I couldn't stop questioning what I was doing. Then there was Eli, who let his objections to my impetuous plans be known. He had whimpered when I put him back into the car seat at the service station, but I had hoped he would settle and finally drift off to sleep. Instead, his tiny, punctuated sobs eventually built up to a crescendo of excruciating, piercing crying. I played music to soothe him, which failed. I already felt overwrought, and his wails had me feeling even more on edge. I had to stop myself compulsively looking at his screwed-up red, tear-covered face in the mirror monitor and focus on the road, fearful I would lose concentration and veer into another vehicle. All I wanted to do was pull off at one of the junctions and find somewhere to park so I could settle him. I was terrified that something was wrong. I had to keep reminding myself that he was fine, rationalising that he was out of sorts as this wasn't part of his daily routine and that once I reached Plymouth, I could take him out and comfort him.

I kept focusing on needing to be as far away as possible before Tom finished his surgery and realised what had happened.

***

The drive through Plymouth's historic city centre, traceable back to Saxon times, was a stressful blur. I desperately wanted to be on board the ferry, watching as Drake Island became a dot in the distance. But I was terrified I wouldn't make it. I had crossed into the wrong lane, ending up in the opposite direction and losing time while the satnav attempted to reroute to Millbay Road.

When I reached the ferry port, it took me some time to decompress and accept that despite my misgivings, I had got here ahead of the passport control booths opening.

I was aware from history lessons at school that the most noted ship to set sail from Plymouth was the Mayflower in 1620, embarking for the New World, finally docking in Plymouth Harbour and founding Plymouth, a coastal town in Massachusetts. It made me think of Tom's childhood town, Marblehead, north of Boston and Plymouth. I imagined Tom would have wanted to visit the Mayflower Steps if he had been here. A pang of sadness, combined with regret, overwhelmed me. I struggled to accept that my marriage had come to this.

I jumped as a call came through the Audi's Bluetooth system.

I quickly answered on my iPhone before Eli woke up, having finally drifted off. I wanted to get on the ferry before he started to surface.

'Hey,' I whispered.

'Great that you're there in plenty of time. I didn't want to say anything, but I was worried you might not make it,' Oli admitted.

I had texted him when I arrived to say I was here and with time to spare.

I suddenly shuddered as if someone was watching me.

'Hey? You still there?' Oli questioned.

'Yes. Just—' I faltered as I turned and looked at the other cars in the adjacent lanes. But I couldn't see anyone watching me. It was odd.

'Alice?'

'It feels as if someone is watching me,' I said. 'Do you think I've been followed?'

'By whom?'

'I don't know... Maybe Tom hired someone to keep track of me.'

'Sure, he's got a lot to answer for, but I doubt hiring a detective can be added to that list. You haven't given him cause to suspect you would leave, have you?'

'No... No, I haven't,' I answered.

But the uneasy feeling didn't disperse. Who could possibly be watching me here, and why? It made no sense. Yet, I'd had the same unsettling feeling at Taunton Deane Motorway Services. But no one knew where I was heading, apart from Oli.

I shakily breathed out, trying to steady myself. I was so close to getting away with escaping that I couldn't cope with the stress. I couldn't stop the terrifying thoughts spinning out of control in my mind. I only had to get through passport control, but if Tom's surgery had finished earlier than anticipated, he would now know I had fled with our son.

Damn... What if Tom has finished early, Alice? What if the police have alerted Border Control?

It felt as if hundreds of wasps were trapped in my stomach, frantically buzzing and stinging in a bid to escape.

'Oli?' I questioned, my voice barely audible.

'I'm here,' he answered.

'I don't know if I can do this. I can't stop shaking, and I feel sick. I... I think they'll guess when I'm called forward for them to inspect our passports.'

'And what will they see when they look inside the car? Huh? A mother with her baby going on holiday,' he assured me.

'And what do I say? Why am I leaving the UK with an eight-week-old baby, Oli?' I questioned, hearing the hysteria in my voice.

'Alice, take a few deep breaths. Okay? You have this! You booked a return ticket, didn't you?'

'Yes,' I answered.

Oli texted on my drive home yesterday to make sure I had booked a return ticket to avoid any questions at Border Control regarding my journey. The story was straightforward: I was travelling to see my brother for a week's holiday with my baby. It was a simple plan, but at this point, I was unsure I could answer any questions coherently, let alone convincingly. I was sure they would see straight through me. I felt like a criminal.

Aren't you, Alice? You're leaving the country with your baby without your husband's knowledge or consent. What does that make you, if not a criminal? The police will find you eventually...

I panicked and craned my neck to see if I could somehow pull out, turn the car around and leave before it was too late. Before I did something I would later regret. But I couldn't. I was jammed in on both sides. I couldn't help but notice that the occupants in the other vehicles looked happy, even excited. I flipped down the driver's visor and looked at myself in the mirror. I was horrified at how pale I looked. I nipped my cheeks to try and add some colour, flattened down my dark hair and adjusted some stray strands, tucking them in place to make myself look less bedraggled. However, there was nothing I could do about how tired I looked. Then again, I reasoned, that wouldn't surprise anyone as I was travelling with a tiny baby.

A car behind beeped. It took me a few moments before I realised I was being waved to the vehicle embarkation check-in booths.

Oh God...

'Are you all right?' Oli questioned.

'I've got to go, Oli. Talk later,' I instructed before cutting him off and throwing my phone on the passenger seat.

I put the car in first gear and crawled forward as dread filled my body.

You can do this, Alice...

I glanced at Eli's sleeping face. I needed to remind myself of why I was doing this.

I braked and buzzed my window down. I passed the two passports and my booking reference to the grim-looking official in the booth. I had also brought Eli's birth certificate as evidence that I was his mother since his passport was American. I waited as he looked at my photograph and then studied my face.

'Can you lower the back window so I can see him?' he asked.

I did as he requested and watched as he looked at Eli.

Without another word, he scanned both passports. I held my breath, expecting his computer to alert him that I was fleeing the country with my baby. Relief flooded me when he returned our passports with the boarding card, which acted as my room key, without any incident.

Fingers trembling, I dutifully hung the boarding card on the rear-view mirror so the port staff could identify me. I couldn't believe my luck when I was waved on to join the car lane designated for security checks. I had convinced myself that I would be apprehended when they checked our passports. But the Border Control check hadn't raised any suspicion.

I breathed out. I had made it through passport control. Tom hadn't managed to stop me. I was about to call Oli and tell him I was through with no issues when two Border Control officers ahead signalled for me to pull the car over.

Oh my God...

I tried to swallow but couldn't. My fight-or-flight response had kicked in as cortisol flooded my body, throwing me into a blind panic.

They know, Alice... They know you've taken your baby, and you're attempting to leave the country with him.

31

'Oh God, Oli...' I said as I relived the car being searched.

'Hey, you're fine now, Alice.'

I looked at Eli, still asleep in his car seat, now attached to his pram. I was cross-legged on the sofa in the cabin. I looked out of the window. I was surprised by the ball of red fire dramatically descending from the heavens towards the tranquil blue water. I hadn't even acknowledged the cloudless skies on the drive to Plymouth, focused only on arriving here ahead of time. However, I recalled wearing sunglasses on the drive because of the glare from the sun.

'Yeah... Now I am,' I answered.

'Look, they do random spot checks all the time. It's more common now. There'll even be armed French police marshals on board.'

'What! Why?'

'Plain-clothed officers are being posted on ferries because of fears of terrorist action. There's nothing to worry about. I spotted two marshals on my ferry to Santander. They're there to keep you safe,' he stated.

I slowly exhaled, closed my eyes and leaned against the back of the sofa. I was exhausted. I had expected to feel safe in my cabin and for the tension over the last couple of days to disperse. Instead, my anxiety levels had notched up to a new level as the ship powered its way out of UK waters. I may finally be on the ferry, but what I had discovered when they searched the car had changed everything and shaken me to my core.

'And the tracker, Oli? What of that? I would never know if they hadn't stopped and searched the car.' The vision of standing on the top deck with Eli and relishing the liberating view as we sailed from Plymouth had quickly evaporated when the two Border Control officers had asked about the small tracking device underneath my car. The only valid explanation was that Tom had attached it. The question was when and why. I had so believed I had succeeded in escaping, only for Tom to have outwitted me. I had somehow managed to keep it together and shrugged it off as if I knew all about it, claiming it was in case of theft. But inside, I was reeling from the shock of finding out Tom had been tracking my every movement.

'Christ!' cursed Oli. 'I'm still trying to get my head around it.'

'You know what's odd,' I began. 'I don't understand how I managed to get on the ferry without Tom having me apprehended. It doesn't make sense.'

'He's in surgery, though,' Oli pointed out. 'What did you say the procedure was?'

'An awake craniotomy,' I numbly answered.

'He surely doesn't know yet,' Oli suggested.

I didn't reply. Something about this felt wrong, as if I had walked into a trap. But I couldn't explain why Tom would do that unless to prove that I couldn't be trusted with Eli. Fleeing to Europe with him on the eve of Noah's death wasn't rational. Given my actions, Tom would have no problem gaining full custody of Eli.

'You're definitely sure you destroyed the tracker?' Oli asked.

After the security officers had waved me on, I had discreetly removed the tracker before joining the line to board the ferry. I had waited until no one was watching and dropped it out of the driver's window, watching in the side mirror as the large 4x4 vehicle behind me drove over it. But it was too late. I knew that. If I could have turned and driven away, I would have done. But that wasn't an option. I had no choice but to board the ferry and act nonchalant, knowing what awaited me when I disembarked the following afternoon in Spain. But at least Oli would be there. That was one advantage.

'Yes. I watched as it was crushed,' I replied. 'But Tom will still have the data up to that point, won't he? With real-time locations and full location history. Which means that he can pass the information on to the police.'

I heard Oli sigh. 'I suspect so,' he reluctantly conceded. 'Unless, by some miracle, it wasn't transmitting. I mean, it wasn't hardwired into the car. So, we don't know whether it was still operational. It depends on when he fitted it. The battery life can span from seven days to six months. I had a battery tracker for the Transporter and got one hardwired because it kept losing power. We've just got to hope it had run out of battery and didn't transmit your location.'

'Oli,' I began. 'If he'd been tracking the car, surely he would have known that I drove to Reading yesterday and—' I faltered before continuing, 'And he would have received notification alerts. Yes?'

'Christ! Of course!' Oli replied. I could hear the palpable relief in his voice. 'See? It must have run out of battery; otherwise, Tom would have known something was up yesterday. It wouldn't have taken much for him to figure out why you were at the motorway service station in Reading. That you were heading to Croyde. But he didn't say anything, did he?'

I remained silent.

'And you said that Florence wasn't suspicious when you returned home yesterday,' Oli added.

'No, she wasn't. She had some friend over,' I answered, recalling that, if anything, Florence was the one who looked jumpy.

'Alice, I don't think you have anything to worry about. If that tracker was working, Tom would have known from your movements yesterday that you were planning something. There is no way he would have let you leave this morning.'

'But Florence saw me take Eli and leave,' I pointed out. 'She... she saw the luggage in the car and knew something was wrong. She tried to stop me, but I sped off.'

I refrained from adding that I had sent Florence the video of her and Tom, deciding to wait until I was with Oli before sharing that with him.

'Even if Florence suspected you had taken Eli and left Tom, she couldn't alert him because he was in surgery. Otherwise, if she had, you would have been apprehended when you checked in.'

I didn't reply.

'Hey, come on, Alice. You managed to get away. You're safe now.'

'Yeah... You're right,' I answered, slowly breathing out, feeling the unease lessening.

But whatever relief I felt was short-lived. Again, the question of how long would it be before Tom reported me and Eli missing to the police hit me. But what really troubled me was how long it would take before Tom realised the passports were missing. If the tracker hadn't worked, his first thought would be that I had fled to Croyde. It wouldn't be until he found out Oli was in Europe and the passports were gone that he would inform the police of his suspicion I had taken Eli out of the country. The API online form I completed stated who I was and where I was travelling to, but I had lied and given a hotel in Santander that I had booked and paid for online for a week rather than Oli's address in Nazaré. And now I was in a cabin on a ferry for the next twenty hours, bound for Santander, where Spanish police could be waiting to detain me.

'Oli...' I fearfully whispered.

'You'll be fine, Alice. Trust me. Stay focused. You only have to get through tonight and tomorrow morning. I'll be at the port in Santander when you arrive. Okay?'

'If he contacts me, what do I do?' I questioned.

'Don't answer,' he firmly instructed. 'I'll talk to him tomorrow when you're safe with me. All right?'

'Okay.'

'Look, go get something to eat and drink, then have an early night. You must be exhausted,' Oli advised.

I had told him that in my panic over the tracker, I had left the supplies I had bought at Taunton Deane services in the car. The vehicle area on the ferry was effectively locked down until it was time to disembark. Oli was right. I should get something as I hadn't eaten today, but I had no idea if I could stomach something as the dread that had consumed me as I fled Chiswick for Plymouth hadn't left me. I couldn't stop the scenarios playing in my mind of being arrested by Spanish officers as I disembarked the ferry.

'Look, I'll talk later. Yeah? Try to relax. You've made it this far,' Oli stated.

I stared around me at the deluxe twin-bed cabin, which suddenly felt like a prison. I couldn't escape if I wanted to, as there was nowhere to run. I looked past the chair and small table with the complimentary fruit basket and out of the large window. I could feel the tension in my body at the sight of the sea. I struggled to catch my breath as a sharp pain shot through my tightening chest. I reminded myself that I could do this. I had spent countless sessions with Dr Samuels, facing my fear. But now was the actual test of whether I had indeed overcome the trauma of my past. For I was surrounded by miles and miles of water.

32

FOUR HOURS LATER

I looked around the self-service restaurant and was surprised to see it was still quite full. I felt conspicuous and out of place. I still couldn't dispel the feeling of being watched, not that anyone was looking at me. I edged Eli's pram forward and picked up a tray. I hadn't booked the à la carte restaurant for obvious reasons. All I wanted was to grab something to eat and then leave.

Eli had woken up later than I expected. I had fed him, then changed him into his sleepsuit and put his blue knitted cardigan on. He seemed perfectly happy as he sat in his car seat, absorbing the bright, noisy surroundings. I had noted that the ferry's movements from side to side were becoming more pronounced. I didn't typically suffer from seasickness, but I was starting to feel queasy. Also, the captain had announced earlier that we might encounter turbulent waters as we entered the Bay of Biscay. I hadn't thought to bring seasickness tablets, so the next best thing was to find something light to settle my stomach.

I had left my phone on charge in the room; for some reason, the battery kept rapidly draining. I was relieved to have some respite from constantly checking it to see whether Tom had contacted me. I had left the cabin at 8.07 p.m. At that point, he still hadn't been in touch. I suspected he might still be in surgery. Oli had suggested that I turn my phone off until I reached him in Santander. That all I was doing was driving myself insane. The anxiety I felt as I waited for Tom to reach out as soon as he discovered I had disappeared with Eli was ripping me apart. I kept expecting to hear an authoritative knock at my cabin door and to open it to be met by two armed marshals.

My legs felt like jelly, and I was grateful to have the pram for support as I tried to act normal. But I couldn't help feeling jumpy. My mind kept replaying when the security officers had found the tracker on the wheel well of my Audi as I wondered how long Tom had been tracking me and whether the battery-operated GPS tracker had run out of charge or had uploaded my journey. If he had the details of my drive to Plymouth ferry terminal, he would figure out I was on this ship. There was a heliport on the top deck in case of medical emergencies, and I began to fear UK police boarding to arrest me. I accepted that I was now being ridiculous. My mind was in freefall, spinning out in all directions.

I jumped as a red-faced toddler ahead let out a high-pitched scream. I breathed in slowly to try to focus on why I was here. I needed to eat. Then, I would return to my room with Eli and eventually manage to hide from the anticipated outcomes awaiting me while I was asleep.

I instinctively felt for my bag. It was still there on my shoulder. Even though there was a safe in the cabin, I didn't want to take the risk of somehow losing our passports. I managed to balance the tray and push the pram forward. I stopped and scanned the beverages on display and eventually picked up a plastic bottle of Coca-Cola. I contemplated a small bottle of red wine to help take the edge off but discounted the idea. I was overwrought, over-tired and feeling queasy: not a good combination. However, the thought of tomorrow and what might happen to me, to my baby, made me want a drink to block it out. I felt sorely tempted.

Don't, Alice! You're not her... You're not your mother. You don't need to get drunk to cope.

I moved on past the alcoholic beverages and the lure of respite from the fear relentlessly gnawing at my insides. I was deciding on something easily digestible, like saltine crackers, to ease what might be the start of seasickness, when someone banged into me, unbalancing my tray. I let out a small, startled cry of shock.

'*Mis más sinceras disculpas*,' the person behind me apologetically said.

I turned around to see them bent down, retrieving the plastic bottle of Coke that had fallen off my tray.

'*Perdón, perdón*,' she repeated, looking up at me and offering the bottle back.

I smiled as I took it from her. 'It's okay,' I assured her.

The long, curly-haired woman nodded as she straightened up, pushing a stray auburn lock from her dark brown eyes. I couldn't tell whether she returned the smile as a black mask hid the rest of her face. She looked down at Eli, her eyes crinkling at the corners before turning her attention to a man who looked to be in his eighties behind her, also wearing a face mask. I had noticed a few travellers on the ferry with them, preferring to be cautious. I heard her speak something in Spanish to him as I moved forward. When I looked around again, she was helping the elderly gentleman, who I assumed was her father, choose something to drink.

I eventually found some crackers, added them to my tray, paid and then pushed the pram through the restaurant, searching for an empty table. Finding one at the other end, I sat down and looked out of the window at the all-consuming blackness. I turned away, feeling even more queasy at the thought of the rough waters ahead. I opened the lid of the Coca-Cola, which was released without much effort. I assumed that the fall had loosened it. I had forgotten to pick up a glass. I sighed, not wanting to get up and walk back to retrieve one. There was no one here to care what I did, so I took a much-needed mouthful straight from the bottle, suddenly realising how thirsty I was. I was hoping the sugary drink would help quell my nausea.

A few minutes later, I was feeling slightly better. I turned and smiled at Eli, who was gurgling away, fascinated by two little girls playing nearby. I opened the crackers and nibbled on them, washing the saltiness away with the Coke.

Again, I stared out of the window as time disappeared, drawn to the darkness as thoughts of tomorrow tormented me. I found myself counting in my head to four and repeating it four times to try to ward off the threat of something terrible happening to Eli. Again and again, I religiously counted. I didn't want to be alone with Eli tonight, scared that some harm would come to him. I had made a dreadful mistake bringing Eli on this ferry. One that I was certain I would regret for the rest of my life.

I needed Dr Samuels to reassure me that Eli was safe with me and that I wasn't a danger to him. She had made me list my fears in order, highest to lowest. Then she had used Exposure Response Prevention therapy alongside medication. She had forced me to face up to my fears, starting with the least fearful and remaining with it until my anxiety level was tolerable, repeated three times a day to retrain my brain. I had spent months working on my OCD, preparing for when Eli was born. The psychiatrist had suggested that I no doubt always had OCD, but the trigger for it becoming so dominant, so debilitating to the extent that I stopped taking care of myself and was at high risk of suicide, was Noah's—

I stopped myself; I couldn't go there. Not now. Not tonight.

Tomorrow... Oh God, Alice... You'll be on your own with Eli tomorrow morning... And a year ago, you were on your own with Noah and—

'One, two, three, four. One, two, three, four,' I muttered under my breath, tapping my thumb and index finger as I counted.

Again and again.

'Oh, he is adorable,' a woman's voice loudly trilled, cutting through my thoughts.

Startled, I looked up, surprised to see a young, attractive couple holding hands approach my table. Her partner was carrying a baby, protectively wrapped in a sling against his chest.

'How old?' the woman asked as she crouched beside Eli.

'Eight weeks,' I politely answered, wishing they would disappear.

'Oh gosh! My Joshua is five weeks old,' she replied as she beamed at Eli. 'And he would just love you!'

I watched as her fingers touched his knitted blue cardigan, fighting back the urge to tell her to leave him alone.

'You are just the most gorgeous baby ever! Doesn't he look like Joshua, Rob?' she asked her partner.

He nodded as he rubbed his thick, black beard and looked down at the baby hidden in the sling against his chest.

'How are you finding it?' she then asked, turning her head to look up at me.

'Fine,' I replied.

'Oh, we're just loving having a baby,' she enthused. 'We're taking Joshua to see my parents. They retired last year and decided to move to northern Spain. And so, our *bambino* is making his first trip to see his *abuelo* and *abuela*.'

I took another mouthful of Coke as she looked adoringly up at her partner.

'Gosh, I could just eat you up!' she beamed, turning back to Eli and stroking his cheek. Before I could object, she stood up.

I attempted a smile, relieved that she was leaving, but failed. My skin suddenly felt cold as beads of sweat gathered on my forehead, and my mouth filled with saliva.

'Are you all right? You don't look so well?' she questioned as she frowned at me. Then she looked at the empty red wine bottle and half-full glass beside it.

'No... It's not what you think. The bottle was there when I sat down. The table hasn't been cleared.'

'Okay...' she hesitantly replied.

But I could see she didn't believe me.

I pushed my chair back and tried to get up.

'Here, let me help you,' she suggested.

'No... I'm okay,' I insisted, holding my hands out for the young woman to keep her distance.

I found myself having to suddenly lean on the table to steady myself. The room was spinning around me. I shakily breathed out in an attempt to stop the sensation.

I turned, knocking over the crackers and Coke bottle as I did so, and lurched sideways for the Silver Cross handle. I gripped Eli's pram to stabilise myself and somehow started pushing it.

'I think she's drunk, Rob. What should we do? She can't look after him in that state,' I heard her say behind me.

I wanted to refute what she was saying and state that I was suffering from seasickness, but I could barely walk, let alone speak. I could feel eyes judging me as I wheeled the pram past the other tables.

I heard someone say, 'Do you think we should follow her to make sure he's safe?'

It took all my willpower not to swerve and to keep putting one foot in front of the other, passing the toilets and heading for the lift. I was on the seventh floor and needed to go up to the eighth. All I wanted was to reach my cabin before I threw up. I could hear my stomach gurgling as it attempted to reject the crackers and Coca-Cola. I repeatedly thumped the lift key, desperate to get to my en-suite bathroom. The doors finally closed. I covered my mouth with my hand as my stomach lurched when the lift ascended.

The doors pinged open, and I somehow pushed the pram out of the lift. I was suddenly aware that someone else was behind me. I hadn't noticed them when I'd entered the lift, too concerned with trying to keep the contents of my stomach down.

'Are you okay?' I heard them say.

I flapped my hand behind me to shoo them away. All I wanted was to get to my cabin. I felt horrendously discombobulated. It felt as if my body no longer belonged to me. I reached my door and fumbled in my bag for my boarding card. Grasping it, I yanked it out, but my hands were trembling so much that I dropped it. I groaned as it landed by my feet.

The person behind me quickly bent down, picked it up and handed it to me. I slurred some acknowledgement without even looking at them as I took it and attempted to unlock the door. I then noticed that the young couple with the baby in the sling were running down the corridor towards me. I realised they must have taken the escalator at the other end of the floor.

'Wait! WAIT!'

Finally, hearing the lock release, I hurriedly pushed Eli's pram into the cabin. Relief seeped through me as the door swung closed behind me on the voices outside. I stumbled to the bathroom, collapsing in front of the toilet and lifting the lid just in time before I was violently sick.

I had no idea how long I remained there, passing in and out of consciousness as waves of nausea came over me, accentuated by the room closing in on me and the floor tilting.

Then Eli started crying. At some point, his wails became more frantic and piercing.

Alice... Do something... Get up.

I tried to move, to crawl to him on my hands and knees. Then, as suddenly as he started crying, he abruptly stopped. The silence was terrifying. I knew something was wrong. Very wrong.

33

THURSDAY: 3.03 A.M.

I felt groggy and disorientated, unsure of who or where I was. The compulsion to descend into the numbing black abyss I had surfaced from was overwhelming. But something didn't feel right. I gasped as I suddenly lurched to one side. I gripped onto the edge of what I realised was a wooden bed, terrified I would fall. I tried to swallow back the bile that had risen to the back of my raw throat, but my tongue was too swollen and my mouth too dry.

I struggled to open my eyes, but the explosion of fireworks in my head thwarted my attempt, the booming throbbing, accompanied by strobing white lights, making me cry out in agony. I lay perfectly still, holding my breath, fearful of another onslaught.

When the pounding started easing off, I felt myself disappearing into oblivion. But again, the feeling that something was wrong hit me – louder and more forceful this time. Confused, I tried to remember who I was. Nothing came.

WHO ARE YOU?

I am... I am...

I couldn't recall.

I tried to swallow. Again, failed.

I forced myself to think, despite the flashes of searing white pain that tried to block my quest. But my mind was blank. I couldn't get the neurons to connect, to charge up and retrieve the information I needed. The electrical storm in my head had short-circuited everything. Something had happened to me. Something terrible. But what? What had happened to me? What had happened to—

Eli...

The name came to me, calling out ever so softly. Teasing me. Tormenting me. Terrifying me.

Eli... Eli... Elijah...

The room suddenly dipped to the opposite side as my stomach flipped in protest. I fought the urge to heave. Failing, I leaned over the bed and dry retched. Panting, I lay back against the pillow and wiped the spit from my lips with my hand, giving in to the exhaustion that swept over me.

Then I remembered.

Oh my God, Eli... His car seat was empty. He was gone.

Oh God... NO!

No... He wasn't gone. He was on the bed.

Remember? You crawled into bed to be near him. To hold him. To keep him safe.

Groaning with the exertion, I reached my hand out for him, fumbling around for the reassurance of his body next to mine. My stomach protested with every movement I made, as did my thumping head and feverish, aching skin. I groped blindly behind, hoping to silence the sense of disquiet screaming at me that I had committed my worst fear.

Terror took hold when my hand touched something. I snatched it away in horror.

Eli?

Is it happening again? Are you too unwell to even realise?

Holding my breath, I forced myself to turn around and look – at Eli. To prove to myself that it was all in my head, that my baby was fine. I was fine. Tom was wrong. The psychiatrist who stated I was mentally unwell and needed to be sectioned was wrong. There was nothing wrong with me.

Oh my God... Alice?

I stared and stared, not entirely understanding what I was seeing. It wasn't Eli next to me, it was—

Noah?

I let out a guttural, wounded, strangled sound as I was thrown back to that morning, precisely a year ago, when my life changed forever.

34

THURSDAY: 3.33 A.M.

I opened my eyes and was startled to see a woman in her late thirties crouching beside me between the twin cabin beds. Her unusual cerulean blue eyes caught me off guard as she cautiously watched me. She wore her blonde hair scraped back in a tight bun and her handsome face unblemished by make-up. I noted that she seemed to be wearing a uniform, a dark skirt suit with a white blouse and a name badge pinned to the lapel of her jacket, suggesting she was part of the ship's personnel. My eyes were too tired and blurry to make out her name or position.

'Madame Fitzpatrick?' she quietly questioned with the trace of a soft French accent.

I blinked groggily at her in confusion. 'What are you—' I whispered, my voice trailing off.

'Alice? Do you mind if I call you Alice?'

'How... How do you know my name?' I hoarsely whispered.

She smiled at me as if I were a child. 'Your name is registered with your cabin booking.' She looked down at my arms. 'How old?'

I followed her gaze. I was surprised to discover I was holding Eli. I realised I had drifted off, sitting upright against the small wooden headboard.

What happened, Alice? Before you fell asleep?

I couldn't recall. My head hurt too much to attempt to remember, and I was struck by a disquieting feeling of disorientation. A sense that something terrible had occurred managed to break through the brain fog that had me in its grip.

To Eli?

I resisted the compulsion to wake him, needing the reassurance that he was all right. That nothing had happened to him.

'How old?' she repeated.

'He's eight weeks,' I found myself replying.

'Can I hold him?' the woman asked.

'Who are you?' I questioned, nervously pulling my legs away from her and pressing Eli tighter into my chest.

'My name is Sophia,' she replied with a reassuring smile.

I heard someone clear their throat. Startled, I looked past the woman to the cabin door, where an official-looking man in a dark uniform stood with his hands behind his back, watching me. He was positioned in front of the door, which I couldn't fail to notice was closed behind him. It immediately crossed my mind that he was blocking my escape route.

'Why is he there?' I questioned, unable to hide the fear I felt.

Scared, I tried to swallow but failed. I could feel my swollen tongue cleaving to the roof of my mouth. Panic coursed through my body at the thought that Tom had sent them.

'What are you doing in my cabin? You've no right to be here,' I challenged as I gripped Eli even tighter.

I could hear the high-pitched hysteria in my voice, aware I sounded unstable. I didn't want to play into their hands by presenting as psychologically unhinged and neurotic. I had been here before and—

They've come for him. They know that you took him... That he's not safe with you, Alice.

My eyes darted back over to the tall figure guarding the door. He must have been in his mid-forties with cropped, receding hair. His impassive expression was chilling as he silently held my gaze.

I looked back at the woman. 'Who are you? What right do you have to be here?' I demanded again. But I could hear the anxiety in my voice. Tom must have called the police, and they had alerted the ship's captain. He must have told them I had taken our baby and left our home and ran.

But how does he know you're on this ferry?

Then, I recalled the small tracking device that security had found underneath my car. Tom had been tracking my movements. I didn't recognise the man I had married. The stranger who messaged me, calling themselves 'a concerned friend', knew about my husband and his plans – plans he had intentionally never shared with me. The sense of betrayal was horrific. He didn't trust me with our son. Did that mean he blamed me for Noah's cruel and untimely death? After a year of denial, his actions had proven otherwise. I had talked about my fear that Tom blamed me with Dr Samuels. She had assured me that he didn't, that Noah's death was a tragic event that had nothing to do with me. I needed to accept that fact and let go of the strangling guilt that clung to me. Then I remembered what today was. A year ago, Noah—

'Alice? Did you hear me?'

Her voice cut through my dark, disruptive thoughts.

'Sorry,' I apologised, feeling confused. 'Why are you here again?'

'That's what I was trying to explain to you. The occupants in the cabins on either side heard you—'

'Heard what?' I asked as dread took hold.

Eli?

I held him close to me, not wanting to let him go.

'You were screaming that something had happened to your baby. When they couldn't get any answer from knocking on the door, they searched for help. Two crew members couldn't get an answer from you either, so they radioed for Officer Barnaud here, who opened your cabin door when you failed to respond. You weren't making any sense when he entered the cabin, and you refused his help, so he requested my medical assistance.'

I had no memory of calling out.

Screaming, Alice. She said you were heard screaming...

I hesitantly looked up at the officer standing guard as he stared back with cold indifference. I didn't know who these people were; for all I knew, they were here to steal my baby.

I turned to the woman. 'Who are you? This isn't right. You shouldn't be in my cabin. He shouldn't be in my cabin!' I argued, gesturing towards the ship's officer by the door. 'This has to be breaking the law. It's an infringement of my rights!'

'Sophia,' she gently answered, smiling to reassure me. 'Remember I told you my name is Sophia?'

I frowned.

'I'm the ship's duty nurse. Officer Barnaud sent for me because he was concerned about you and your baby.'

I heard the hesitation in her voice despite her calm expression.

I stared at her, filled with distrust and fear.

'Alice—' She suddenly broke off and looked down at the beige carpet.

I followed her gaze. An empty wine bottle had rolled by her feet as the cabin dipped. Her eyes also rested on the temazepam blister pack. She picked up the empty medication and examined it.

'I have trouble sleeping,' I explained, heat radiating from my skin.

'These are twenty-milligram-tablets of temazepam. How many did you take, Alice?'

'I... I... I didn't take any,' I uneasily replied.

The truth was I couldn't remember.

Perhaps that was why I couldn't remember?

She looked at me. I could see the suspicion in her bluest of blue eyes. 'And the wine?' she asked, picking up the bottle and placing it with the empty blister pack on the small bedside cabinet.

I shook my head. 'I... I don't remember drinking it...' I admitted.

Yet my unbearably dry mouth, churning stomach and thumping head suggested otherwise.

None of this was making any sense. I would never take sleeping pills, let alone with alcohol, but the evidence was damning.

I tried to hold back the tears that were stinging my eyes. I must have swallowed back those tablets with a bottle of red wine. Why else would I have blacked out? I had no memory of what had happened. No recollection of placing Eli on the bed, of—

Eli? You thought Eli was Noah. Remember?

I felt as if I was going to throw up. I could feel the water pooling in my mouth as my skin became clammy, and I suddenly felt light-headed. I closed my eyes for a moment and shallowly breathed out, then in, trying to resist the urge to let Eli go and run for the en-suite bathroom.

'Alice? Are you okay?'

I couldn't even shake my head for fear of being sick.

'Alice?'

I blocked out her voice. My body's physical symptoms screamed at me that I had overdosed on sleeping pills and alcohol. The question was, why? It made no sense.

Eli...

I could feel the weight of his body in my arms, but I couldn't bring myself to look down at his sleeping face. Something in the dark recesses of my mind whispered that something was wrong.

He wouldn't wake up, Alice. He wouldn't open his eyes.

'Alice, why don't you let me check your baby over?'

'No,' I mumbled.

'Please, Alice. Do you believe there's something wrong with him? Is that why you were shouting for help?'

'I want you both to leave me alone,' I stated, turning my head away. 'I want to lie down.'

'I can't do that. I need to make sure you and your baby are both all right before we leave.'

'Go away!'

Before I could react, she reached across and touched Eli's neck.

'He's cold, Alice. Let me just check that he's okay.'

'He's cold?' I questioned, looking down at him.

His face was turned into my chest as he slept. His tiny hands balled into fists, resting against my white cotton sweatshirt.

'Please? Let me just check his breathing.'

Then it came back to me. The memory: cruel and terrifying.

He isn't Eli... This isn't Eli, Alice.

I wondered whether I was experiencing postpartum psychosis. It was something I feared and had discussed at length with Dr Samuels. Perhaps the events of the past forty-two hours had led to this, for what other explanation was there, other than I was having some kind of psychotic break from reality.

I didn't resist when I felt her lift him from my arms.

Numb, I watched as she carefully laid him on the bed on his back before bending over his head and placing her ear next to his mouth and nose. I knew she was listening for sounds of breath. But there were none. I had already tried.

Failing to hear anything, she pulled back and studied his chest for the up-and-down movement of his breathing. Not seeing any signs, she lowered her cheek to his mouth and nose to feel his tiny breaths against her skin. I knew she wouldn't feel anything. I hadn't.

I waited for her to realise. This baby wasn't Eli. Someone had taken Eli and left in his place a baby that looked like his brother, Noah.

'Alice?' she abruptly questioned. 'Where's your baby?'

I dragged my head up from the baby's face, identical to Noah's. But I knew that couldn't be possible. Noah was gone. And now Eli…

I looked at her, taken aback by the confusion on her face.

'Alice? This… this isn't real. This is a Reborn silicone baby. It's startlingly realistic, and I imagine it would have cost a lot for this level of artistry.'

I gaped at her. 'I… I don't understand.'

'It's not alive, Alice,' she explained. 'It's an expensive doll, which looks like a real baby. The arms and legs are weighted to make it feel like a human baby. It even has real hair.'

'But that's Noah. Noah's real. He's not a doll,' I stated, confused.

'Noah? But isn't your baby called Elijah?' she questioned.

I nodded.

'Who is Noah then?' she asked.

'He died.'

'When? When did he die?'

I could hear the edge of panic in her voice.

I shook my head. None of this made any sense.

'Alice? When did Noah die?'

'One year ago,' I answered, staring in horror at the baby lying on the bed. The baby that looked identical to Noah. How? How was that possible?

'Alice? Your booking states that you travelled with your baby, Elijah?'

'I did,' I mechanically answered.

'Then where is he, Alice? Where is your baby?'

'I don't know...' I admitted. 'I woke up and found... found that lying next to me.'

Hot tears spilled down my cheeks.

She looked at the discarded teddy bear lying next to the empty Moses basket and turned to her colleague, who was equally uneasy. They glanced across at the empty Silver Cross car seat attached to the pram with the changing bag, then at the changing mat with baby wipes, rash ointment and nappy sacks laid out on the sofa. Next to the coffee- and tea-making facilities, a discarded baby bottle with remnants of formula milk: all telltale signs that a baby – my baby – had existed.

'Alice? Listen to me,' she instructed, her voice cutting through my sobs. 'You need to tell us what happened.'

'I don't know!' I cried out as I wrapped my arms around my trembling body. 'All I know is my baby is gone.'

'Is he real, Alice? Your baby? Or is this in some way connected to your baby who died? Is that why this Reborn baby looks like your son, Noah?'

'He's real!' I yelled out.

I could see the sympathy in her eyes as she evaluated me.

'My bag... I have his passport in my bag,' I said, looking around the cabin.

'Is this it?' Sophia asked, reaching over and picking up my leather tote bag, which was abandoned on the floor next to the sofa.

I grabbed it from her and started frantically searching for Eli's passport. I found it. Hands shaking, I opened it to ensure I wasn't going insane. That it was Eli's baby face and not Noah's inside.

'See! There! That's proof! Elijah Oliver Fitzpatrick,' I declared with satisfaction, shoving the passport at her.

I watched as she looked at it. I heard a barely audible gasp of acknowledgement that another baby did exist. She handed the passport to Officer Barnaud.

'Where is he, Alice?'

I noted that her sympathetic tone had disappeared.

'Alice? Where is your baby?' she firmly repeated.

I shook my head. 'I don't know...'

Her eyes narrowed as she took in the empty wine bottle and the blister pack of temazepam lying next to it. She turned her head round to her colleague and mouthed something before returning her attention to me.

Oh my God... She thinks you're drunk and... and what, Alice? What happened to you?

35

THURSDAY: 3.43 A.M.

I pushed the heels of my palms into my eye sockets as I pulled my knees up to my chest and started rocking backwards and forwards. None of this was real. It couldn't be. I had to be hallucinating.

Wake up! WAKE UP!

'Alice... Alice?'

I felt my shoulders being forcibly shaken.

I blocked it out.

Then again, but even more aggressively. 'ALICE! I need you to focus. You need to help us find your baby!'

Someone grabbed my wrists, pulling my hands away from my face.

Shocked, my eyes snapped open. The woman with the startling cerulean eyes was now sitting on the bed directly in front of me. I dropped my gaze to her name badge pinned to the lapel of her jacket.

'Sophia?' I read aloud, tears slipping down my cheeks as I stared at the identification badge.

I was sure this had to be some form of psychotic episode. None of it made sense.

The doll... It has Noah's face. How could that be possible?

'Yes, Alice. It's Sophia. Remember, I'm the ship's duty nurse,' she reassuringly replied.

'I'm a nurse,' I whispered. 'I mean, I was a nurse before I had... Before...' My voice trailed off.

She turned her attention to the officer guarding the door. 'Get her some coffee, will you? We need to sober her up.'

He walked over to the kettle, ensuring there was water before switching it on.

I shook my head. 'No... I'm not drunk. I'm not!' I insisted.

But as I did, I caught her glancing at the empty wine bottle.

'I... I didn't drink it. It's not mine. I don't know why it's here,' I pleaded.

She looked back at me, her expression doubtful.

'Please?' I begged. 'You have to believe me!'

She didn't reply.

'Take a blood test! That's what you can do. It will prove I have no alcohol in my system,' I frantically insisted.

She gently touched my arm. 'I can do that if that's what you want. But right now, I'm concerned about your baby. About Elijah. He's missing. Remember?'

I choked back a sob.

Where is he, Alice? Where is your baby? What has happened to him?

I tried to block out the frantic, terrifying thoughts assailing me.

'Someone must have—'

'Must have what, Alice?'

I frowned as I tried to recall the events of last night. But they were too hazy. The memory was so tenuous that I was terrified I would lose it.

I slowly replied, 'I... I went down to the seventh floor to the self-service restaurant.'

'Go on,' she gently encouraged.

'I was unwell. I felt really sick... I... I then returned to my room.'

'Did you talk to anyone?' she asked as her colleague handed me a steaming black coffee.

'Thank you,' I quietly said.

He didn't look at me. Instead, he directed his attention to Sophia. 'I need to inform the captain.'

'Of course. I'll stay with Mrs Fitzpatrick.'

Then, an image came to mind, powerful and terrifying.

'No, wait! I know who took my baby!' I cried out, jumping up and simultaneously spilling the coffee over the white bedding. 'They were there, right outside my door,' I exclaimed, pointing to my cabin door. 'You must have cameras in the corridors? Yes? Security cameras?'

Sophia turned and looked at her colleague.

'All passenger areas are monitored and recorded. I will have to check with the security staff if that includes the corridor outside,' he replied in a deep, gravelly French accent.

'They were out there!' I insisted. 'I heard them... They... They must have followed me.'

'Sit down,' Sophia gently instructed as her colleague stepped away from me towards the door. 'Alice, you need to try to keep calm.'

'Keep calm?' I incredulously questioned. 'How can I keep calm when someone has stolen my baby?' I spluttered. 'I know who took him! That's what I am trying to tell you!'

I looked over at the officer's figure as he approached the door.

'Please, wait. They have my baby. You need to know who they are so you can find them.'

He stopped and turned around, waiting.

'Go on,' instructed Sophia.

'They were young... In their early twenties... And... They had a baby!'

I noted that Sophia looked over at her colleague. Something passed between them.

'No... No, they have my baby! You don't understand.'

'Alice—' Sophia began.

'No!' I snapped, cutting her off. 'I don't think their baby was real. It was a ruse to talk to me. To get close to Eli.'

'Why don't you sip some coffee,' she suggested.

I looked down at what was left in the cup. I shook my head. 'I'm not drunk!'

'Okay. Tell me why this couple's baby wasn't real,' she said.

I heard her colleague impatiently clear his throat.

'This woman's partner, he had the baby in a wraparound sling. But I couldn't see him. He was completely hidden by the sling...' I faltered.

Oh, Alice... They took Eli...

I dropped my gaze to the Reborn doll. To a doll that looked like Noah... But how was that possible?

What's happening to you, Alice? Are you imagining things because of the significance of today?

'Alice?' Sophia said. 'Look at me. Focus!'

I dragged my head up to her face. 'That doll,' I said, gesturing to it. 'They must have hidden it in the sling. They swapped it with Eli. They took my baby...' My voice trailed off as I shook my head.

Sophia squeezed my hand. 'Alice, we'll find him.'

I wanted to believe her, but I was terrified that she was wrong. That they wouldn't find him.

Oh God...

'Did they say anything about who they were or where they were travelling to? Anything that could give us an idea about their identity,' she asked.

I chewed my bottom lip as I tried to recall. But nothing came.

The officer made a move to leave when I suddenly remembered something.

'The baby... She said he was called Jo... Josh... No... No, it was Joshua. Yes, that's it. Joshua.'

I looked back at the Reborn doll. I remembered undoing the poppers on the sleepsuit, searching for evidence that it wasn't Eli. The haemangioma wasn't there. They had swapped my baby...

'Eli has a physical anomaly that they won't be able to disguise,' I hurriedly shared. 'You'll be able to identify him by it. He has a haemangioma on his left chest.'

'Okay, that's good to know,' Sophia answered.

I desperately wanted to go back to sleep and wake up to find this was all just a horrific nightmare. That Eli was safe – with me.

'What was Eli wearing?' Sophia suddenly questioned.

I jabbed a trembling finger at the doll. 'That! Eli was wearing that. That blue and white striped fox sleepsuit. I changed him into it before we left to go to the restaurant.'

I saw her eyes widen in disbelief as she shifted her gaze to the Reborn doll.

'I strapped him in the car seat attached to the pram,' I explained, looking over at the empty car seat. I couldn't silence the hornets frantically buzzing around in my head, adding to my confusion. I felt dread stirring in my stomach come over me as I remembered. 'I pulled on his baby blue knitted beanie hat, fastened the buttons on his matching blue knitted cardigan and... And then I placed his pale blue blanket around him.'

I looked back at the Reborn doll. It seemed so natural. It was identical to Noah, but it was wearing Eli's adorable little fox sleepsuit. A pain so visceral that it made me gasp seared through me.

Why, Alice? Why had they changed Eli out of his sleepsuit? Why put it on the reborn doll? Had they done that so you wouldn't realise until it was too late? Until they had disappeared with your baby?

'Alice?'

Startled, I looked at Sophia.

'Do you recall anything else about this couple?' she questioned.

I swallowed, then nodded. 'Rob. The woman called the man Rob. They were travelling to...' I faltered as I tried to remember. But the memory was too elusive.

'Where?'

'I'm sorry,' I apologised. 'I can't remember. I know that when she crouched down to see Eli, I started to feel really unwell. They must have drugged me... I don't know how... But I started to feel really shaky and light-headed, as if I was going to pass out. It happened really suddenly. I initially thought it was seasickness, but—' I stopped as her colleague walked out the door.

'Why has he left?' I questioned.

I could feel my cheeks burning with shame, as if he had slapped me. His disgust at me that I would make up such an elaborate lie to cover for the fact I got drunk while in sole charge of my eight-week-old baby was palpable. The empty wine bottle was damning evidence against me.

'He has to inform the captain so search procedures can be initiated. He'll return when he has an update,' she assured me. 'In the meantime, I'll stay with you.'

I nodded, then noticed my phone lighting up on the bed.

Sophia waited for me to answer it. I didn't.

'Who's Tom?' she questioned, picking it up and reading the name on the screen.

'My husband,' I uncomfortably replied.

'Can you speak to him?'

I shook my head and shuffled further back against the headboard. I couldn't talk to him. How could I tell him our baby was missing? That something had happened to him because of me.

'Shall I answer it? Let your husband know what's happening?'

Before I could respond, Sophia had stood up and turned her back to me.

'No... Please,' I objected.

But she either didn't hear me or chose not to listen.

'Hello, is that Tom Fitzpatrick? Alice Fitzpatrick's husband? Yes... Yes. She's here.' Sophia looked at me. 'Can you give me a moment, please? Yes... Yes... I will explain what's happening.' Sophia then clicked the mute button on my iPhone. 'Alice, I'm just going to update your husband outside in the corridor. Try to think of anything else that you think will help. Okay?'

I shook my head. 'I need to look for Eli. That couple have—'

'No! Alice, you need to stay here. My colleague will be informing the captain, who will no doubt announce for passengers to muster in a designated area to account for all guests—'

'What?' I exploded. 'He said that the cabins would be searched. Eli's here! Somewhere. They need to search all the rooms,' I implored her.

She patiently nodded at me. 'The ship has an electronic manifest of all crew and guests. Officer Barnaud and his colleagues will check it against the details of the young couple you gave him.'

'And if they lied about their names?'

'We have dedicated security staff who will be reviewing all recorded CCTV—'

'But what if no surveillance cameras exist on this corridor?' I interrupted.

'As far as I'm aware, all passenger areas are monitored. You said that you were on the seventh floor?'

I nodded. 'Yes, I took the lift down and went to the self-service restaurant with Eli in his pram. That's where this couple came up to me.'

Sophia nodded. 'Officer Barnaud will make sure the security staff take a look at the CCTV recordings.'

I shakily sighed, using the cuffs of my top to wipe my damp cheeks.

'Alice, the captain and the crew will do everything to find Eli,' she sympathetically assured me.

'And if you don't find him? What happens when we arrive at Santander?'

I couldn't stop thinking about this couple: they would leave with Eli and disappear forever with my baby.

'If we haven't located Eli by then, the immigration authorities in Santander will conduct a full check of all passengers as they disembark from the ship. We don't have enough crew to search the entire ship, but whoever has Eli will be apprehended before leaving, Alice. I can assure you of that.'

Fresh tears came as reality started to kick in. This was a year to the morning I lost Noah. How could it be happening all over again?

'Tell my husband... Tell him I'm sorry...' I murmured.

Sophia gave me an odd look. I suddenly realised what she was thinking.

'No...' I panicked. 'I... I... haven't hurt my baby...'

She turned her back to me as she put the phone to her ear. 'Mr Fitzpatrick... Yes,' she began.

I helplessly watched as she left the room.

I looked around the empty cabin. I saw the empty blister pack of temazepam and the wine bottle.

What have you done, Alice? You knew Eli wasn't safe with you. And yet, you ran with him, placing his life in jeopardy. All because you refused to acknowledge that you needed help and that you were a danger to your baby. And now he's gone...

* * *

When Sophia returned, I knew something had changed.

'Alice,' she tentatively began.

I stared at her as dread filled me.

'Your husband told me that you have a history of...'

I felt my stomach flip.

No... NO!

'Of mental illness,' she continued carefully. 'And that you recently spent a significant period in a psychiatric hospital after a suicide attempt.'

I lowered my gaze to the Reborn doll. I knew what she was going to say. But she was wrong. She was so wrong.

'Your husband explained that you were very unwell after you lost your son. And you were scared you would hurt the baby you were pregnant with at the time of hospitalisation. That you were fearful of giving birth in case something terrible happened to the baby.'

I tried to swallow, to rid myself of the dryness in my mouth that silenced me. Failed.

'As part of your treatment, your psychiatrist suggested a Reborn doll to help you with your OCD. Your husband said that you received Exposure Response Prevention therapy, using the doll so you could challenge your fears about hurting your baby.'

I shook my head. It was all wrong. Tom had got it wrong. 'No...' I muttered. 'That doll isn't the same one. I specifically requested a doll that bore no resemblance to Noah. Mine was much smaller, like a newborn. It had no hair, and its eyes were blue and open. But this one... It looks identical to Noah... As if he was sleeping...'

'Alice, Tom told me you took your baby yesterday and left the UK without his knowledge. Is that correct?'

'He was going to take Eli from me. I had no choice. He was trying to gaslight me. Lying to me. Telling me I wasn't well again—' I abruptly stopped, silenced by the look in her eyes, which told me she believed my husband, not me.

'Alice, where is your baby? What have you done to him?'

I dropped my gaze, unable to stare into her eyes, which suspected me of the worst crime a mother could commit – murdering my baby.

36

THURSDAY: 10.11 A.M.

'I want to return to my cabin!' I pleaded, my voice trembling.

I looked at Sophia, who was sitting to the side of me. She didn't respond. I then looked at the person across the table from me. Officer Barnaud was seated beside them. We were in a small office situated on the deck. A few hours ago, I had been escorted here by Officer Barnaud and another member of the crew. The atmosphere was unbearably tense, and I had noted a discernible change in the way they acted towards me as if they suspected I had done something terrible to my baby.

'I've already explained that it's being treated as a crime scene. The police will want to examine it when we dock,' the official-looking man opposite me repeated. He had the subtlest trace of a French accent. 'Let's go over these questions again.'

I sighed. I was exhausted and felt horrendous. I was experiencing the worst hangover of my life. But I knew I hadn't consumed any alcohol.

Or did you? How do you account for the empty bottle of red wine on the floor in your cabin room, Alice?

I looked back at him. The master of this ferry, Captain Guillaume Laurent. He was in his mid-fifties, short and slim, with intelligent hazel eyes and short blond, wavy hair with flecks of silver. His demeanour was similar to Officer Barnaud's: tight-lipped, impassive, and with a glint of coldness in his eyes. It was as if he had already made up his mind about me.

I had initially assumed Captain Laurent wanted to see me because he had an update on Eli's whereabouts, but this wasn't what I had anticipated. Nor did I expect him to be recording our 'talk'.

'The couple you believe—'

'They're lying!' I interrupted. 'They have to be.'

'I personally questioned them,' he calmly replied.

'But they're lying!' I repeated. 'They drugged me! I did not drink any alcohol last night. How many times do I have to tell you?'

He placed his hands on the table. I noticed the gold wedding band on his left hand and his neatly trimmed, immaculate nails. 'I've seen the CCTV footage of them talking to you in the restaurant. At no point could they have drugged you, Alice. They both say that you were acting very drunk. And other guests have substantiated their claim that you seemed intoxicated. I've seen the security footage of you pushing your baby through the restaurant, and you appear—'

'I was drugged!' I hissed at him. 'Why won't you believe me? They drugged me to take my son!' I insisted, unable to hide my frustration at repeating myself. I didn't understand why they weren't searching the boat for Eli or questioning this couple rather than wasting crucial time.

'Security officers have searched their cabin and found nothing. However, you are correct. They do have a baby. Joshua. And they have all the official documents to substantiate that he isn't your son, Alice.'

'Did you check for a haemangioma?'

'Yes. There was no identifiable mark on his body.'

I shook my head. 'No... No... NO! They're hiding Eli somewhere. They have to be! Why else would they have followed me? They came running down the corridor to take him from me. I ran into my room to get away. But I could hear them outside my cabin door.'

'The couple said they were talking to another guest. This guest had also followed you back to your cabin because of concerns over the welfare of your baby due to your physical condition.'

'No...' I muttered uneasily. I had no memory of anyone else there.

'She was in the lift with you, and you were swaying and seemed unwell.

She was heading to the deck for fresh air but followed you to floor eight to ensure you were all right.'

'So where is she? Have you questioned her?'

'I've put out a request for her to come forward. But I don't believe she will be able to help us at this stage.'

I narrowed my eyes. He wasn't making any sense.

'What? You need to talk to her. Surely, you can see her face on the CCTV footage?'

He shook his head. 'No, unfortunately not. The position she was standing in the lift and the fact she had her head down looking at her phone means we don't have a clear image of her features.'

'Maybe this person took Eli? Have you thought of that?' I suggested. 'I mean, what the hell are you doing sitting here questioning me when you should interrogate the other guests? Especially this woman in the lift and the couple who... who...' I faltered, hearing myself.

Captain Laurent picked up the jug of water next to him, poured some into a glass and pushed it across the table towards me.

'I don't need a drink! I need you to find my son!' I snapped.

'That's what I am trying to do, Alice,' he quietly replied.

But there was a lack of reassurance in his voice. It was as if he already knew something.

'I was drugged,' I repeated. 'Can't you check if anyone accessed my room?'

'No, we don't have the passenger's Key Access details,' he answered.

He watched my reaction.

'I know I didn't leave my cabin after I returned. I was too unwell. I couldn't sit up, let alone stand up,' I defensively stated.

'But we do have security footage.'

I stared at him. There was something in his tone that scared me.

'So, you'll see if someone entered my cabin?' I uneasily questioned.

He shook his head. 'The camera on your corridor was blacked out.'

'Blacked out?' I repeated, not understanding.

'The lens was covered with spray paint.'

'What? When?'

'Approximately when the ship left Plymouth port,' he answered.

'Doesn't that show that this was planned?'

'Yes,' he agreed.

I breathed out heavily, not understanding him. 'So, why are you sitting here?'

'Alice, show me your hands,' he instructed.

I froze.

'Why?' I asked as beads of sweat gathered at the nape of my neck. I instinctively curled my fingers into my palms.

I noticed Sophia, the duty nurse, catch Officer Barnaud's eye. It was evident that they knew something I didn't.

I felt like a criminal. 'I haven't hurt my baby despite what my husband has said. I would never do anything to harm him. Someone has taken him. You have to believe me,' I desperately pleaded.

Captain Laurent nodded, never taking his eyes off me. 'I know you believe someone has taken him, Alice.'

'They have!' I countered. 'I haven't done anything. I was drugged.'

'So, show me your hands.'

I turned to Sophia, but she wouldn't look at me.

'Alice?' repeated Captain Laurent. 'Show me your hands.'

I reluctantly placed my clenched fists on the table.

'Lay them flat and turn them over, please.'

I dropped my gaze to my hands. I slowly turned them over as requested and unfurled my fingers. 'I... I don't understand,' I said as I stared in disbelief at what appeared to be specks of black paint on them. 'No... No... No. No,' I stuttered, shaking my head.

This can't be happening, Alice...

I looked up at him. 'I... I didn't do this... I swear.'

There was a knock at the door.

'Enter,' Captain Laurent ordered.

I turned to see a young woman dressed in a uniform similar to the others. She walked over to the captain, bent down and discreetly whispered something into his ear. He nodded, then logged onto the laptop in front of him. I watched as she waited while he uploaded something. I realised it must be surveillance footage.

'What is it?' I nervously interrupted.

Neither one spoke as they both studied the screen. I noted that Officer

Barnaud was also watching. I could see from their eyes that whatever they were witnessing was disturbing. I watched as a terrible feeling of foreboding took hold as the young woman turned away, unable to look at the screen.

'I want to talk to my brother!' I cried out. 'You can't just keep me here! I haven't done anything. Someone took my baby! And... And...' I stared at them. It was as if I wasn't even in the room. 'I'm a qualified nurse, and I was drugged,' I continued in desperation. 'I... I must have been administered something without realising... Maybe something like Rohypnol? It would have the same effect of making me feel so ill and out of sorts before blacking out...' My voice trailed off as I realised no one was listening. 'Did you hear what I just said? Someone could have drugged me with Rohypnol! The date rape drug used to spike a victim's drink!'

The room was suddenly silent.

Captain Laurent looked at me. 'Is there anything you want to tell me, Alice?' he quietly questioned.

I stared at him. Confused, I shook my head. 'No...'

'Can you explain this CCTV footage?' he asked, turning the laptop to face me.

The surveillance footage was already playing. I watched, feeling as if the walls were closing in on me. A woman, wearing a denim baseball cap and a black face mask that completely obscured her face, was pushing Eli in his Silver Cross car seat stroller. Her dark hair hung out the back of the baseball cap in a familiar ponytail. I instinctively touched my dark hair, which I had pulled back in a similar messy knot. I realised the woman was wearing a long, padded North Face coat – identical to mine – zipped up so you couldn't make out her clothes underneath. I was surprised that she also had classic, tan-coloured Ugg boots, the same as I was wearing.

'I don't understand,' I stated, confused.

Terrified, I continued watching. I noted the time on the tape: 1.01 a.m. I could feel Sophia studying the footage over my shoulder.

'Why is she on deck?'

My question was again greeted with a disquieting stillness.

'I can't...' I whispered, pushing the laptop away as the woman unclipped Eli and picked him up, his blue blanket falling as she did so. He was wearing his knitted blue cardigan and beanie hat.

I heard myself let out a sob. I squeezed my eyes shut against the horror of what was unfolding. I turned and bent over and started to retch.

I heard the lid of the laptop snapping shut.

A few minutes later, I straightened up. Tears blurred my vision as I looked at Captain Laurent. 'Why? Why did you show me that?' I hoarsely whispered.

'My security officers found the same coat captured on the CCTV recording in your room, Alice. The face mask was in the coat pocket with the baseball cap, and the aerosol can of black paint was in the changing bag attached to the pram. The baby blanket was recovered earlier this morning on deck.'

I stared at him, open-mouthed. It then hit me that he had been waiting for the CCTV recordings on the deck of the woman with Eli about to—

I stopped myself.

I looked in horror at Captain Laurent. He had wanted confirmation of his suspicion, and now he had it. 'You think I did it? Do you really think I would hurt my baby? That I would... I would...' But I couldn't say the unthinkable.

None of it made sense.

'Why... Why would you think I would get drunk then? If this couple and the other guest are right? That I was intoxicated in the restaurant and could barely make it back to my cabin room? That must have been before nine last night,' I stated. 'The CCTV camera recording shows this woman on deck just after one in the morning. I was in my room, passed out. I... I... I couldn't have done it,' I pleaded with him.

Captain Laurent stared straight at me. 'I'd suggest you got drunk to give you the courage to carry out your intentions.'

'NO!' I vehemently cried. 'That's not possible. Why not do it when I left the restaurant? Why not go straight to the top deck and...' I couldn't bring myself to say it.

'Because you were too intoxicated, and there would have been too many witnesses. Someone would have stopped you. You returned to your room, sobered up enough to make it to the deck early in the morning when the other guests would be in their cabins and—'

I shook my head. 'No.'

'You used a can of aerosol paint to obscure one of the surveillance cameras where you were standing on deck. But you didn't spot the other

CCTV camera that recorded you committing—' He abruptly stopped and cleared his throat.

I waited, terrified of what was left unsaid.

Oh God, Alice...

'Otherwise,' he then continued, 'we would never have known what you did. I have never witnessed anything like this in thirty years of service, and I hope I never will,' he stated, unable to disguise his disgust.

'If I did something so heinous, don't you think I would have taken my own life? It doesn't make any sense,' I despairingly argued.

'You attempted to when you returned to your cabin.'

'What?' I spluttered. 'I didn't!'

'How do you explain the empty packet of temazepam tablets and a bottle of red wine?'

I gaped at him. 'I didn't do it... Someone drugged me. They took Eli and they—' I couldn't say the unimaginable.

'And why would someone do that, Alice?'

'I... I... don't know,' I admitted, my voice trembling with uncertainty. 'But someone did. You have to believe me,' I pleaded.

He didn't respond.

Then I remembered why Sophia and her colleague were in my cabin.

'Why would I scream so loudly that my cabin neighbours could hear me? Sophia said that I was heard shouting that something had happened to me, my baby. Surely I wouldn't do that if I was responsible for hurting him. It doesn't make any sense.'

Captain Laurent sighed. 'I can't answer why you were screaming, Alice. Maybe you realised what you had done.'

I shook my head. 'No... NO! If you're so sure that I did that to Eli, why haven't you turned the ship around to search for him?' I demanded. 'He's on board and you know it!'

'As soon as I was aware of the situation, I radioed the French Maritime Rescue Centre in Gris-Nez. They are currently conducting a search for your baby.'

'No...' I murmured, feeling light-headed. 'No... I didn't do that to him. I wouldn't. Someone has taken my baby!'

His countenance remained inscrutable as his eyes bore into mine. 'Out of the two thousand passengers I have on board, can you explain why another guest would take your baby and go to such elaborate lengths to make themselves look like you and then attempt to kill you with an overdose, staging it as a suicide?'

Lost for words, I could only stare at him.

'Sophia informed me that your husband had no idea until the early hours of this morning that you had taken your baby and left the UK. You booked your tickets for this ferry just over twenty-four hours before departure. Please elaborate on who, if your husband had no knowledge that you were leaving him, and you booked your journey so late, would know to target you?'

'I… I was drugged…' I repeated, confused.

'Sophia also explained that you have a history of mental illness…'

No… No… NO! This is all wrong. You would never hurt Eli… Would you?

Tears slid down my cheeks. Numb, I sat there, not hearing what they were saying to me – about me. Nothing mattered any more. I didn't care what they did. I was pure evil. I deserved to die.

Your father left because of you… Then your mother drowned because of you… And Noah. Alice? You know he died because of you as well. But Eli… How could you? How could you have possibly done that to him? HOW COULD YOU?

I gasped out loud as terror ripped through me. I remembered…

I remembered walking with Tom along the banks of the river Thames and holding Noah because he was crying. And a terrible impulse to throw my baby in the water came over me. Not that I did. Instead, I held him against my chest so tightly to protect him, so terrified of the fleeting but overwhelming compulsion.

But it must have finally happened…

You know those thoughts are in you. And those thoughts are powerful. So powerful. You know it, so why did you pretend everything was all right? Why did you take Eli and run, Alice? Why…

37

THREE HOURS LATER

Two Spanish police officers escorted me back to my Audi to retrieve some belongings. I had begged them to let me collect what I needed – primarily my medication, not that I was a threat to anyone. I was formally arrested with my hands cuffed behind me: I wasn't going anywhere. I was in the custody of the Spanish police, due to be processed. I assumed that at some point, I would be returned to the UK to await trial.

Even though I had accepted that I was responsible, deep down in my core, I struggled to believe that I would hurt Eli. Not just hurt him, do something so horrific, so unimaginable that I was terrified the knowledge would drive me to insanity. If I wasn't already insane. No matter how hard I tried to remember, I couldn't recall any of the events I was accused of or witnessed on the CCTV surveillance recordings.

How, Alice? How can you not remember anything? The black aerosol paint on your fingers? The empty bottle of wine and temazepam blister pack? And Eli... Eli...

I heard myself give out a strangled sob. I hated myself even more for daring to feel sorry for my situation. I had no right to feel grief, or self-pity. I had no right to anything. Not now. I thought of Oli, the pain this would cause him and how he would struggle to make sense of it. And Tom, the excruciating loss he would feel, for hadn't he tried his utmost to keep Eli safe and me away from him?

I waited while one of the officers held my arm, and his colleague opened the boot and started unloading my bags, searching for my medication. I turned and looked at the other passengers sitting in their cars, getting ready to disembark and begin their journeys. I dropped my head when a driver looked at me, ashamed to be witnessed handcuffed and restrained by a police officer. I felt as if he knew what I had committed – the worst crime imaginable for a mother.

I wondered if someone would drive my car off the ferry so it didn't block the cars parked behind or if they would simply divert the vehicles into another lane when it was empty. Not that it was my problem. There was a police car waiting in the ferry port for me. Everyone would pass it as they disembarked, none the wiser that it was waiting to escort a baby killer to the police station.

I gasped as the pain that thought elicited stabbed me through the heart. For that was what I was and would always be known as, the mother who killed her baby. It was immaterial that I had no memory of it. The police had the CCTV footage, which was so incriminating there was no denying it.

Then I heard something. A cry. A baby crying. It was faint, but I was attuned to it – it was Eli.

Oh God, Alice... You've lost your mind...

Then again, only louder. I looked at the police officer holding my arm, but he was oblivious amid the noise of the other vehicles waiting to disembark and the staff shouting to one another as they started waving cars in the outside lane to move forward.

Again, I heard the cry. It was a high-pitched wail now. I knew it was Eli. The hairs on the back of my neck stood up as my body screamed at me that this was my baby crying. And he was crying for me.

Oh, Alice...

I started to tremble. I hadn't taken my medication this morning. Maybe that was why I was hearing things.

But you don't suffer from psychosis, Alice!

I shook my head. I knew I did. At its most dominant, my OCD could persuade me to believe in anything. To hear anything.

Then again, that frantic wail. I looked around, desperate to know whether it was in my head or if—

I didn't want to think the impossible – to have hope. I had seen the CCTV recording.

My eyes caught sight of a vehicle in the lane next to me. Someone was watching me. A sense of disquiet descended on me. I turned and looked at them. It took me a moment to register. I thought I recognised her.

Alice... ALICE! It's your neighbour... It's the same black BMW SUV...

How?

Frozen, I stared at her as she, in turn, stared at me. I couldn't see her eyes as they were hidden by sunglasses, but I could still feel her hatred boring into me.

She knows what you did... What you did to your baby...

I felt my flesh burning with shame.

Then it hit me. The baby crying. It was coming from her vehicle. The passenger window was down.

I shook my head.

No... She was pregnant. Remember, Alice? It must be her newborn baby...

But the cry. I would recognise that cry anywhere.

'Help!' I pleaded, turning to the officer beside me. 'She has my baby...'

He frowned at me.

'That black BMW there. Right there.' I frantically gestured with my head.

I watched as my neighbour saw my reaction and buzzed the window up as if she was taunting me. Letting me know she had taken my baby and left me framed for his disappearance.

His murder, Alice...

Some primal instinct caused me to snap. It happened so quickly that I didn't have time to process what I was doing. All I could think was that my neighbour had my baby, and a staff member was signalling for her to pull into the outside lane to disembark.

I yanked my arm out of the officer's grip and ran as fast as I could towards the car.

I heard shouts behind me from the two police officers.

Not that I cared. All I could think was she was driving away with my baby. With Eli...

Head down, trying to balance myself with my hands cuffed behind me, I sprinted between the other waiting vehicles and ran in front of the black

BMW. I didn't stop to look in the window at the car seat or the baby strapped inside. I didn't need to see him to know it was Eli. My primitive instinct screamed and screamed at me that the baby crying was him. It was enough. Enough to know that the voice deep, deep inside me was right. I could never have possibly committed the unthinkable.

She suddenly braked as I jumped in front of her car.

'SHE HAS MY BABY!' I screamed as loud as I possibly could.

She stared at me, and then her car screeched in reverse, and before I saw what was happening, she drove straight at me, striking me and driving my body into one of the pillars. I felt my head ricochet off the steel structure as my body crumpled to the ground.

A member of staff ran over to me and bent down.

'She has my baby...' I pleaded.

The frantic voices surrounding me started to fade away as I began to lose consciousness.

My baby...

* * *

Three Days Later

I moaned, feeling disorientated. I could feel my eyelids frantically fluttering, trying but failing to open. In the background, I could make out the beeping of a machine. Constant and somehow comforting.

'Alice?'

I groaned in response. Again, I tried to open my eyes but failed.

'Alice? Honey? It's me... I'm here,' someone beside me whispered.

'No... No...' I croaked in horror, recognising the voice.

'Alice, shh,' he soothed. 'You're safe now.'

'No... No...' I fearfully stammered.

I fought with all my might to open my eyes. Finally, I managed to will my eyelids apart, immediately narrowing them as the unexpected, painful glare blinded me. All I could see was intense white. Incrementally, I divided the solid mass of sterile colour into walls, then white Venetian blinds with beams of dusty white light streaming through, and finally, a white door.

Slowly, a face came into focus. It took some time for me to recognise that it was Tom, my husband. He was why I ran. The reason that I took Eli and...

Oh God, Alice...

'No... Get away from me,' I hissed in terror.

'Alice, honey. It was all lies. I would never do anything to hurt you. I love you more than anything,' he pleaded, his voice cracked with emotion.

His eyes glistened with pain as he searched mine for some kind of recognition that I believed him.

'You... You wanted to have me put away.'

'God, no! Never. It was all lies, Alice. Please? I love you.'

I scowled at him, scrutinising his face for proof he was lying. But all I could see was despair and desperation.

'Alice, I have proof that I was set up. That everything you think I did was all fabrication. Please, you have to trust me.'

I suddenly became aware my mouth was parched, but I couldn't summon saliva to ease the dryness.

'Water?' I hoarsely whispered.

'Here,' Tom offered as he attempted to place a straw in my mouth.

I clamped my lips tight against it.

'Please, Alice? I would never hurt you,' he begged. 'Just take a sip. It's only water.'

Desperate to quench my unbearable thirst, I parted my lips to accept the straw and bent my head forward to reach it, only to be greeted with an explosion of white, searing pain.

'Ahh...' I cried out.

'Careful. Try not to move,' Tom gently instructed. 'Let me get this glass tilted so you can get a drink.'

I sucked on the straw and was filled with such relief as the water flowed into my mouth.

'Not too much, okay?'

I took a couple more sips before Tom removed the straw from my lips.

'You can have some more later,' he assured me.

I licked my lips and was surprised to find them cracked.

'I have been rubbing Vaseline on them, but—' I felt him grab my hand and squeeze it tight.

I tried to pull it away, but I didn't have the strength to resist his hold.

'I thought you weren't going to make it, Alice,' he whispered, leaning over me.

Numb, I looked up at him. He looked exhausted. I was surprised to see days of black, coarse stubble covering his face.

'Eli?' I questioned, searching Tom's face for an answer.

Tears slipped down his face.

'No...' I murmured as it hit me. 'I... I tried to stop her... She had Eli... She had him in her car... They thought I had... That I had—' I stopped myself from saying it out loud.

'Shh... I know... Just rest. We'll talk later,' Tom promised.

'But... The neighbour. Our neighbour...' I gasped, struggling to catch my breath.

'Shh...' Tom gently repeated. 'Rest.'

As if on cue, my eyelids suddenly felt heavy and refused to stay open any longer.

'Eli,' I heard myself cry out before sinking into oblivion.

38

SIX HOURS LATER

'Hey.' Tom smiled, walking into the room. 'The nurse said that you had woken up.'

He approached the bed, leaned over me and brushed his lips against my forehead.

I recoiled at his touch, turning away and staring at the opposite wall.

'Alice? Please, look at me,' he begged. 'I... I would never hurt you. Never. Please? Let me explain. There's so much you don't understand.'

I didn't respond. I didn't know what to believe. All I knew was that Tom wanted to separate me from Eli and have me sectioned.

'Honey? Just look at me,' he insisted. 'It was all false. All of it. I wouldn't do any of that. Please, Alice, I was set up. You've got to accept what I'm telling you.'

Reluctantly, I turned my head. I was surprised to see his deep brown eyes filled with sorrow. I searched his disconsolate face, unsure whether I could trust his words.

Is it all lies, Alice?

'I thought I'd lost you. I... I couldn't cope without you... I... I—' Tom broke off, collapsing in the visitor's chair beside the bed. I watched as he covered his face with a trembling hand.

Neither of us spoke.

'How long have I been asleep?' I finally asked, not ready to hear how the impossible could be possible. For I had seen the evidence with my own eyes.

'You were unconscious for three days,' he explained. 'But you briefly woke up six hours ago before drifting off.'

'Three days...' I repeated, confused. 'Where am I?'

'You're in hospital,' he answered.

'Where?' I questioned.

'Valdecilla Hospital, in Santander,' he clarified.

'Santander,' I heard myself repeat.

'Do you recall what happened? The accident?' he questioned.

'The accident?' I echoed.

Then it came back to me.

'Eli? She had Eli in the front of her car... She had taken Eli...' I gasped.

'She drove the car at you. You sustained some nasty injuries, including trauma to your head. You were in surgery for five hours because the impact had ruptured your spleen, which caused serious internal bleeding. I was scared you wouldn't make it,' he admitted.

I could see the fear in his eyes, which made me terrified of what he wasn't telling me. I tried to move, to sit up, but instead found myself crying out as pain ripped through my left chest.

'No... Don't try to move. You've suffered a traumatic pneumothorax caused by the broken rib you sustained when the car hit you.'

I thought of Eli again.

'Eli... The neighbour, did she—'

'Oh God, Alice... I am so sorry,' Tom hurriedly said. 'I should have immediately told you—'

'Don't!' I cried out as tears filled my eyes. I didn't want to hear Tom articulate it. I couldn't bear to lose Eli all over again. Not after believing he had... That I had...

I tried to stop the horrific CCTV footage replaying in my head. Of the woman on the deck, dressed in my coat, my Ugg boots, taking Eli out of his pram and... And—

But she hadn't hurt him. It was all a ruse. I had heard him crying. I had run to her car to block her from disappearing with him.

My baby was alive—

And now, Alice? Where is Eli now?

More tears came as I knew the answer.

'Hey... Hey, honey, it's okay,' Tom soothingly assured me, stroking my left cheek as the tears slid down. 'Eli's safe. The security officers managed to stop her and got him out of the car. If you hadn't insisted on getting your medication from the Audi. If—' He broke off, swallowed as he shook his head. 'You were so brave, honey. You didn't stop to think about your safety. You just thought of our son.'

'Where is he? Eli?' I asked. That was all I wanted to know.

'He's with Oli back at the hotel. He'll bring him to visit later.'

Relief and pure joy flooded through me.

'Hey? Don't cry,' Tom said. 'He's safe, Alice. Or at least as safe as he can be with his Uncle Oli!' Tom stated, laughing.

'Oli?' I repeated, smiling, 'Oli's here?'

Tom nodded. There was a concerned look in his eyes. 'Remember he was meeting you at the Santander ferry terminal?'

'Oh, yes... Yes, I remember,' I replied, starting to recall the events that led up to the black BMW driver trying to kill me so she could escape with my baby. 'What was she going to do with Eli?'

Tom paused, stroking my cheek. He looked at me. 'You didn't recognise her?' he questioned, surprised. There was a look in his eye that unsettled me.

I frowned. 'She's our neighbour. Florence knows—'

Then I remembered Florence – our nanny.

I pushed Tom's hand away from my face.

'Alice?' he asked, hurt.

'Florence? You and her? How could you, Tom? How?' I hissed at him.

'No... No, Alice, you've got it all wrong.'

'Tell me, how could I have misinterpreted the video that Florence filmed of you two having sex?' I hoarsely questioned.

'She didn't film it,' he answered.

I found myself struggling to breathe.

'Alice, you need to try to keep calm. Take a slow breath,' he instructed.

I glared at him, hating the man in front of me. It was because of him and his actions that I'd nearly lost Eli: I would have been charged with his murder if I hadn't attempted to stop my neighbour from driving off the ferry with him.

I stopped myself from going over the 'what if' scenarios. None of them made sense. How did our neighbour know I was taking Eli to Santander? Or that I planned to board a ferry from Plymouth when I had booked my ticket twenty-six hours in advance? How was it possible?

'It's a deep fake.'

'What?' I asked, confused.

'The video. It's what's called a deep fake.'

'I know what a deep fake is, but you're trying to gaslight me!'

He sighed and shook his head. 'Alice, the police have verified that the video is fake. They are outside,' he began. 'They want to talk to you when you feel up to it.'

'The police?' I repeated, panicking. 'I thought you said Eli was safe. I... I... didn't hurt him, Tom. I was set up.'

'I know. And so was I,' he pointed out. 'The police know all of this. Two police detectives have flown over from the Met to talk to you. They're working in conjunction with the Spanish police.'

The thought of talking to the police filled me with terror, even though I hadn't physically harmed Eli. But still, they would know my mental health history and that I had put Eli in danger by fleeing with him.

'I contacted the Met as soon as I knew you had disappeared and why.'

I stared at him, waiting for him to elaborate.

'When I finished my surgery, it was after midnight, and I had all these frantic messages and voicemails from Florence,' he explained. 'She was in a terrible state. Of course, when I got home, she showed me the video you had sent her. I checked my emails to see if anything had been sent to me or if there was a blackmail threat. And that was when I saw the emails from this alleged Dr Keyes and Blair. At that point, I called the police. I discovered you'd taken the passports. I tried calling your brother, but he wouldn't pick up. So, I checked Oli's latest social media posts to see he had tagged his location as Nazaré. It didn't take much to figure out where you had gone and the means you had taken. You'd also left your laptop behind. So, I could log in and see your emails with the bookings for the ferry.'

'But how were you set up?' I sceptically questioned.

'Think back to the emails you opened sent to my Gmail account on Tuesday morning. The same morning that this "concerned friend" sent you an anonymous text telling you I was having an affair with our nanny. Then she sends you incriminating evidence in the form of a sex video. Didn't this "concerned friend" also tell you to check my emails?'

'How do you know?' I asked, astonished. Then I realised. 'Oli. He told you?'

Tom nodded. 'The UK police called Oli for more information as you were being held on suspicion of—' He swallowed before continuing. 'Of hurting our son. I caught a flight to Santander on Thursday morning from Stansted, accompanied by the two officers from the Met, to be here when you arrived. Oli flew in later, and we were both at the police station waiting for you. Of course, we believed Eli was missing at sea at that stage, and there was an ongoing search for him.'

I rested my head back and closed my eyes for a moment. My head was pounding, and the morphine didn't feel as if it was touching the pain caused by my fractured rib and punctured lung.

Tom remained silent as I tried to process how we had been targeted and why.

'So this Dr Keyes, is he a real psychiatrist?' I asked, opening my eyes and turning to Tom.

He shook his head. 'Fake, as is the email address. The mental health assessment that I had allegedly instigated was all a lie.'

I frowned. 'I don't understand. Our neighbour and the "concerned friend"? Are they the same person? Did she set me up to believe you were having an affair with our nanny and intending on having me sectioned by this Dr Keyes?'

'Yes,' replied Tom.

I shakily breathed out.

'Hey, it's all okay, Alice. The police have her in custody. She's got so many charges against her that she'll be spending years in prison.'

'But the email from Blair? She said you had accepted this new position at MGH and were relocating to Marblehead with Florence and Eli. I... I don't understand. Is that a fake email from this "concerned friend" as well? Our neighbour?' I asked.

'The neighbour, as you call her, wasn't our neighbour. Our real neighbours, Simon and Antony, have been away in Japan for two months. She pretended to be living there. She would park her car in the drive so it would appear as if she resided in the property.'

'But why?' I asked.

'To watch you. *Us.* She wanted a way to destroy us. You found a GPS tracker on your car? Yes?'

Shocked, I nodded. 'She did that?'

But then it started to make sense. It explained how she was able to follow me. But how did she turn up and board the ferry without an API?

'I don't understand how she got on the ferry. How did she know I was intending to travel to Santander from Plymouth?'

'Your laptop,' Tom replied.

I shook my head, confused.

'On Tuesday morning, you went out and gave Florence the time off. Well, our so-called neighbour watched you leave and visited Florence. She had talked to her a few times and exchanged numbers. She even got your number on the pretext of wanting to connect about private nurseries and pre-schools as she was new to the area and expecting a baby. But she wasn't. It was one of those fake pregnancy suits.'

'That's how she was able to text me? Florence gave her my number?' I interrupted. I recalled seeing Florence giving her a number from her mobile.

'Yes. But there's more. When you were out on Tuesday morning, she invited herself over for a chat. Florence didn't know how to say no. They went into the living room, and your laptop was left open on the wooden chest,' Tom explained. 'She asked Florence to get her a cup of tea, and while she was out of the room, she took your computer, then shouted out she had forgotten to turn something off at home and would be back shortly. She returned, apologised and asked for a fresh cup of tea. When Florence returned to the room to ask if she wanted a different herbal tea, she caught her taking your laptop out of her bag. Florence asked her what she was doing, and she reacted as the aggrieved party, and accused Florence of lying to cause trouble. She said if Florence said anything, she would tell us what a terrible nanny Florence was and that she had caught her mistreating Eli. Florence was terrified she would lose her job.'

I nodded, recalling how flustered Florence had seemed when I'd returned home. She said she had a friend in the living room.

'But what did she want with my laptop?'

'She secretly installed spyware, giving her access to all your information, such as browsing history and credit card information.'

'That's how she knew to book the ferry in advance,' I murmured in disbelief.

He nodded.

I thought of my mobile phone and how it had suddenly started draining power.

'Could this spyware have infiltrated my iPhone?' I asked.

'Maybe? I'll get it looked at,' Tom suggested.

'But...' I shook my head. 'I don't understand. That was on Tuesday while I was out. If she hadn't accessed my information before then, how did she know about my stay at The Woodlands Hospital?'

Tom gave me a strange look.

'What?'

'My mom, Alice. She got a lot of information from my mom.'

'Your mom? How would this woman know your mom?' I asked, shocked. 'And you said, "us" Tom,' I stated. 'Who are we to her?'

He gave out a low, dejected sigh. 'I was always worried that something like this would happen,' he admitted.

'Tom... I don't understand.'

'The woman who did all this to you and took Eli, setting you up for his disappearance, was my ex-fiancée.'

'Blair? Blair Worthington?' I questioned. I was sure I had misheard him.

He nodded uneasily. 'I am so sorry, Alice. I had no idea that Mom was talking to her about our lives. None at all.'

'Blair?' I repeated, dumbfounded. 'The beautiful, blonde woman who has it all?'

Again, Tom nodded. 'She's not who you think she is,' he stated. 'She's—'

'She's some super successful neurosurgeon at one of the best hospitals in the United States. And she's married to some guy who's even more accomplished and lauded than her. They have an amazing apartment overlooking Central Park. So why would she risk all that? For what?'

'Revenge,' Tom simply answered.

'No... No, no. This makes no sense. The neighbour, the woman in the BMW who had taken Eli, she had long, dark hair and—' I stopped. I shook my head. She was always wearing oversized sunglasses that hid her features.

Tom waited a beat before adding, 'It was a wig. An expensive one with real hair.'

'No...' I muttered.

'She's been arrested and charged, Alice. They have Blair in custody for your attempted murder and kidnapping of a child. I am sure there will be more charges against her as she went to elaborate lengths to frame you for the murder of our baby.'

'Tom...' I mumbled, struggling to comprehend what he was telling me.

'She drugged you with Rohypnol. She crushed the tablets and added them to a bottle of Coca-Cola.'

I gaped at him. 'I said... I said I had been drugged, and no one believed me.'

'They found a box of Rohypnol tablets in her luggage. She confessed to drugging you. To switching a bottle of soda in the restaurant.'

Confused, I stared at him. 'No... No, that woman had curly auburn hair, and she was Spanish. She had this elderly gentleman with her,' I stated.

'Blair is fluent in Spanish. Her own nanny was Spanish and she continued in school because she excelled at it. That was the point with her; she had to be the best.'

'The auburn hair?'

'Another wig. The police retrieved a pregnancy suit and multiple wigs from her car.'

'And the elderly man?'

'Who knows? He was no doubt just some poor guest.'

'She knocked into me intentionally,' I whispered, working it all out. 'She knocked my Coca-Cola off my tray, and then she must have swapped it. She must have been following me, watching my every move. I took so long deliberating over what I wanted. She had time to see me choose, and she would have picked a bottle up and spiked it, then swapped it for the one that had fallen on the floor. That's why she bent down so quickly to retrieve it, so she could change them over and hand me the bottle with the Rohypnol.'

'And you never saw her face?' Tom questioned.

'She was wearing a face mask. So was the elderly man. I assumed they were being cautious.'

I shook my head. I understood why I had started to feel so ill after drinking the spiked Coca-Cola. I didn't notice it in the drink as the cola was dark brown, and the blue tinge effect of Rohypnol wouldn't be visible. Nor does Rohypnol taste of anything.

'How did she think she would get Eli through Spanish border control? I had his passport,' I pointed out.

'She had a fake passport. Money can buy you anything, Alice.'

I shallowly breathed out as I tried to process everything. 'So, the email from Blair was part of her plan?'

'Yes,' Tom replied. 'And it was all lies to make you believe I was leaving you. To ensure you took the bait. How could you believe I had arranged to have you assessed under the Mental Health Act, Alice? How?'

'You did it before,' I evenly replied.

'Yes, because I had no choice. You were seriously unwell then. Understandably so. But you have been fine recently. You seemed to be coping with Eli.'

'Was I? I remember you suggesting the contrary,' I threw back.

'I... I was stressed with work and with my parents. Mom was constantly on at me for us to relocate back home so that we could be there to support her and Dad.'

'And Eli's passport? When were you going to tell me about that?'

'I did. I got you to sign the forms from the American Embassy. You were so exhausted at the time. You hadn't slept for a couple of nights. Remember?'

'But you didn't tell me you had taken Eli there, Tom. What was I supposed to think?'

He dejectedly shook his head. 'I know... I know... All I wanted was to surprise you. I wanted to take you on holiday. Just the three of us, and no, before you say it, not to the States. I know you've always wanted to return to Rome where I proposed...' He faltered and shrugged. 'It was something Mom had suggested: I should surprise you with a holiday. But now I realise that Blair was playing her to get to us. And it worked. Mom had no idea about Blair. I protected Blair, and now I wish I hadn't.'

'What do you mean you protected her?' I questioned.

Tom dropped his gaze to his hands. I noted, shocked, that they were trembling.

Then it came back to me. Our first night after returning from the States. Tom had said something odd about his ex-fiancée: 'There's stuff I haven't told you about her. I'm scared of what she's capable of...'

39

'Tom? What didn't you tell me? About her? About Blair?'

He dragged his head up to meet me, and I was surprised to see the fear and sadness in his eyes.

'There was always something wrong with her. Even growing up. There was a cruelness in her that I chose to ignore. She... She was...' He stopped and shook his head, struggling to continue. 'The engagement was her idea. I went along with it. Our parents were so happy, and it was expected that it would happen, you know? We grew up together. But she followed me in everything I did, everywhere I went.'

'You mean college and—'

'Yes. And choosing to be a neurosurgeon. She was clever and driven, but it wasn't her passion. It was mine. But it was her way of keeping me, by watching my every move. The college I chose, she chose. The same happened with my med school and then my first residency. My friends became her friends. It was as if she took everything that was mine for herself. Blair inveigled her way into my mom's world, becoming the daughter she never had. But Mom never saw her for what she was. The cruelness, the conceitedness, the jealousy and, above all, the need to control everything and everyone. She would repeatedly lose it with me, accusing me of cheating on her. She put software on my devices and would follow me without my knowledge. It was crazy. Eventually, I caught her screaming at a nurse, claiming she was sleeping with me. I found out some time later that Blair had made her life so unbearable that she ended up attempting suicide. She was stalking her, sending her vile anonymous messages and sticking up explicit images of her on her staff locker that she had photoshopped and—' He stopped, looked at me.

'God, Tom...' I heard myself mutter, aghast.

'There was more, but...' He shook his head. He cleared his throat. 'When I found out what Blair had done, I challenged her, but she denied everything. She then turned on me. She made my life hell, professionally and personally. So I broke off the engagement. I moved out of our apartment in Manhattan. But it just made things so much worse. She had lost control of me. I started getting these anonymous messages on my phone. Death threats. I knew it was her, but I couldn't prove it. It affected my work, so I took time off. Without telling her, I moved to Chicago to stay with a friend. You know how I found out she knew where I was?'

I shook my head.

'Tim's girlfriend, Heidi had this Labrador. He was poisoned. Someone had thrown some contaminated meat into the backyard, and before Heidi could stop Toby, he had eaten it. She immediately suspected something, as all this weird stuff had started happening after I moved in. She took him to the emergency vet, and they managed to save him. But it was hit and miss for a while.'

'Tom...' I muttered in horror.

'Not that we could prove it. But that night, we saw Blair sitting in her car outside the property, watching. She did that for weeks. Every day and night. I eventually begged her to leave me alone. But it reinforced her resolve.'

'Couldn't you go to the police?'

He broke away from my gaze, embarrassed. 'I tried when it got really bad. When my car was vandalised and fake stuff started being posted about me, I mean really offensive accusations, on social media. All from fake accounts. I hired someone to trace them, and they all led back to Blair.'

I gasped. 'Eve Truth? After Noah's funeral? Those posts accusing me of—' I broke off as I saw the confirmation in Tom's eyes.

'Why didn't you say at the time?'

'Because we had just lost our baby, Alice. I... I just couldn't bring myself to talk about Blair... Part of me didn't want to accept that she was capable of something so heinous after we had lost Noah.'

'But you suspected, right? That Blair was behind the X post?'

He reluctantly nodded.

I was astounded. I had first suspected Blair, but her warmth and compassion towards me and her defence of me on X had blindsided me.

'Oh God... The newspaper article about my mother's drowning? She made it sound like she knew I had done something to her. That I was responsible?'

'My mom might have mentioned to Blair that you suffered from survivor's guilt. You told me you and your mother had a huge argument that night. She left you and headed down to the beach and...' He looked at me. 'I'm sorry. I should never have told my mom. Blair took that information, googled it and spun it for her own end.'

Numb, I shook my head. 'Why?'

'Because she couldn't have me, and you did.'

'None of this makes any sense. Weren't you still engaged to her on the first night of our date? She bought her wedding dress and posted photos on Instagram that same day. Maybe she thought I was the reason you broke off the engagement.'

Tom looked at me with surprise. 'Alice, I broke off the engagement a year before I came to the UK. I transferred here to get away from her. I thought she would leave me alone if I was on a different continent.'

'A year before our first date?' I numbly repeated.

'Yes. Do you think so lowly of me that I would take you out on a first date while still with someone else? Engaged to someone else?'

'But she posted all that stuff on the day of our date. The video of her with her bridesmaids and—' I shook my head.

'Oli told me about it. I looked at those posts and have no idea who the women are. Blair no doubt paid them.'

'But how would she know about our date?'

'Because I told my mom. I had no idea that Blair would FaceTime my mom all the time or would call in whenever she was back visiting her parents. Like I said, I never told my parents the truth about Blair and our break-up. When Blair learned about my date from my mom, she posted that stuff to make it look like I had a fiancée in the States and I was cheating on her. No wedding venue was booked, and no wedding dress was bought, Alice. We never got that far. I assume she hoped that whoever I was dating would see it, and you did, eventually.'

I shakily breathed out. I couldn't believe what I was hearing of how far Blair had gone to destroy Tom and to prevent anyone else from being with him. 'And your mom? I always felt she blamed me for you guys not being together,' I admitted, my own guilt weighing heavily on my shoulders.

Tom sheepishly nodded. 'No, I get that. She had a real hard time accepting it was over between Blair and me. She secretly kept hoping we would get back together. And then, of course, I met you.'

What would Barbara make of Blair now after she had tried to abduct her grandson and frame her daughter-in-law for his murder?

'The Reborn doll... The one she left in my cabin room, dressed in Eli's sleepsuit. It was... It looked just like Noah, Tom. I... I wasn't imagining it,' I said, shuddering as I recalled it. I felt my eyes stinging at the shocking image.

Tom leaned into me and gently cupped my face. 'I know... The police showed me a photograph of it as evidence against her. She must have had it custom-made from our photos of Noah on social media and at my parents' house.'

'How did she get into my cabin without a boarding card? And without anyone seeing her?' I asked, stunned at Blair's level of manipulation.

'The security cameras had been obscured with black paint on your cabin's floor. Blair had also booked a cabin on the same floor a few doors down from you.'

'What?' I questioned, shocked.

'She was watching your every move. She followed you down to the restaurant.'

'How did she know I had left my room?'

'She had placed a mini spy camera on the wall opposite your cabin, and the film footage was being streamed live to her phone.'

'But that doesn't explain how she managed to get into my cabin to take Eli and leave that Reborn doll on my bed. Then she must have returned and left the empty pram—' I suddenly remembered something – or someone. 'Someone was in the lift with me. They followed me to my cabin. I... I dropped my boarding card and someone bent down, picked it up and handed it to me. I think she had curly, reddish-brown hair, like the Spanish woman in the restaurant, but without the face mask. But I felt so unwell her face was just a blur. It was Blair, wasn't it?'

Tom gave a slight nod. 'Yes. She said you were so out of it that you had no idea she took the boarding card from your hand as you struggled to open the door and get the pram into the room. She would have followed you into the cabin then, but Rob and Hannah came running down the corridor from the opposite end after taking the lift.'

'The young couple with the baby?' I questioned, guiltily remembering accusing them of taking Eli.

'Yes. They were worried about the state you were in. Blair talked to them, assuring them that you would be fine.'

'She set me up, Tom. She made it look as if I had... I had done something to... to Eli and had then tried to take my life.'

'I know... Blair confessed to the police that she had been planning this for months to coincide with the anniversary of Noah's...' He faltered, unable to say it.

'But why, Tom? Why do something so heinous, so unimaginably cruel?'

'She's ill, Alice. I mean, really ill. To do that, it's... it's...' His voice trailed off.

'But why? She had it all. Her life seemed so perfect.'

Tom stared deep into my eyes as he still held my face. 'It was all a lie, Alice. Yes, she married. But it fell apart soon after. She lost her job at the time. Malpractice by all accounts. A patient's family were going to sue the hospital. It was one of many claims against her, so they cut their losses. She was given a generous severance package to discreetly leave. The medical board was informed, so she could never practice again as a surgeon.'

'So, she had nothing to lose and everything to gain by targeting us?'

He let go of my face, and sighed resignedly. 'She had all the time in the world to implement her plan. Finding out the news that we were having another baby at the time she had lost everything must have pushed her further over the edge. My mom was so excited for us and wouldn't stop talking about it.'

'But... But the afternoon of Noah's funeral... I saw you, the two of you, talking outside the bedroom. You seemed fine with her...'

'Yeah, because I was terrified of what she might do, what she could do. I even apologised at the time for hurting her in the hope that we could move on. She had met someone else and I thought she had finally let me go.'

'When you came into the bedroom, when she brought me up some food, I thought it was because you didn't want me to be alone with her for fear of her telling me you had been engaged.'

'I wasn't terrified of that. It was what she might do to you. In case she tried to hurt you.'

'Seriously?' I questioned.

Then I thought about everything she had done to me. To my baby. She had taken Eli and tried to kill me. I shook my head, struggling to swallow as Noah came to mind.

'Tom?' I whispered in horror.

'What?'

'Do you think Blair could have hurt Noah? Could she have entered your parents' home without their knowledge? I was sleeping and I doubt I would have heard her come into the guest room—' I stopped myself, unable to articulate the unspeakable.

Tom shook his head. 'I had the same thought. I told the police as much, and they questioned her about her whereabouts the morning of Noah's death. And she was at work at MGH in Boston, Alice.'

'But...' I began.

'She has indubitable evidence substantiating her whereabouts.'

I was silent for a moment.

'Why Eli? Why take him?' I questioned.

'I suspect because she knew the pain it would cause me believing my wife had...' He shook his head, unable to say it. 'She wanted me to live with that knowledge for the rest of my life.'

'And what was she going to do with Eli?' I asked, terrified of the answer.

Tom shrugged. 'I don't know. She won't tell the police what her plans were.'

'Do you think she would have... have hurt him?' I asked, dreading the answer.

'No... I think Blair would have raised him as her own. She would always have a part of me then. And the knowledge that she had taken my baby and wife from me. That she had fulfilled her promise of destroying me. Because it would have done, Alice. If I had lost the both of you...'

'Hey, I'm here.' I smiled at him as I reached out and touched his face. I felt an overwhelming rush of love for him. How could I have ever doubted Tom? Worse, how could I have allowed Blair to make me distrust him? But I had. However, I accepted that Blair's level of duplicity and manipulation was beyond anything I could have imagined.

He grabbed my hand and held it against his cheek. 'I'm so sorry, Alice. I should have told you about her. I had no idea of the lengths she would go to.'

'I know,' I whispered. 'I know.'

There was a polite knock at the door before it opened.

'Look, there's Mummy,' Oli said to Eli, protectively cradling him as he entered the room.

I beamed at them as tears filled my eyes. A pang coursed through me at the realisation that, not that long ago, I thought I would never see Eli again.

Oli gently handed him to me.

'Be careful,' Tom said.

I looked up at him.

'Not of Eli, honey. I don't want you to hurt yourself.'

But I didn't care. I gently kissed my baby's cheek, nuzzling his skin as I breathed in his smell, acutely aware of how lucky I was, for it could have ended so differently if Blair Worthington had succeeded with her plan.

'Mummy's never letting you go,' I whispered to him.

I already knew that when I returned home, there would be changes. I didn't want anyone else looking after my baby. I doubted that Florence would be there when we returned home anyway. Not after the video clip of her and Tom. Regardless of the fact it was fake, I was certain I was the last person she would want to see, let alone work for.

I looked up at Tom and Oli as tears cascaded down my face.

'You're meant to be happy, sis,' Oli said, shaking his head as his eyes glistened.

I couldn't imagine what torment he had endured these past few days. But we were all together now: they were my family, my world, my everything. And I had come so precariously close to losing them. I looked down at my beautiful baby asleep in my arms. Oblivious to the drama around him.

'I am happy. I am so happy, Oli,' I simultaneously sobbed and laughed.

40

THREE YEARS LATER

I smiled to myself as the baby kicked. I stroked my bronzed, swollen, fecund bare belly, luxuriating in the rocking movement of the sparkling warm azure water as I sat, legs dangling over the surfboard.

'Mommy! Mommy!'

I turned and cheered as Oli rode a wave in the shallow water with my son, surfing in tandem. My heart felt as if it could burst with pride as Eli managed to jump up from a crouching position on the front of Oli's board with his arms outstretched for balance, like the natural he was in his multicoloured board shorts and life jacket.

'Honey?' Tom called out, paddling over to me on his board. 'Did you see our boy? Goddammit! He puts me to shame! And he's only three. He shouldn't be able to balance like that until he's four.'

'He's a natural. Unlike his dad,' I teased as I leaned over to kiss him.

Tom ran his hand through his wet, black hair when we pulled apart. He had never looked fitter or happier. 'I'll send Oli's GoPro footage of Eli to Mom and Dad. I reckon we've got another world champion surfer in the making.' Tom beamed. 'They can't wait to visit next week. However, it's not us they're interested in. They only want to see their grandson. That is if we can get him out of the water.'

'Maybe this time they'll make the decision to move here. Especially with this little one due in a few months,' I said, stroking my belly.

'Yeah, I hope so,' replied Tom.

His father had recovered well and was as active as ever. We both knew William would relish being a part of his grandchildren's lives, as would Barbara. More so, Barbara. After what happened with Blair, she had made a concerted effort to build a relationship with me. She adored Eli and was desperate to be more involved with him, and consequently, was the driving force behind them leaving Marblehead and joining us, which I also wanted. She had become more of a close friend these past few years, something I never believed possible. But William still needed convincing to leave behind his golf and yachting friends. However, Tom had planned to spend time with his father at the yachting club, where he had finally secured a membership, for their upcoming visit to persuade him to make the move. The Islands offered some of the best sailing in the world, drawing Tom here. He now needed to convince his father of the unlimited possibilities of living here, including the renowned nearby golf course.

I suddenly laughed in surprise. 'Your daughter just kicked me, Tom Fitzpatrick. Feel,' I said, grabbing his large, protective hand and placing it on my stomach. 'She's just like her big brother and loves being on the water.'

Tom looked at me, a sudden seriousness in his eyes. 'We've got it all, haven't we? We're living the American dream,' he stated as if not quite believing it.

I nodded, holding his gaze. He was right. There was nothing more I could want. I had it all.

I looked across the beach to our beautiful house on the North Shore of Oahu in Hawaii. It opened out onto panoramic views of the beach and clear crystal water. It was paradise. Not that long ago, it would have been a living hell for me, and without therapy, it would never have been a possibility. But now, I couldn't envision not being here. I had found my place in the world.

Dr Samuels' words came to mind: You are a good person...

The difference now was I knew they were true.

I breathed in deeply as the water rhythmically swayed me back and forth, watching the sun majestically ascend in the orange and yellow sky. The sunrise, gentler than the dramatic golden hour sunset, was now my favourite time. It offered promises and joy, something I had once believed I didn't deserve and would never experience again.

I glowed as Eli triumphantly high-fived his uncle near the shore.

I had it all and more. Much more. I had been given a second chance. I had found peace. Noah would always be with me wherever I was in the world. He was in my heart, my soul, my very being. He was in the sun as it rose and the water as it flowed.

I closed my eyes and smiled as the sun's rays delicately kissed my skin and the water gently lapped around me.

I know I am a good person.

ACKNOWLEDGEMENTS

As always, thank you to my mother and sister for their unwavering support and for being my most valued readers. Thank you also to Francesca, Charlotte, Gabriel-Myles and Ruby.

Thank you to Peter Dempsey.

Thanks to Caroline Raeburn and Craig Raeburn for your fabulous advice at the beginning of this journey.

Thanks also to Tom Avitabile.

Thank you to my wonderful literary agent, Annette Crossland – I don't know what I would do without you.

Thanks to all at Boldwood Books for your brilliance and for being such an amazing team. Thank you to my incredible copy editor, Jade Craddock, and proofreader, Susan Sugden. And, in particular, huge thanks to Francesca Best for being such an exceptional and fabulous editor – thank you.

ABOUT THE AUTHOR

Danielle Ramsay is the author of the DI Jack Brady crime novels and other dark thrillers. She is a Scot living in the North-East of England. Always a storyteller, it was only after first wanting to be a filmmaker and completing a Degree in Media Production that she then went on to follow an academic career in literature. It was then that she found her place in life and began to write creatively full-time. Danielle fills her days with horse-riding, running and murder by proxy. She is also the proud Patron of the charity SomeOne Cares.

Sign up to Danielle Ramsay's mailing list here for news, competitions and updates on future books.

Follow Danielle on social media:

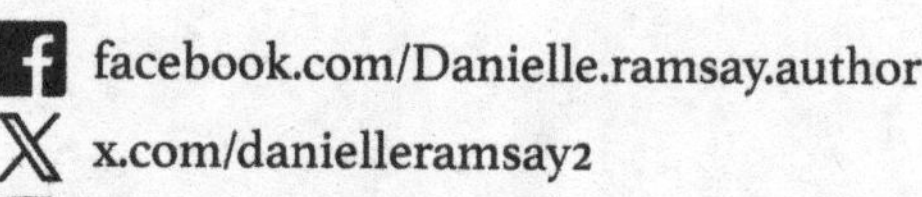

facebook.com/Danielle.ramsay.author
x.com/danielleramsay2
instagram.com/danielle.ramsay.author

ALSO BY DANIELLE RAMSAY

The Perfect Husband

My Best Friend's Secret

The Other Wife

Taken

www.ingramcontent.com/pod-product-compliance
Lightning Source LLC
Chambersburg PA
CBHW010746310726
48980CB00004B/382

* 9 7 8 1 8 3 5 6 1 6 4 6 8 *